Return

TO SENDER

NICOLE BAZLEY

Cover design by Katie Jaspersen @k.jaspersen Designs

Developmental editing by Alyssa Matesic

Copy editing and production by The Self-Publishing Studio

Internal artwork by Iryna Kopyrina.

Dedication

This is going to get sappy, so if you aren't into that, skip ahead. But I mean... you bought a romance book so you're probably into it.

TO MY HUSBAND

Without you this book would never have progressed past a dream written in a word doc.

You encouraged me to carry on writing it. You gave me the confidence to send it off to be reviewed, even though I felt like a total imposter. You sat and brainstormed with me to help it evolve and you encouraged me to publish it.

Your belief in me when I thought it was an unrealistic goal and your complete lack of fear of failure gave me the confidence to finish and publish this book.

You have always been my biggest hype man, no matter what I do or how crazy the idea, I can count on you to say, 'What do you need from me? I'm In.'

I can honestly say I would never have even considered that I could publish a book if I didn't have you in my corner.

So Thank you.

I am also going to force you to read it and make you give me detailed notes as proof that you did.

1

Love is only a feeling

SCARLET

I can feel his presence, his energy. Feel his eyes boring holes into me. It is so real that I swear I can hear his voice as it fumbles over the syllables that form my name. The hairs on my neck stand up, pin prickles tickling my skin from within. Goosebumps roaming my arms. I don't have to see him to know he is here. I can just tell.

I know that sounds so hocus pocus. But I believe when two people suffer a trauma together, they connect in a way that cannot be explained. Almost like their souls become intertwined. They become in tune with the other's presence, feelings and emotions without a word being spoken.

Bonded…

Although, it had always felt like this for us. From the moment I first laid eyes on him.

I remember the moment, the pull, as we drove down the driveway to our new home. I was just eleven years old. We had moved town for a job my mum had taken.

We locked eyes for the longest time as my mum turned the car into our new driveway. His image was burnt into my mind like a hot branding iron to skin.

His eyes were the most amazing shade of green I had ever seen. Even from a distance, they shone bright, like green emeralds in the sun. He was climbing a tree in his front yard.

"The neighbourhood looks nice," my mum said as she put the car in park and turned the engine off. She turned to face me with a soft smile. "I wonder if he goes to your new school," Mum continued once she had noticed what, or rather, who I was looking at.

She was trying to make small talk to lighten the mood. I had been crying the entire drive. I remember feeling nothing but misery. I didn't want to move towns, leave my school, my friends, the only home I had ever known.

Yet despite my every protest and reasoning, here we were. Pulling up to our new house. In a new town, where I was to start a new school the next day.

In reality, it was only an hour away from our previous hometown. My mum had been offered a promotion within her aged-care facility. It meant more money. But it also meant a transfer to a bigger facility, in a different town.

I knew that being a single mum whose partner had split at the mention of a baby being on the way, she had to make sacrifices. More money and less hours meant more time to-gether. Just the two of us, the way it had always been. But to me, we might as well have been moving to another universe.

I looked out the window and across at the house next door. The lawn was perfectly manicured in strips of light and dark grass.

There were flower beds that lined the house with explo-sions of colourful flowers pouring out of them. A large tree in the middle of the yard. I looked up at the boy now sitting on a branch in the tree that rose high up from the ground.

His piercing eyes were staring straight back at me. We were locked onto each other for what felt like a lifetime.

I was shaken from my daze and his hypnotizing eyes by yelling coming from his house.

"Vin!" A deep, dark grumble. "Vin!" Louder, more frantic. "VIN!" almost a roar.

The boy jumped off the branch, landing on the ground, and ran to his front door. A man stood in the doorway. He was tall and wide, taking up most of the entrance space.

The boy stopped briefly and looked back at me, a shiver coursing down my spine. Then he squeezed past the man and ran into the house. I sat in the car staring at the front door, thinking about the question my mum had asked.

Would I see the boy at school tomorrow? The boy with the long, wavy caramel hair. The boy that looked way too tall and gangly to be my age. The boy with the emerald-green eyes.

If only I had known then what I know now.

So here I stand, water drops sprinkling my skin. The sprays from Niagara Falls are raining down around me. My skin goose-bumped and pin-prickled. I can feel the earth shift. Like my world is about to be flipped on its axis. I have been living upside down for years. Right at this moment, I can feel it, I know it is about to change…again.

2

SCARLET

"Coffee?" His voice is deep, but somehow playful. It wakes me from the trance I am in. I turn to look at him. Dark features, short jet-black hair and eyes like tar, skin tanned dark. He is smiling at me and holding out a paper cup with what looks like a strong black coffee.

"Thanks," I say as I grab the cup from his hand. The paper cup does absolutely nothing to lessen the heat coming from the boiling-hot water, and I almost drop the damn thing right there on our feet. I quickly recover, somehow managing to place the cup down on the small side table next to me, wondering how he even managed to keep a hold of it for so long.

"Oh yeah, it's hot," he says with an apologetic smile on his face.

"Ya think," I spit out, full of sarcasm. He doesn't seem taken aback by my snarky comment. Instead he smirks, a small little laugh escaping his closed lips.

"Can I get you some milk?" he asks in a polite tone. Too polite, almost condescending. His face looks sincere, but the tone was definitely fake, forced even.

"That's ok, I saw a cafe down the street, I might just head there and grab a coffee before we start," I say as I start towards the door. "Instant burnt coffee really isn't gonna cut it today."

He laughs, thinking I am joking. I laugh because I am dead serious.

This is my way out, my escape. I can tell my mum that I came, and in truth, I did. I was here for a full ten minutes before sneaking out. I will come back in an hour and make out that I have been here the whole time. She will be none the wiser.

"I will come with, if that's ok? I could actually use a decent coffee myself," he offers, almost like he can read my mind and knows my plan.

I clench my teeth. "Sure," I reluctantly huff under my breath. I force myself to be polite. Part of me doesn't want to scare away a potential new friend, but the other part really does not want to be here. Let alone drinking burnt Blend 43 with some church do-gooder.

My mum had dropped me off at the church to attend a group counselling session. We have been in town for about four months now. On the outside, I appear to be making strides. I have just secured a hairdressing apprenticeship. Getting up and going to work every day has helped. But on the inside, I am dead. I know it. Mum knows it.

She has been suggesting that I speak to a counsellor or psychologist nonstop. Finally I agreed to these group sessions, purely as a way to get her off my back and let me rot in peace. Mum said the sessions would be a great start. A way to help me cope with my grief.

HA! It's almost laughable. There is no coping with this. There is no way out of this grief, not for me at least. Mum seems to think that talking about what happened with others that have had losses or dealt with trauma will help me heal.

I am sure that would be true for some, but I can never talk about what happened. I can never tell the truth of what we went through. What I did. No one will ever understand. No one except the two of us. He and I. Me and the boy with the emerald-green eyes. The boy I lost…

3

Do you believe in fresh starts?

He holds the door to the church open for me and gestures me through before him.

"Thanks," I say as I walk past and down the couple of stairs that lead down to the garden path. It is lined with an array of coloured roses. He follows close behind me.

"I'm Blake, by the way." He holds out a hand to shake. "My parents help run the church events; my mum organises most of these sessions." He continues chatting as I weakly shake his hand, kind of shocked by his confidence.

No kids my age at twenty shake hands. They high-five, or fist pump or try to hug you, copping a feel on the way. He looks a similar age to me, but his mannerisms and energy seem so much older.

"I'm Scarlet," I say as my hand drops back down to my side. We keep walking towards the coffee shop my mom and I drove past on the way here. He seems to know the one I am leading us to.

We are silent for a while, but strangely, it doesn't feel awkward. He has a calming presence, and he leads the way with a quiet confidence.

"Are you new to town, or just the church group?" he asks, breaking the silence that I was peacefully enjoying.

"Both." He looks sideways at me while we walk, waiting for me to elaborate. I'm not going to.

"Where are you from?" he finally asks, gently prying further.

"Over east." I pause, deciding how much about my life I actually want him to know. He is half watching where we are walking, half looking sideways at me. Something about him makes me relax, and I almost involuntarily start talking again.

"We just moved to Western Australia from New South Wales. We lived around the Sydney area, but we needed a fresh start so…" I pause, hoping he will jump in and I can stop talking. He doesn't. "Here we are, in Mandurah. All the way on the opposite side of the country."

He doesn't say anything back. We reach the coffee shop, and he opens the door, moving to the side again so I can enter first. I stand there awkwardly for a moment before going through. There is a bit of a line, so we stand and wait our turn to order.

"What made you need a fresh start?" he asks as we wait. There are lots of people in the coffee shop. People are standing directly in front and now also behind us as the line fills up.

I really don't want to be talking about this while people can overhear. I really don't want to be talking about it. Full stop. It was the reason I came up with this damn coffee run in the first place. To get out of talking about it.

Now here I am. Being slapped with the very questions I am desperately trying to avoid, left, right and centre.

"Are you a counsellor, like your parents?" I ask somewhat sarcastically, completely ignoring his question. He starts laughing. A slow chuckle that turns into a full-on belly laugh.

"No!" he finally spits out, trying to control his laughter.

"What's so funny?" I ask once his laughing has subsided.

"I am probably the most messed up out of everyone in the group sessions, and my parents aren't counsellors either. They just volunteer with the church."

"Oh, I see."

We reach the front of the line, and the cashier asks us for our order.

"Cappuccino for me please, and a," Blake motions to me to add to his order.

"Oh, a latte for me please, large," I add. She takes Blake's name, and before I can even get my wallet out of my bag, he has paid.

We stand off to the side to wait for our order, and our conversation picks up again.

"So what made you so messed up then?" I ask, trying to deflect the line of questioning away from me and my painful life. He looks down at me for the longest time.

He is handsome, I suppose. I don't really pay that much attention to guys these days. I have no interest in anyone else. Something about him is very attractive to me, though. His skin looks like it browns really easily over summer. I can see different shades of brown over his arms from different tee shirt lengths.

He has a strong jawline covered in patches of dark stubble and really calming eyes. They looked so dark from afar, but up close when the light hits them, they almost look like they are swirling with streaks of lighter brown and yellow. Eyes you kind of get lost in. I stare back at him, waiting for him to tell me more.

"ORDER FOR BLAKE!" The lady yells it so loud it makes both of us jump. Like she is expecting us to be waiting outside as opposed to right there, where they told us to wait. We don't say anything else as we grab our coffee and start the walk back to the church.

"I'm under a lot of pressure to be a certain way, act a certain way. A lot of high expectations, and I am not sure I live up to them all, " he finally replies to my earlier question after we've been walking for a while.

"Like what?" I like that we are not talking about me anymore. So I aim to keep him talking.

"Well, for one! Extremely religious parents."

"You're not a believer?"

"I love the community that the church stands for, and I love a lot of their values, but no, not really. Some of the things my parents believe." He pauses like he is going to elaborate, but he doesn't. He just stops talking altogether.

I am not a religious person. In all honesty, today was the first time I have ever stepped foot in a church. I have never read the Bible or even really thought much about how the world was created. I celebrate Christmas and Easter, but we always celebrate the, I suppose, Hallmark version of it rather than the religious version.

We set up a Christmas tree and exchange presents on Christmas Day. We give Easter eggs and eat our fair share of them too. But I can quite honestly say I don't know the traditional celebrations for these events. Jesus was born, died, was reborn. I'm not sure. Maybe to people's distaste, but this is just how it is with my mum and me.

I have no idea how to respond to that question. I don't really know what he is talking about, what beliefs he doesn't agree with.

"Like what?" I finally ask. He looks over at me and gives a bit of a forced smile.

"Never mind," he says as we reach the steps to the church again.

4

If you could go anywhere, where would you go?

SCARLET

Blake opens the church doors for me again and I walk through to the foyer. Everyone is already sitting down in a giant circle. Damn, no way out of this now.

Blake motions me to some seats and I sit down. He follows suit and sits right there next to me. Ok, I am starting to panic now. I haven't really thought much about what happens at these group counselling sessions. Will I be forced to share? What would I even say? I can never tell the truth about what happened to me, to him, what I did. I feel the heat washing over me like a tidal wave.

I look up from my coffee to see the counsellor standing there. She is holding a large beach ball, bright-coloured pie sections with black writing scribbled all over it. I can't make out what any of it says from where I am seated. She asks all of us to stand.

Ah, worse than sharing. This is one of those awful get-to-know-you games. The ones where they force you to stand up and say what your name is and why you're here. I cannot think of anything I want to do less right now. I start praying. If there is a god, please let the ground swallow me whole. RIGHT NOW!

The counsellor introduces herself. Her name is April. She looks kind and approachable; she could look like a goddamn Care Bear and it still wouldn't make me want to play this ridiculous game.

She starts to explain that, as this is the first session for the majority of us, we will be doing an icebreaker. She then goes on to start explaining the game.

She looks genuinely excited. What's worse than her enthusiasm is the level of eagerness from everyone else. Aren't we supposed to be depressed here guys? Come on.

This game is based around the beach ball. It has a heap of ridiculous questions scrawled all over it. Most of which I probably cannot answer truthfully. We all stand around in a circle and then have to throw the ball to someone. Whoever catches the ball has to say their name and read out the question that their right hand lands on. They then have to answer the question.

My praying has just escalated from getting swallowed by the ground to lightning to strike and turn me to stone or glass or whatever is supposed to happen. I would rather do anything, ANYTHING! than answer a personal question in front of these people I don't know.

I purposely try to avoid eye contact with whomever has the ball. Surely someone won't throw it at me if I am not looking, right! I look down at the ground, at the back wall, the snack table, anywhere except at who has the ball.

I listen to a heap of questions like, 'Where are you from?' 'What are you hoping to get from these sessions?' Then some lighter questions like, 'If you could go anywhere in the world, where would it be?'

I know they are not going to stop until everyone has had a turn. If I go last, I will be the last thing everyone remembers. I don't want that. NO, I need to get this over with and then be forgotten.

I have heard enough questions now to know I can cheat and say it landed on a light and breezy one. One I have heard before. Like the 'If you can go anywhere question.' That was easy. I would answer Niagara Falls. I've always dreamed of going there. It will be the truth.

That is not the question I land on. It is the question I answer in front of this crowd of complete strangers. It is not, however, the question I am meant to answer.

I move my hand over the writing to reveal my question. I read it in my head, then start to recite the one I have rehearsed, for which I have an answer prepared. So when I say, "If you could go anywhere in the world, where would it be?" I should have said, 'If you could talk to anyone, dead or living, who would it be?'

When I answer, "Niagara Falls," I should have said, 'Vin Henderson!'

5

Lightness in my chest

BLAKE

*M*an, I hate these sessions. It's a Tuesday, my only morning off from university besides the weekend. And my parents force me to come and help at the church for their counselling sessions. As if I am not here enough.

I have to be here at a completely unholy hour. Set up the chairs, put the snacks out and make the coffee. The awful coffee. I don't know why we can't find the cash to get a decent coffee machine. Instead we have an ancient urn with instant coffee in it. No one likes it.

"They don't come for the coffee," my mum had said when I suggested the idea of an actual machine with good coffee. Blah. We have come to this church for as long as I can remember, each and every Sunday and to every single damn event they run in between. Now my parents have put their names down to help with a church community group therapy session.

Fantastic.

So here I am on a Tuesday. When every other twenty-two-year-old is sleeping or relaxing or traveling the world, I am at a church therapy session with a bunch of damaged people.

I know I shouldn't be so harsh. So many of these people have suffered loss, pain or trauma of some sort. But fuck, why do I have to be the one to care?

I mean, I do care, that's the hard part. I actually do care. But I also have my own problems, my own shit to deal with. Shit that I don't get the luxury to actually deal with because I am supposed to be the poster child for all that is holy and righteous.

Everyone who normally comes to these sessions is over the age of fifty, and every session just leaves me feeling even more trapped and depressed than the last. At least my folks don't make me share. HA, that would be a wild ride.

Suppose they think I have no need to. On the outside, I am a wholesome, good young man with a bright future following in my dad's footsteps as a surgeon. On the inside, I feel like a caged animal, shoving the roar down with each and every breath I take.

I have been here for what feels like forever already. I have swept the floors, placed all the chairs out in a big circle. Set up the trestle tables. Laid out all the flyers with further resources and help available. Printed the sign-in sheet and placed it in the clipboard next to the cards. Set up another table for snacks, tea and coffee.

I have made a batch of instant coffee and gagged at the thought of actually drinking it. Set up another thermos with boiling water for tea, put the tea bags, sugar and milk out. I am now setting up the cups for the tea and coffee. When she walks in.

She is the youngest person we have had at a group session this far—that I have seen, at least. She doesn't look like an addict, nor homeless, like some of the younger ones I have seen before. She is dressed in jeans and a printed tee with sneakers. Everything looks new and clean. Long brown wavy hair hanging loose well past her shoulders.

She doesn't look thrilled to be here, but she doesn't look broken like some of the people coming in. She has a pretty face, but she looks entirely bored to be here. She walks in the doors, her eyes darting around, then she steps to the side and keeps looking back out the entrance to the car park.

She looks like she is about to do a runner. Runnnnnnn, trust me. Don't get sucked in…RUN! But that is the caged animal in me talking, feeling my own fate so chained down. I tug at his leash. Shhhhh, she may need to be here and need the help this church offers. Not everyone is in your shoes Blake! Go be kind, help her.

I take a deep breath and swallow down my own frustration at being here. I pour a cup of coffee into one of the cups. It smells burnt, but who knows. Maybe she is into crap coffee. It is the gesture of kindness and welcome that I am trying to provide, just like I have been taught my entire life.

I walk over and offer it to her. She takes it and almost drops it straight onto the floor. Oops, should have told her it was hot. My hand was burning holding it, but I had nowhere to put it and didn't want to seem weak. She is quick-witted and full of sarcasm, and I like her already.

Turns out she was trying to make a run for it and she shares my hatred for the coffee. I shamelessly invite myself on her little coffee run, needing the escape as much as she does, apparently.

We walk to the coffee shop together, and I buy her a decent coffee along with one of my own. It's from the church fund anyway. I laugh at the irony. She really doesn't seem thrilled to be going to the session, but something in me tells me she needs to be here.

She has somewhat tried to deflect my questions, which I understand. But she is the first person in a really long time to actually ask me questions about my own life. Which feels entirely strange.

Like a tiny little bit of water being splashed on a raging internal fire. I choke on what to actually say to her line of questioning. I can't be completely honest. I also don't want to scare her away if she needs a friend. So I tell the truth, divulging little parts but being careful to not spill the entire tea. She seems to have a good sense of humour, and every little quick remark or chuckle she makes seems to create a little lightness in my chest that I haven't felt before.

Don't run, I think. Stay! But it is for entirely selfish reasons.

6

The lies we conceal

SCARLET

"How was it?" My mum asks as I hop in the passenger seat and buckle up.

"It was ok." My mum and I have always had a good relationship. We have always been close, always been honest and open with each other. Well, for the most part.

But once a lie creeps into a relationship, the lies never stop coming to protect the first. It drives a wedge between you. One lie to cover another. Down and down the rabbit hole you go, until you have told so many lies to cover the truth you actually don't know which way is up and which way is down.

It is like that with my mum now. There are times when she looks at me with those loving eyes. So much patience and acceptance, and I feel myself start to unravel. I know she feels the divide. I know she so desperately wants me to open up to her. To confide in her. But I can't. Not now, not ever.

Little lies started creeping into our lives from the moment I met him. Lies to protect him, lies to protect us. Now it's all too big to unpack. Too dark, too deep to ever find a way out of it.

Sometimes I start to feel the truth bubble up inside of me. About to boil over if I don't put a lid on it. So I turn away, I swallow it down. I push it back into the box and force the lid shut. I turn cold towards my mum. It's the only way I can keep the truth from her. It's the only way I can keep this secret.

She smiles softly at me as she places a gentle hand on my knee.

"I am glad it went well." She starts to pull the car out of the parking spot. "The more you talk about things the easier it will get hun," she continues, turning into the street to head home.

I blankly stare out the window. Thinking about the session. How I can't imagine it being easier. How I can't imagine this pain or guilt ever lessening, let alone going away. I nod, returning her smile, and we drive the remainder of the way in silence.

7

The animal within

BLAKE

My alarm goes off at six a.m. Instead of my usual antics of hitting snooze every five minutes for a solid thirty minutes, I jump out of bed and quickly shower. I want to get set up and go get her a coffee before she arrives.

With each session, I have found myself more and more drawn to Scarlet. I can't explain it, but whenever I am with her, the tiny cage that holds the real me locked up tight seems to get a little bigger.

I seem to have a little bit more room, space to stretch my legs and arms, stand and even roam. A freedom I have never had before. It seems to grow with each and every smile, every laugh, every quick-witted reply she makes to my own humour.

It feels effortless with her. There is no forced conversation, no expectations. Just fun and easy. Jokes and stories. Laughter and playfulness.

My mum is already there when I arrive at the church. She makes a comment about me being earlier than usual. I brush it off and get straight to work, going through my normal Tuesday routine. Chairs out, check. Tables, check. Flyers, cards, sign-in sheet, check. Coffee eww, check.

"You're in a good mood today," Mum says as she helps me move the giant urn of coffee around on the table so we don't spill any of it. Let it spill, I say.

"Always." I give her my biggest fakest smile reserved for especially annoying tasks. She has absolutely no clue. " I'm headed to Beach Bites to grab a coffee." I don't wait for her reply. Before she can even register what I've said, I am out the doors.

I am back with her latte and my own cappuccino within fifteen minutes. Ten minutes until the session starts. She is usually early, and I find myself waiting on the front steps to see her mum pull up and drop her off. A smile creeps over my lips when I see her step out of the car and wave goodbye to her mum. Only this time, the smile is as real as it gets.

8

Fight or flight

SCARLET

"Thanks," I say as he hands me a latte in a takeaway cup from the coffee shop. The lid has a large letter L on it. I take a sip, and it is just as good as it was last week, and the week before that, and the other weeks before that. Strong, creamy and not too hot. Just the way I like it.

He laughs under his breath as he takes a sip of his own.

"You're starting to warm to these sessions, aren't you?"

"I'm not trying to bail out anymore, if that's what you're asking."

"It's an improvement for sure," he chuckles. "Surprisingly, you wouldn't be the first person that has used going to get a coffee as an excuse to skip out." I have to laugh now as well.

"I thought it was a clever plan." Guess people with trauma act the same. Fight or flight, right?

I realised the first week that they don't force you to share. Once that ridiculous game was over, I could just sit and listen to other people's experiences and grief.

That sounds even more depressing, I know. A bunch of people drowning in heartbreak and pain, sitting around talking about who has it worse. But it wasn't like that. It was kind of a relief to know I wasn't the only person who ever suffered loss. I wasn't the only person to have their heart ripped from their chest and smashed into a million pieces.

Everyone's story was different, but each had a theme. Loss, pain, trauma! So, I decided that I would keep coming. If only just to listen. I came to learn a few of their stories.

There's Brian. He is in his eighties, and his wife has just passed away. He has a permanent look of heartbreak and confusion on his face. Every week he brings up something new he doesn't know how to do because Beatrice used to do it.

Today he has a stain on his shirt that he has apologized for three times. He doesn't know what his wife used to do to get them out. He can't find where she used to keep the starch to iron his shirts crisp or the recipe to his favourite meal she used to cook.

Not that it would help if he found it, because he doesn't know how to cook, clean or even wash his clothes. He says his son has been visiting. He lives about three hours away and has been coming to help over the weekends. But how long can he continue doing that? He has kids of his own, a job and wife he needs to be home for. I wonder how he will survive once his son can no longer come every weekend.

Then there's Rebecca. She's in her thirties and lost her baby to SIDS. She is so stricken with grief and heartache and blame that I don't even know what to say to her.

Mark, he's youngish. He looks older than he is, I think. Despite his constant proclamations of being sober, the way he is constantly jerking and chewing his inside cheek off tell a different story, or maybe years of substance abuse has left him like that permanently. Who am I to judge?

I could go on. Each person seems slightly more broken than the last.

Blake's claim when we first met of being the most messed up doesn't seem to be all that accurate to me. He never speaks in the group sessions, but then again, neither do I. I know eventually I may have to, but today isn't the day.

However, I do feel these sessions are helping. My mum was right in making me come, and I am glad I did. Blake is a refreshing change, and I have enjoyed our sarcastic banter and laughs each week. I have even found myself feeling a glimmer of excitement to come. Just to see him.

9

Withholding truths

BLAKE

I have decided today is going to be the day. I tossed and turned all last night, weighing up the different options in my mind. I've considered telling her the truth, the whole truth. But I'm not sure I'm ready to face that beast yet. Not sure I ever will be, to be honest.

What I do know is that I love being around Scarlet. She makes me smile. Like real smiles. Not the fake shit I reserve for my parents, professors and friends at university.

When I am with her, I feel like I can breathe deeper. The burden feels less intense, and I can feel more of the real me coming alive than I have ever felt in my entire life thus far.

My caged animal has woken up, and he is roaming around, held back by a leash that grows longer with every minute I spend with her.

We have only really hung out at the church groups, and I want to ask for her number to see if we could hang outside of the church. But I also don't want to lead her on or give her the wrong idea. I don't want to date. Even though his cage is broken, I need to keep that animal on a leash. At least for now.

We decided at the last session that this week we would meet early at the coffee shop. I rush to set up the church foyer and make my way to the cafe to meet Scarlet. She's already there when I walk in.

She is waiting in line. Long dark hair falling in big loose waves around her shoulders. She smiles when she sees me, and I feel that lightness again. Yep, today I will ask. Just be honest. Being honest doesn't mean I have to disclose everything. Tell her you want to hang out, but just as friends.

I take a deep breath and walk to meet her in line.

10

What's the best that can happen?

I am waiting in line for Blake. We decided to meet at the cafe this week so we could hang out a bit before the session. He's the only friend I've made so far in town, and I enjoy his company.

I don't see the girls I work with outside of work, and I haven't met anyone else.

I have been coming to the group sessions at the church for six months now. We sometimes hang back afterwards and chat or come early and get coffee, like today. It feels easy with Blake. There is always lots of laughter, and he makes me feel so at ease. I considered asking him to hang out on weekends or after his classes or my work, but I didn't want him to get the wrong idea.

I don't want a boyfriend. Period! A friend, yes, but boyfriend, nope. I am not ready to move on yet. I don't think I ever will be.

I have only been in the line a few minutes when Blake comes in, a big smile across his face, and I find myself doing the same.

We order our usual coffees and go find a table outside.

"How was your weekend?" Blake asks, taking a sip of his coffee. I worked all Saturday and spent Sunday doing a whole lot of my usual, which was absolutely nothing.

I have no friends to do anything with, hence asking Blake to hang out more. Blake tells me he spent Saturday studying and most of Sunday at the church.

"We live such exciting lives," I say. Blake almost spits his coffee out across the table in laughter. I start laughing at him, choking on it as he tries to calm down enough to swallow his mouthful.

"One of the guys in one of my classes is taking a break from uni; he is traveling all over Europe for the summer," Blake says once his laughter has subsided.

"That sounds amazing. I always dreamt of travelling. Take off for a while. Forget all my problems."

My mind starts to flash back, back to a different time. Flashes of green eyes and wavy hair. Big hands with long arms wrapped around me.

Feelings flowing through me, accompanying the images. My purple floral bedspread as we sat together talking about traveling and where we would go. The feeling of his arms wrapped around me as he sat behind me. His hair tickling my neck and shoulders. I could feel the colour draining from my face, heat covering my body and a lump rising in my throat.

I can't let myself go down that black hole. I shove the memories back to the far depths of my mind, forcing the door shut on that part of my brain that so badly wants to remember him.

Blake seems to notice the reaction my thoughts are having on my body. Breath getting shallower, jaw tightening, colour draining. He places a gentle hand over mine on the table.

"Hey," he says, leaning his head down but looking up through thick black lashes. "I know you're not ready to talk about it. But you're going to be ok." And at this moment, I believe him.

I turn my hand over and wrap my fingers around his hand, not interlocking our fingers like you would do with a lover, but palm to palm, hands wrapped around each other's. It feels safe and peaceful, and for a brief moment, I want nothing more than to curl up in his arms and cry.

To tell him everything I've been holding in. Cry for what I have lost, cry for loneliness, cry for the guilt that crushes me. But also cry for the moments of happiness that being with Blake gives me. The sense of calm and peace and the laughs. It feels like the only times I smile these days are when I am with him.

It makes me forget about the pain and guilt. It makes me forget the truth.

We sit in silence for what feels like forever. Just holding hands and drinking our coffees. Then he starts talking again.

"I remember you saying you always wanted to visit Niagara Falls, our first session, remember?" I nod, and he keeps on talking. "I've always wanted to travel. Just seems impossible with the life my parents have planned out for me. School, university, church, work, more church, marriage, kids, more church, die!"

"Sounds like a wild ride," I say, chuckling.

"I know right," he says, joining in on the laughter.

"You don't have to do it that way if that's not what you want, you know."

"Ha!" he chokes out, "have you met Marion and Jeffrey?" I start laughing again. He always calls his parents by their first names around me. He is so polite and formal to their faces, but in front of me he seems so angry at them. Angry at his life. He masks it with humour and sarcasm, but I can tell.

Because I do the same thing to hide my own pain.

"What would happen if you didn't do it that way? You are twenty-two, what is the worst thing that could happen if you don't follow their plan?" I sit and wait for him to think. I can see his brain ticking over. Going one way and then back the other with the scenario, but he says nothing.

"Maybe that's the wrong question. Maybe you should be asking yourself what's the best that could happen," I add, feeling quite proud of myself for this little snippet of wisdom I have learnt from April at the sessions.

He starts to smile. "The best, huh."

"Yyyiip," I say, smirking back at him, raising my eyebrows.

If only I could take my own advice. What's the best that could happen? If I let myself feel again, if I let go of the guilt, if I told the truth. I shake the thought from my mind. Small steps. Then I let myself take that first one forward.

"Do you want to do something this weekend, like outside of the church and the counselling sessions? Something fun. Let's go bowling or ice skating, or I dunno. We may not be able to travel to Europe for the summer, but we can get out of this town for a day."

I barely even finish my rambling sentence before Blake says yes. I didn't realise the nerves were making me talk so fast.

"Let's do it."

I don't add anything more. Anything about it not being a date or me not wanting a boyfriend. Somehow, I just know he feels the same. We put each other's numbers in our phones and make our way to the church.

11

What is normal?

SCARLET

"Hey," I say as I walk into the cafe to meet Blake. It's early Saturday morning. I'm headed to work, and Blake is planning on staying at the cafe to study. He has completed a Bachelor in Medicine and is now doing his Doctor of Medicine. His parents want him to go on to become a surgeon like Blake's dad, who is a cardiothoracic surgeon, although I know it isn't what Blake wants.

He doesn't like to talk too much about his parents and what they expect of him. He hates talking about his university and studies even more.

I know he doesn't enjoy it and that it's not what he wants to do, but he never really told me why or what he wants to do instead.

Blake is already sitting down with our coffees. He slides mine across the table as I sit down, along with a ham and cheese croissant that he has ordered for me.

"Mm thanks," I say as I start ripping into it. He starts chuckling at me and my excitement over the croissant as he takes a bite of his own bacon and egg sandwich.

We started hanging out a lot more outside of the church these last six months. These quick morning breakfasts on Saturdays have become a regular thing for us. We meet here at the crack of dawn, talk about our week and scoff down breakfast before heading off on our days.

35

"Sooo, Claire from my work is having a party tonight at her house. Do you want to go?" I am not really sure I even want to go, if I'm being entirely honest with myself.

"To a house party?" He raises his eyebrows, and his voice gets higher pitched with the last word.

"Yeah, why not?" I have been in town for almost a year and a half now. Blake is really the only friend I have made. I am friendly with the girls at work, but they never invite me to things, and we never really speak outside of work. This is the first thing I have been invited to, and there is a small part of me that desperately wants to feel like a normal twenty-one-year-old again.

Even if I would be faking it for a while. I mean, I didn't even have a twenty-first birthday party. That's how sad my life is. I worked on my birthday, and Blake brought me a cupcake and coffee on his way up to uni in the morning.

Blake never goes out either. I never see him with other friends. He is either at home with his parents, at university or at the church. Or, I suppose, now with me. Blake is a couple of years older than me and has told me all about his twenty-first birthday party. We laughed about it for hours. His parents hosted it and invited all their long-term family friends and people from the church. He said he died of boredom and snuck off to his room before they even got the cake out. I can imagine Claire's party will be a completely different ball game.

"My parents will never let me go to a house party," he replies.

"What, you are twenty-three," I say in shock. "Why will they care?"

He gives me an exasperated look. Like I just don't get it. "Why do you let them dictate your life so much? They are making you miserable. You're an adult, if you want to go to a house party you can. Legally they can't do anything to stop you."

The exasperated look changes to a flash of anger. I have never seen him look like that. He stops chewing and puts his coffee down on the table hard. A bit of the liquid gold splashes over into the saucer.

"It's not about letting them do anything to me Scarlet, it's about respect. They are good people, and they just have strong ideas about what they expect from their only child."

"Well, shouldn't they respect you and what you want as well? You do everything the way they want. Abide by all their crazy, weird rules and ideals; half the time I can see you don't agree. Why are you so afraid of them?"

"I am not afraid of them, I just…" The anger drains from his face, replaced by heartbreak. He looks like he is going to cry. I slide my chair around the table to sit next to him as I grab his hand.

"You just what, Blake, what are you so afraid of?"

I feel terrible now, I can't believe I spoke to him like that. My own fears and insecurities are bubbling up and spilling over. Maybe I don't get it. Just like I am sure he doesn't get me all the time. The way certain things trigger me so badly that my body freezes up.

The way I sometimes just zone out during a conversation, flooded with memories I don't want to share. He never pushes me. He just grabs my hand and lets me ride it out or makes me laugh to bring me out of it.

I love him for that. And yet, here I am, pushing him and questioning him about things I know he doesn't want to talk about. I know his parents are extremely religious and very strict. They have very strong opinions about a lot of things that don't make much sense to me.

If I go to Blake's house to visit, I'm not allowed in his bedroom. Like not even in the middle of the day with them around, door open and all. I'm not allowed to be there past nine p.m. He's not allowed to come to mine unless his parents speak to my mum and they know exactly what he is doing.

His mum asked my mum to enforce the same rules with the bedroom and curfew if he comes over.

I find it entirely strange considering we are both adults and legally old enough to drink, drive, have sex and marry. But I never questioned it until now.

He smiles at me weakly, but the heartbreak is still swirling in his eyes. "I am afraid they won't like who I really am. If I let them see. They won't… They won't love me."

"And who are you really, Blake?"

"I don't even know, Scarlet."

"Well, when you figure it out, I will still love you." I say it tongue in cheek. I don't love him, I mean, not like that. He is a friend, and I am really starting to care for him, but I want him to know that it won't change our friendship.

He gives my hand a squeeze, and I know he knows exactly what I meant.

"Can we just watch a movie tonight?" he asks.

"Sure, I'll get the snacks after work, come to mine for six. We will have more privacy at mine."

He nods, and we finish our breakfast in peace, hug goodbye, and then I head off to work for the day while he sits back down with his computer to study for the day.

12

Fuelling fires

She opens the door before I even have a chance to knock. My hand sits in a fist an inch from where the door was right before she opened it.

"Hey," she says with a big smile as she moves to the side so I can come in. We walk into the kitchen, and I see the kitchen bench where she has laid out a huge array of snacks.

Sour worms, Clinkers, Maltesers, popcorn, Starbursts.

"Omg Scarlet, overboard much," I say, and she starts laughing.

"I didn't know what I was in the mood for, sooo, I got it all," she replies, smirking as she waves her hand in front of the snacks as if she is a hostess on *The Price is Right*.

"Well, we won't need dinner with all this."

"Too late, I've already ordered us Chinese." She is flat-out laughing now, and I can't help but join in. We match each other's decibels, growing louder and louder until neither of us can stop. Fuelling each other's fire.

After a while, we have zero clue what we are even laughing about and are purely laughing at how hard the other is laughing. I am sure I even heard her snort.

I have never had this with anyone before. The uncontrollable laughs, the comfort, the ease. No one else would find any of our shit funny, or even understand what the hell we are going on about. But we always seem to end up in absolute hysterics over the dumbest shit. I love that about us. Love that about her.

"Where's your mum?" I ask after we calm down and make our way to the couch.

"Oh no, she's at work till ten," she says with such fake shock horror.

"Oh dear, whatever will your parents do?" she adds as she places the back of her hand on her forehead in pure dramatics.

"Shut it," I say, throwing a cushion at her head. Then we start cackling again. We are interrupted by the door and our Chinese arriving. We make our way back to the lounge and start flicking through the movies, opening up the Chinese containers as we go.

She is picking absolute trash, so I snatch the remote from her. I flick through some selections before landing on one.

"Oh, remember this movie, yesss, let's watch this," I say as I click the icon to go into the movie.

13

5,4,3,2,1

*S*uddenly I am frozen, locked in my seat as if I am paralysed. I don't fully understand the way the human brain works. How a sound or a smell can trigger an old memory that unleashes a wave of emotion. Emotions and feelings that have your physical body frozen.

They are giving us steps to help with this in group therapy. The counsellor has given us some tips to deal with this kind of anxiety. I can't calm myself down enough to remember. Was it five things I can see, four I can hear, or shit, was it feel, or colours? Supposedly it makes you aware of your physical body again.

The only colour I can see is the green of his eyes. All I can smell is grease mixed with his cologne. All I feel is his rough, big hands on my skin, burning me up alive. He is everywhere but nowhere at the same time. It feels like I am back there. It is me and him, he and I. Just the two of us.

It plays out in front of me as if Blake just selected the movie that is my past. Little pictures of us dancing across the screen.

I had just turned twelve and had asked my mum if I could go to the movies with a couple of friends for my birthday. The local cinemas were doing a month of re-runs of older movies. My friends and I were dying to go. It was one of the first things I remember Mum allowing me to do by myself since we moved to the new town.

She had been so excited about me making friends, she practically jumped out of her skin. She had dropped me and two girlfriends off at the local cinemas in the afternoon, loaded up with a heap of home-made snacks so we could avoid the lines and not have to spend a fortune that I knew we didn't have. A Ziplock bag each with a couple of brownies. Another with popcorn and another with lollies.

We had been chatting and laughing so much that I almost didn't see him. He was sitting with a couple of friends a few seats in front of us. The lights from the projector flicked colours through his wavy hair.

His friends were loud and obnoxious, throwing popcorn at a group of girls in front of them. He sat quietly. He was like that at school too. Vin, I had learnt his name was. He was in my year, but besides the two friends he was with now, I never saw him talking to anyone else.

I had been living next door to him for just over six months, and aside from stolen glances that lingered a little too long, sideways smirks or nods of acknowledgment in the hallways, we had not spoken a single word to each other.

But there was a faint electric pull between us. Something that always had us making eye contact in the halls or across the driveway. Something that always had me finding him in the large school cafeteria crowded with others.

As if that current buzzed between us, calling him, he turned around and locked eyes with me. I could have sworn there was a little sparkle in them when they connected with mine. His hair had gotten longer since we first arrived, like he hadn't cut it since. Chunky curls framed his face.

He gave me a side smile before turning back to the screen. Then he got up and walked back down the steps. My eyes followed him as he went down and around the corner to head out the doors. I didn't say anything to my friends, who had not even registered that he was there.

I was lost in my own thoughts, barely watching the lights start to dim and the screen open wider as the ads started. He came back up the stairs, his long legs taking the steps two at a time. He was holding a massive box of popcorn. Only he didn't stop at the row with his friends. He walked straight past them, headed towards us. Towards me.

I started to feel my cheeks heat up and thanked the stars that it was now dark enough that he would not see. My palms started to feel sweaty, and I wiped them on my jeans, trying to dry them off.

We had never spoken before. I saw him each and every day at home and at school, and not a word. Yet now he was headed straight towards me.

"Here," he said as he stretched his arm towards me with the box of popcorn.

"What's this?" I said, having to crank my neck to look up at his tall frame from my seat.

"You can't come to the movies and not get popcorn," he said as he stretched his arm further, forcing me to grab the box before it dropped right in my lap.

"We have snacks," I replied shyly, holding up my Ziplock bag with the popcorn in it. That looked somewhat pitiful now in comparison to this giant box of hot, buttered popcorn.

He simply chuckled at me, then turned around to walk back to his seat. My friends started to giggle.

"I didn't know you were friends with him," Janelle said.

"I didn't know either," I replied.

"Who cares, it's free popcorn," Mikaela said as she grabbed a massive handful and started shovelling it into her mouth.

We all started laughing as the ads finally finished and the movie started. I smiled at him as he turned back around one last time. Although I spent the majority of the movie staring holes into the back of his head, I didn't see his face again, not until later that night.

14

Animals within the stars

SCARLET

*M*um had picked me up and dropped my friends off, and as we turned onto our street I saw him again, riding his bike home. The sun was starting to set, as it was May and coming into winter now. The weather was cooler, and I could see him pedalling fast, fighting against the wind, his hair blowing back, tangled up in it like a storm cloud.

I didn't know Vin's dad's name, but I knew he was a big guy whose face always wore a scowl. He seemed to have a beer can permanently fixed to his gigantic hand, and he liked to yell. A lot. My mum had often made comments jokingly about him being a ray of sunshine after she bumped into him in the driveway. 'What a pleasant fellow he is,' she would say in her most sarcastic tone.

He didn't seem to work. Mum said something about him being on a pension. He kept to himself, and he kept our patch of lawn on his side of our driveway cut to perfection when he did his own. So, Mum wasn't complaining.

He was standing out on the driveway with a beer in one hand and his other in his jeans pocket. We turned into our driveway, and I watched as Vin slowed down on his bike. He pulled up into his own driveway. His cheeks were flushed, and for a brief moment I thought I saw a look of worry slide over his features.

Vin chucked his bike down by the tree in the front yard and walked up towards the house. His dad followed close behind him as they disappeared into the house. The door closed behind them with a slam.

"Scarlet," Mum said, shaking me from the glare I had on the now closed front door. She had been asking me a heap of questions about the movie the whole way home and listened intently as I explained the story play by play.

Without even realizing, I had gone completely silent once I saw Vin riding his bike.

"Sorry Mum," I said as I shook my head, shaking the image of him from my mind.

"Do you speak to him much at school?" she asked.

She had noticed who I was staring at.

"No, he keeps to himself," I replied as I grabbed my bag and got out of the car before heading for our own front door. We ate dinner and talked about nothing in particular.

I don't remember when the conversation stopped with mum or when we finished eating and moved from the kitchen table to the lounge. Or when I finally said goodnight and got into bed. But I do remember the rest of the night as clear as a cloudless sky. As if I am still sitting on that couch watching it unfold on the screen.

I was woken later that night when the noise had died down, the TV was off and the crickets were chirping outside my window. I always loved to sleep with the blinds open. I loved looking out and up at the stars.

The moonlight cast shadows over my room, and I looked out to see light flashing and dancing across the sky. It was coming from next door, from what looked like the backyard. The light was green and looked like a laser pointer. A strong single beam, dancing in the sky above.

I threw a jumper over my tank top and tracksuit and crept out my room down the hall to the back sliding door. The grass was cold and dewy under my feet. I had no idea what time of night it was. I walked down to the side of the yard where there were breaks in the fence between the wooden panels.

I could see his outline lying on a trampoline, a mass of black darker than the rest, knees bent over the edge with his feet dangling down. He had a small laser light in his hand that he was shining up, moving it around, tracing stars.

He seemed smaller somehow, lying there in the dark. I turned to walk away. But my foot tripped on the garden edging, and I banged into the fence with a thud. He turned towards the fence, and even though I knew he most likely could not see me, it felt like he was looking straight at me.

I froze, unable to look away, unable to move, unable to breathe. He, however, did not share my deer-in-the-head-lights response as he jumped from the trampoline and walked towards the fence with long strides. I held my breath as he approached, wanting to turn and run and deny ever being there, but something was making me stay. Something had my feet glued to the ground.

"Scar," he said softly, far softer than I remembered his voice being at the movies what felt like a lifetime ago now. No one had ever called me that. Scar. I liked it.

I let out the breath I had been holding in. "Yeah."

"What are you doing up so late?"

"I could ask you the same thing."

"I couldn't sleep. When I can't sleep, I like to make patterns and shapes out of the stars in the sky with the light."

"What kind of patterns?"

"Come, I'll show you," he said as he kicked one of the wooden panels hard enough for it to finish coming away from the frame. It made a loud noise, but he didn't seem to flinch as he pushed it across, opening a section big enough for me to slide through into his yard.

I know I probably should have just gone back to the house and back to bed. But something in me couldn't move anywhere but towards him. He put his hand out to help me through the gate. I placed mine in his, and he steadied me through the little gap in the fence into his backyard.

He didn't let go of my hand as he led me towards the trampoline.

He dropped my hand as he pulled himself up backwards to sit on the edge. He made it look so easy, and when I tried to do the same, I almost fell flat on my face. I tried again, this time opting to climb up forwards, and he held his hand out again for me to grab to help haul myself up.

My hand felt tiny in his, and he pulled me up with little effort until I was seated next to him on the trampoline. It was dark, but I could see him easily enough, a light from the back patio shining a glow over us. I could see welts all over his upper arms and shoulders, exposed by his singlet, and what looked like small bits of blood drying across each one.

Almost like he had been splattered with a paint brush. Something in me instinctively reached out to touch where it looked swollen. He jerked away from me, creating a space between us that hadn't been there before.

I froze, unsure of what I was even trying to do. My hand remained stuck in mid-air like I was holding an imaginary object in my fingers. He looked away from me and let out a deep breath that had been holding him rigid. Then he re-laxed and turned back towards me. A crooked smile split across his face, like he didn't have a care in the world.

I moved my hand again, sweeping my fingers across his arm. I could feel the raised bumps and lumps.

"What happened?" I asked, my words a whisper I wasn't sure he could even hear.

He huffed and shrugged his shoulders, amused almost. "He likes the belt, guess cos it's always on hand," he said with such ease, like it was the most normal thing in the world. Like I would know exactly what he was talking about.

I didn't; I was so confused. "What! He hits you?" I asked, my voice shrill and breaking, shocked by his admission. He didn't say anything in reply, he just looked up at the sky. I moved my hand over the welts again, and he didn't shy away. This time he almost moved closer. Into my touch. Like it soothed his pain.

These were not from a normal belt. These were stripes of welts, maybe marks from the leather, but the ends were rigid, and the skin was ripped and bleeding. Like he had used the metal buckle of the belt rather than just the leather. The pin had dug holes in Vin's skin.

A sharp breath caught in my lungs, and my lips moved to start to speak. But I had no idea what I would even say. Instead, I ran my hand down his arm and placed my hand in his. Our fingers intertwined, and he squeezed gently in what felt like a thank you.

Then he let go, like he had never been touched so gently and didn't know what to do with such affection. He flopped back on the trampoline, aiming the laser at the sky again.

"I'm getting pretty good at connecting the dots with the stars to make animals, wanna see?" I lay down next to him, going with the change of subject.

Our legs touched before our knees bent and dangled off the trampoline. His were so much longer than mine.

"So, what did you think of the movie Twister?" He asked as he started using the laser to connect lines from star to star. We started talking about the movie, recalling our favourite parts. He laughed when I told him I was scared.

I had no clue how long we were out there for. The last thing I remember was him making an animal with the stars and me guessing it was a horse before I fell asleep where we lay. When the morning sun started to rise and woke us both, *we were almost in the same position. Although at some point, without me realising, he had slid his arm under my head for me to use as a pillow. In the morning light, his arms looked so much worse. They were red and swollen, with dried blood crusted all over them.*

"We must've fallen asleep," I said as he started to get up, helping me up as well.

"Sorry," he said, looking worried.

"It's ok. Are you ok?" I asked, reaching my hand out to touch the raised skin again.

"I'm all good," he said. "You better go, if he sees you here it'll be worse." He jumped down from the trampoline. He extended a hand for me to take, and I used it to help myself down. He walked me back to the fence and pulled the panel across.

"See you at school," he said as I slipped through the opening and back into my yard. The wood crashed back into place as he let it go, and I quickly snuck back into my bed until it was time to get ready for school.

Now I sit frozen, like the couch is trying to swallow me whole. A different man sitting next to me, a similar comfort. I try to shake the image from my mind. The welts and dried blood and the truth of what he said to me in the dark of that night. The feel of his ripped skin under my fingers, which I swear I can still feel on my fingertips. My hand in his and the warmth where our legs touched.

My own mind feels exactly like I am stuck in one of those twisters from that movie, images and thoughts spinning around and around and around, unable to settle. How he was so ok with what had happened to him. How he still laughed and joked. How we talked and how easy and comfortable it felt even at that age.

I blink at the TV now in front of me. The screen with the image of a large twister, two people clutching each other running and the large *TWISTER* writing in red across the top. I let out the breath I have been holding and lay my head back on the couch cushion behind me.

I can feel the burn of tears start to form behind my eyes, and I squeeze them shut tightly, willing them to disappear.

They oblige, and when I open them again, I am all too painfully aware of Blake staring at me. He has placed a hand on my knee, and he gives it a gentle squeeze.

15

Relishing in honesty

BLAKE

"I didn't realize you were afraid of twisters." I say it with a smirk, but I keep gently squeezing her knee with my hand for comfort. She looks like she is gonna throw up. It isn't uncommon for her to zone out.

Sometimes we will be midway through a sentence and she will just totally space out. Go white, blank stare. I never probed her for what was happening. Obviously it has something to do with why she was in group sessions in the first place.

She was never able to talk in those sessions, so I don't want to push her to talk to me now. But this time looked different. More intense; she seemed to completely disappear from her own body, like she was somewhere else entirely.

She doesn't answer my question, but her colour is starting to return to her face, and her breathing is starting to return to normal.

"Where do you go Scarlet, when that happens? What happened to you?"

She lets out a stifled breath. It sounds like she is going to burst into tears, but then stops herself. She brings her hands up to cover her mouth and rubs them over her face. I grab both her hands with my own and pull them down to her lap. She shifts to face me a bit more, and I do the same.

"Talk to me, Scarlet," I say.

"Why, it's not like you talk to me Blake?" she snaps. "You are a puppet who just does whatever your parents say, and you seem miserable doing it, so don't talk to me about opening up or talking about my feelings, we don't need to get that deep."

I've never heard her get upset before. Especially not directed towards me. The forcefulness of it shocks me, and to be honest, makes me a little angry myself. Before I can fully register what is happening, I snap back, which is so unlike me as well.

"I am not a puppet Scarlet. I think I am gay!" I blurt it out before I can even register what is happening. I fold my lips in and bite them down with my teeth, as if I can suck the words back in and swallow them whole.

I expect her to pull her hands away from me, I expect her to say 'WHAT THE FUCK!' To yell, to tell me to get the fuck out of her house. To call me a freak. Tell me how disgusting I am. I have never uttered these words about myself out loud before.

What I don't expect is for her face to soften, the anger to drain. For her to squeeze my hand in hers.

I also don't expect the tension that releases from my body as those words slip past my lips. It washes over me, and I can feel my chest unknot. Muscles uncoil. The caged animal in me looks like he is relishing in this honesty. He is now pacing back and forth with long strides, enjoying his newfound freedom, raising his front legs as if to claw his way free.

16

Buried truths

I do not know what to say or do. I spent pretty much my entire childhood comforting another hurting human. But that was so different.

That was Vin; I knew him better than I knew myself. We basically grew up together. I knew what he needed, how to react, how to make him feel better. It was easy to be there for him.

Blake, I have no clue. I feel like I have known him forever. Truth be told, I have not; it has only been a year. A great year of friendship. Best friends. But we never really got that deep. I didn't know if he needed to be left alone, to be comforted, to hear a joke; hell I had no clue. But he said, I THINK I am gay. So is he or isn't he?

I am so confused, and the look on his face makes me realise he is just as confused by his feelings as I am. I mean, being gay is a non-issue for me. It doesn't change the person he is. The friend he has become to me. The feelings I have for him. In fact, it makes a hell of a lot of sense.

Why I never saw him date. Some of the things he said over the course of the year starts flooding back to me, all clicking into place in a bit of an aha moment.

In my mind and experience, there are far worse people in the world than some dude who likes other dudes. I don't understand why Blake is so worked up about telling people. Why it affects him so much. So, I stay still, not saying anything, just holding his hand.

My mind is racing with what to say, how I can help him. All I can come up with is, "What do you mean you think?"

He stares at our hands together for the longest time.

"Do you feel anything?" he finally asks.

"What do you mean?"

"Do you feel anything, between us I mean. I am holding your hand and we often do this, or hug, sit close together. But do you feel anything, lust, a spark, anything?" He pauses for a minute, then keeps talking.

"You're beautiful, Scarlet. I look at you and I think, yeah, she is attractive, gorgeous really. I see the way other guys look at you. But I don't feel butterflies, or anything…you know…" He stops like he is really struggling with the conversation.

"You don't want to have sex with me." I feel like he needs help with the words.

"No, I don't. I don't feel anything at all besides the fact that I can acknowledge that you are attractive. I don't feel any other urges or excitement towards you."

I am not sure if I should be offended or appreciative. I feel the same, but I am damaged goods.

"Maybe I am just not your type. Try blondes, I hear they have more fun." He starts laughing as he pulls his hands from mine and flops back on the couch.

"I've always felt different about it. When the other boys started talking about porn and girls, honestly, it just wasn't there for me. But I've been too terrified to explore it more."

"So, you've never had sex with a guy?" I ask.

"I've never had sex full stop," he replies.

"So what have you tried?" I am less shocked and more curious. My sexual experience has been limited to one guy and one guy only, and I'm not sure I will ever feel ok with anyone else.

"I've kissed girls, that's it. But it did nothing for me."

"What about gay porn? Have you tried that?"

"No."

I am not sure where I am going with this line of questioning. I really care about Blake, he is the only friend I have made in town. He is funny, smart and kind. I also think he is attractive.

Dark features with a bright smile. He doesn't look typically gay, I suppose. Although I am not sure what that even looks like. But he is manly looking, and he doesn't care about fashion or skin care. But is that a token of being gay? I really have no clue.

I also can't fully understand why he hasn't tried to explore it more. Why he hasn't been with a guy at his age yet.

"WHY NOT?" I blurt out a bit more forcefully than I intended.

"My parents, my upbringing."

He starts snacking on the snacks laid out around us, and as he does, he starts telling me about how in his family it is considered a sin. How his parents and the church community he grew up in would never accept him. How he watched a girl who was caught kissing a girl be shipped off to some boarding school church camp to have the gay supposedly taught out of her. Like that is a thing. He tells me how she came home, a shell of the human she once was. She committed suicide three months later.

He truly, wholeheartedly is afraid of what his family will think and do. He is convinced he could never tell them the truth or even explore what that truth is for him. He tells me how he has always felt different, and deep down, always knew but felt sick to his stomach about it.

How he felt like he was doing something incredibly sinful just for having the thoughts he had about other guys. He tried to bury the feelings and push them aside.

He tells me how he thought that maybe if he spent enough time with girls or eventually got a girlfriend, he would develop feelings towards them in that way. As if it is a shitty vegetable that grows on you if you force it down enough. Just like when your parents tell you to keep trying different foods because your palate changes as you grow older. Nope! Pretty sure everyone still hates Brussels sprouts.

He talks about how, as he got older and realised his feelings weren't changing, he just distanced himself from people. To make sure the truth never slipped. So that no one could get close enough to know the real him. On the outside, he was a good, god-fearing young man, on his way to be a doctor. Inside he was gagged. Afraid he would never live up to his parents' expectations. In love and lust with things he believed his family would never understand.

I want to share in his openness, to talk to him, to trust him the way he is trusting me, but my secrets are too deeply buried and too dangerous.

So I tell Blake parts, carefully curated parts. Parts that I have never shared with anyone. It feels all too vulnerable, and I can feel myself slipping. Feel it bubbling up inside me about to spill. I have to shut it down. I tell Blake how I felt for Vin, that he is gone, and that I lost the one love of my life.

I truly don't believe I will love again, and I don't want to. If not Vin, I want no one.

Maybe a little emotional, maybe a little high on sugar, we decide we will be each other's beards. That we will go traveling and eventually get married. That we will never have to tell these truths to anyone else ever again.

We convince ourselves that this is the only way forward for us. Two best friends. We tell each other it will be enough.

By the time Blake's curfew rolls around and he grabs his stuff to leave, we have planned a whole Contiki tour, a lavender marriage, and a whole life that would be a lie based on two people's unfortunate buried truths.

17

Break mine, I'll break yours

SCARLET

Step one of our plan is to save for our trip and wedding. We are not planning on telling anyone and just coming home married. Eloping in Vegas. Blake says his parents will absolutely lose their minds when we do tell them, but he feels this is the best way.

A wedding here would be too much. Firstly, his parents would try to talk him out of it. Stage an intervention or something along those lines. Secondly, if they do come around, they would want it in a church with all the bells and whistles. Blake wouldn't feel comfortable lying in front of a room full of people and God. Elvis in a little white chapel would be far more our style. We assure ourselves it won't feel like as much of a lie that way.

I don't earn a great deal as an apprentice, and I pay Mum rent and utilities, have my phone bill, a small car loan, fuel, insurance and a Netflix subscription. I don't do much else with my money, but it doesn't leave a lot to save each week.

Blake's parents have him on a pretty short leash. They earn enough to support him and want him focusing on his studies and his volunteer work at the church. They pay for everything at home, including his car, fuel and phone. He has a card he can use for any other expenses, but they go through the statements with a fine-toothed comb. They would notice if he draws money to save it. He may be able to take out bits and pieces of cash here and there, but large amounts would be questioned.

His parents definitely would not approve if he tells them he wants a job, as it would disrupt his studies. He has, however, managed to get a job behind their backs. It's at a busy cafe just down the road from his university, which is about an hour's drive from where we live. He commutes back and forth each day.

It's easy enough for him to tell his parents he is at the uni library or studying with classmates while he is actually taking afternoon and early morning shifts at the cafe.

We try our best to work out a little budget to see how long it would take us to save what we need.

"At this rate, we will be going on our trip when we are ninety," I say, feeling defeated.

"Come on, it's not that bad." We worked out that we need about eleven and a half thousand just for flights and accommodation for the trip we want to do.

It would consist of a twenty-one-day Contiki tour from LA to Miami, then we would make our own way to New York, then to Buffalo to see Niagara Falls, over to Vancouver, then back to Vegas to get married, and then home.

We need spending money as well. It's going to take us years to save the amount we need.

"Maybe we should just do a smaller trip. Less days, or try and book it all ourselves without the tour group. It might be cheaper," I say as I start to flick through some of the other Contiki options.

"We can have a look at costs to do it all ourselves, but the whole thing of the Contiki tour is that you meet people straight away. I know with my parents, I am going to get one shot at this. They are going to be pissed, so if I am doing it, I want to do it properly. I'd rather wait and save what we need and do it exactly how we want."

That makes sense. The most expensive flight is getting to LA from Western Australia. Once we are over there, internal flights and buses are relatively cheap, and we can save on accommodation by sharing rooms and staying in mixed dorms at hostels. But the Contiki just covers it all. Flights, accommodation, breakfasts and dinners. All with a group of people.

"What if we get stuck with someone in the group we don't like?" I ask, chuckling.

Blake starts to laugh. "It will be fine, we will have each other, and if it takes us two years to save the amount we need... Well, we also have each other in the meantime."

I suppose he is right. It would give us time to start 'dating' for all intents and purposes. Allow people to believe the narrative when we come home from our trip as husband and wife.

We look down at the final figure. "I could get a second job," I say.

"I saw McDonald's are hiring," Blake says, taking a bite of his sandwich. Just the sound of that name makes my skin crawl.

"I don't know if I can work there," I reply, suddenly feeling very off my own lunch.

"The hours would work well for you, as you could do nights and weekends around your apprenticeship." I take a deep breath, trying to force the lump that has formed in my throat down a little bit. A lump that wasn't caused by the food, but rather by a very morbid memory that is threatening to be revived.

The last time I had McDonald's.

My mind starts to swarm with the memory. My breath is catching, and I swear I can hear his deep voice yelling. As if he is right here. It sends a shiver down my spine.

"WHO BROKE IT?! WHICH ONE OF YOU ASSHOLES WAS IT?! HUH? LOOK AT ME, DON'T LOOK AT HER, WHO THE FUCK BROKE THE FUCKING VASE?!"

It was just a vase, and it wasn't even an expensive one. I had seen the exact same ones in Kmart. They were like fifteen dollars including some fake flowers.

I remembered it because I thought it was pretty. I had seen it while hanging out at the shops with some friends a few weekends ago. White with little ridges in three lines around the neck. It had a handle and a little spout like a water jug. The letters 'F L O W E R S' engraved on the front. Just in case you weren't sure what to do with it, or people needed reminding of what was in it.

Now Mike, Vin's dad, was screaming as if we had just broken an ancient artifact. One he had been keeping safe to eventually take on an antique road show and sell for millions.

Vin and I were standing next to each other in the lounge room. I was looking at Vin, trying to follow his lead on what to do.

After that night on the trampoline, we started talking and hanging out more and more, until we were basically inseparable. Small conversations at school and climbing his tree out the front or hanging on my hammock talking out the back of my house. Until there was hardly a moment where we weren't together.

We tended to hang at my house far more often. Mike was a bit of a loose cannon, and my mum didn't particularly like him. I had learnt that Mike would go from zero to one hundred on the anger scale in a matter of seconds. Truthfully, he scared the life out of me.

I never told my mum what Vin had told me that night. I never told anyone, not that Vin asked me to keep it a secret.

Honestly, I had no idea what to do with that kind of information. Vin had seemed completely fine the next day. Besides wearing a long-sleeved top or jumpers for a while, he hadn't seemed bothered. It was also coming into cooler weather, so no one questioned the warmer clothes.

I was too young to understand how bad it actually was or to really understand how problematic it was, that Vin was so used to it, that such a thing didn't even seem to affect him anymore.

Mike had been drinking heavily most of the day. Vin and I had been back and forth between our two houses. Mike had been watching TV, football or something with giant-looking men running around chasing a ball.

Mum had been home all day as well, cleaning and organising things around the house. She had said she needed to duck to the shops for a bit, and I said I was happy to stay. I was almost fourteen, so she was happy to leave me home for small amounts of time while she ran errands or did shopping.

Vin had told me more about Mike over the last year and a bit. I had witnessed enough at this point to understand what he was like. Vin had never shied away from showing me the aftermath or talking to me about what had happened, things he had always hidden from others.

On the surface, you would have never known what Vin was like on the inside. He showed me a very different side than what he showed at school or around others. To them, he was broody, quiet, even standoffish. To me, he was open and honest, playful and kind. My friends never really understood why I wanted to hang out with him so much, and my mum always just called him shy and reserved.

Vin had told me that Mike was ex-Army. We didn't completely understand then that Mike had PTSD from things he had seen and done, which caused him to be the way he was. To us at that age, he was just a crazy asshole.

Vin had told me that most of the time Mike would have a fit, scream and yell abuse, get distracted and lose his train of thought. Then he'd just leave it alone. So now we were trying to wait it out.

But Vin had also said that sometimes, Mike would be so engulfed in anger that he wouldn't even register what he was doing until it was too late. Well, today was the latter.

I think Vin realised his dad wasn't going to back down before I did. Which is why he did what he did. Vin was only just fourteen, but to me, he always seemed so much older. Maybe it was everything he had lived through that made him wiser. More savvy. More cautious.

Maybe he just knew Mike better. After all, it was his dad. He had years of dealing with this alone before I came into town.

We had only come back to Vin's house so he could pack a bag, as he was supposed to be headed to a friend's birthday later. Vin had stepped in front of me, as if his skinny frame could protect me from a missile. He was tall but lean, and I stepped closer to him, following his lead. I could see the thin muscles in his arms flex. He pinched his shoulder blades together and pushed his arms backwards, as if to encase me in a backwards hug, shielding my front with his body and my sides with his arms.

I took a deep breath, and as if we were in sync, I felt him do the same. I had no idea what was coming, but something in me told me Vin did.

Vin spoke confidently, unwavering.

"I did," he said. He must have done this dance a million times before, because he seemed so fearless. I, however, was shaking. My heart was pounding, and I wanted to grab Vin and run. I had always seen the aftermath, heard the yelling or the stories Vin told me, but I had never been right in it before. Not like this.

It happened so fast, I barely had time to even register what was going on. One minute Vin was standing in front of me, the next he was on the ground with Mike standing over him.

It ended pretty quickly once Mike heard the crack of the bone in Vin's arm. He stood frozen, as if the sound of the bone breaking had flicked a switch and he had come back from wherever he was in his mind to the present situation. He looked over at me, and I froze. Was I next? I wanted to run, but something wouldn't let me leave Vin.

His eyes flicked from me to Vin on the floor. Vin was holding his arm, crying out in pain. Mike looked down at him and simply said, "You break my shit, I'll break yours." Then he turned and walked off.

I collapsed on the ground next to Vin and pushed his wavy mop of hair from his eyes. He looked up at me through his thick lashes, wet with tears. Three words spilled out like he had rehearsed them.

"I'm all good," he said as he started to get up off the ground.

We knew his arm was broken, but Vin didn't want to go and tell my mum or ask for help. So, we stayed at his house for the afternoon, hiding out in his room.

Vin told his friend something came up and he wasn't going to make his party. We waited until we were sure Mike was well and truly passed out on the couch, in front of a blaring TV and an empty bottle of Jack's.

It was late afternoon, and I ran over to tell my mum we were going to ride our bikes into town. We both got on our bikes and rode the six kilometres to the emergency department, Vin with a broken arm.

He told the triage nurse he had fallen off his bike while trying to master a tail whip on his BMX. Of course the hospital called Mike, who didn't answer. They took Vin through and x-rayed his arm, and I was able to sit with him while they put his arm in a cast.

It was now getting late, and my mum had been messaging me nonstop, asking me when I was coming home. I finally caved and told her where we were. She had gone next door, woken Mike up and driven him to the hospital.

We left our bikes at the hospital to collect another day and all loaded into Mum's car. Mike didn't say a word. My Mum tried to make small talk, which fell on deaf ears. Vin and I sat in the back, the silent truth between us.

In an attempt to lighten the mood and because it was well past dinner time now, Mum suggested getting takeout. I quickly chimed in with my request for McDonald's.

Vin and I both ordered large cheese burger meals with extra nuggets, giant chocolate milkshakes and McFlurrys. I don't remember what Mike or my mum ordered, but I watched him eat in the car, like nothing had happened. Like hours earlier he was not pinning his fourteen-year-old son to the ground, breaking his arm for smashing a damn stupid Kmart vase worth fifteen dollars.

We ate our food as if it was our last meal. It didn't do much to quell my guilt and worry, though. Once we were home, Vin and Mike walked across to their house with not much more than a bye and thank you.

Mum mentioned how irresponsible Mike was for being too drunk to collect his son, and she told me she didn't want me over there when he was drinking.

I nodded, but I didn't tell her that he was always drinking. I went straight to my room to bed. Although I couldn't sleep, I lay in bed full and warm. Unharmed. I stared at the ceiling, playing what happened over and over in my head.

I could almost feel Vin doing the exact same thing in his room in the house across the lawn. I swear I could feel his energy, restless, unsettled and in pain.

Even though we never spoke the words out loud, we both knew that broken arm should have been mine.

In the safety of the pitch black, so that the darkness could carry the words away with the night, I spoke the words that escaped me earlier that day. When the sun rose, they would be far, far away.

"I broke the vase." I had swung Vin's backpack over my shoulder while he was headed back to his room to grab something else. As I swung it up, it knocked the vase off the hall table.

I was a coward, and I had caused that broken arm. Vin was hurt because of me!

A single tear escapes and starts running down my cheek. I only notice when Blake swipes a gentle finger across my face to wipe it away. I reach up and take his hand in mine, not saying a single word for the longest time.

Finally, I can feel the emotions start to wash away as I focus on the kind brown eyes in front of me. A different face, softer. I focus on the life we are planning together. The trip of a lifetime.

"I'll go grab an application when we leave here."

18

Return to sender

"You writing a letter?" Blake asks me as he walks over to the table I am sitting at. I work every Saturday at the salon, but it is closed every Monday, so I have a rostered day off. Blake only has one lecture on Mondays but has told his parents it's a full day. He then works the rest of the day at the cafe.

On Sunday night, I worked the night shift at McDonald's. Waking at midday on Monday, I decided to catch the train and a bus to Blake's cafe to just hang out till he finished. He could then drive me home.

It has been a quiet afternoon at the cafe, so his boss said he could knock off early. We are now going to head to the shops in the city to buy some things for the trip.

We still haven't told either of our parents about it, and now it's getting closer and closer. We have booked and paid for the Contiki tour through the USA as well as the additional flights and accommodation to head to Canada and then back to Vegas. We also added a wedding package at The Little White Chapel.

I'm starting to panic about the whole thing now. We've never blatantly said that we are a couple, but it is definitely implied. Blake's parents don't seem thrilled that he is spending so much time with me. They don't want him dating until he finishes his studies. They've never said anything, but I get the impression they don't love the fact that I am in group therapy and am a hairdresser and not at university working to get a more 'honourable' job in their eyes.

My mum tried to talk to me about Blake, but I shot up my wall so fast she was propelled back like a crash test dummy. I couldn't start down that line with her, or my whole web of lies would start to unravel, unearthing truths I could never share. Not even with Blake.

"I know it's stupid," I reply, somewhat defeated. "But it's somehow therapeutic. It's like journaling, I suppose." He nods like he understands.

"Are you going to write while we are away?" he asks.

I sigh.

"I don't know yet."

Blake doesn't say anything. He just smiles at me.

Blake is like that, though. He never forces me to speak more than I want to. He never tries to get me to talk about things I don't want to.

I love that about him. About us.

"Vin would love that I'm doing this trip though. We always planned to travel," I say.

I feel hot, and my stomach drops at the thought of it. Planning this trip with Blake, a trip I had planned to take with Vin, is bringing up a hell of a lot of feelings.

I remember Vin and I used to talk for hours about where we wanted to go. How we would leave Australia and go and snorkel in the Bahamas, gamble in Vegas and go shopping in New York. We used to buy travel magazines from the deli down the street.

We would ride our bikes home and sit on my bed for hours, cutting out pictures of beautiful people sipping beautiful drinks on beautiful beaches. We would make up stories as if that was us and we had just returned from a shopping spree on the boulevard, relaxing with a drink in our hand and our feet in the white sand.

Some of the wild scenarios we created had us talking in different accents and laughing until we could not breathe.

I squashed these dreams under the mattress and buried them deep down in the very pit of my soul. I didn't speak or even dare think of them again for a long time. I never believed it would be a reality. My reality. Just a reality with a different guy.

The red-hot guilt washes over me again. The closer the trip gets, the more I start to feel it. Blake senses me getting uncomfortable.

"I think you should tell him, tell him all about it."

April, the counsellor at the church sessions, actually gave me the idea to write to Vin. I eventually started to see her individually, and while I never told her even half of the truths I'm hiding, I told her enough for her to help me with some healing techniques.

She said it would be a healing experience to write it down and post it. Like getting it all out and then sending it away. It sounded ridiculous if I was being honest, but I decided to try it anyway.

So now I have been writing these letters every month for almost two and a half years. Twenty-eight letters in total. Each and every one came back to me with a big red, 'RETURN TO SENDER!' stamped across the envelope.

I definitely was not expecting them to come back to me. I don't know what I was expecting, to be honest. The first letter I got back felt like a stab in the chest.

I had come home from work to find it on the kitchen bench. My mum must have checked the mail. I was grateful she had respected my privacy enough to not open it nor ask questions about it.

I picked it up and turned it over and over in my hand. I then slept with it under my pillow that entire week. I don't know why, but in a strange way, it made me feel close to him again.

Then I put it in a box and put it under my bed. The next month, I grabbed a pen and paper and wrote him again, almost as if I had forgotten the pain of receiving the first letter back.

I counted the days. I dropped the letter at the post box early on a Monday morning. Worst case, it went over east in Tuesday's batch from our local post office. A day to get to the city sorting centre. Five days to get across the country. Add in some sorting days in Sydney, plus some days for contingency.

I marked it on the calendar and checked each day off with a red pen. One down, two down, one week, two weeks. Sure enough, just like before, it was returned with a big 'RETURN TO SENDER!' stamp in bold red block letters.

I continued to write.

Each and every letter was returned. RETURN TO SENDER!

With every return, it felt like a piece of me died all over again. Then somehow, I don't remember when exactly, it started to become a form of therapy, exactly like April said it would. Like keeping a diary. I would write the letter:

Vin,

You have to know how sorry I am. If I could take it all back I would. You have to know that I never forgot about you. And I never will. I will never stop loving you.

I began each letter the same way. Then I would write about my life, what was happening. How I was going. Sometimes the letters would read like a very mundane autobiography in real time.

Only he never got them. He never knew how sorry I was, and I can't take it all back. But still, like clockwork,

I would drop them off in the red post box and wait with
bated breath for them to come back to me. Then it would
join the others in the box, collecting dust under my bed.

Only now a little piece of me doesn't die when I get
these letters back. Now it is like a little piece of me is being
returned and put back in place.

19

Playing the long game

BLAKE

I know who she has been writing to. I see how it's help-ing her get her feelings out and deal with her past. I've never really asked what she writes about; I've never tried to read the letters or ask to see them. That's her business.

Just like I have my own demons and issues. I don't want her poking around in my head, that's for sure. I just let her be her and do her thing and vice versa.

Our friendship, our fake relationship is perfect. We have the best time together, but it's also so much more than that. We truly understand each other. We have shared our pains and truths, although I still feel Scarlet holding back at times. But I know she will tell me in her own time.

She is truly the only person I can be myself with. My true self. She has helped me come out of my comfort zone so much over the last few years, even helping me sneak out and meet guys. Slowly but surely, she freed the caged animal inside of me. Even though he still has to be locked up around my parents, she has created so much freedom and space for me to be me.

I will never be able to thank her enough for that. We are playing the long game. I know it seems crazy, but I know I will never be able to show the real me to my parents and the rest of the world. So, a lavender marriage to Scarlet is the perfect cover. The perfect way we both get what we want and need. It will work.

It has taken us two years to save for this trip, but that's ok. We got through it together, and now it is within reach. We are really doing this.

Once I am married, I know my parents will back off a bit. I will be able to move in with Scarlet, and then I will finally have some sense of freedom and space from them. Maybe even be able to move out of town.

They expect far too much from me, and it's soul crushing. Be kind, be smart, be faithful, become a doctor, work hard, be charitable, get married, have kids, white picket fence and all that shit.

It just isn't me. I hate every waking minute at university. I am smart; years of private education, tutors and no social life will do that to you.

I have no interest in being a doctor. I don't know what I want to do, but it isn't to volunteer at the church and work every moment until I die.

Don't get me wrong, I don't hate the church completely. I just hate that it makes me feel so conflicted with my own feelings. That it makes me hate who I really am.

I want to get away from it all, and I feel like once I am married, my parents will finally see me as my own man, and I may be able to make my own decisions.

Scarlet walking into that church has been the best thing that ever happened to me. I feel bad thinking that, due to the circumstances that led her to me. But if that makes me selfish, then so fucking be it. I will be selfish. Because I need her. My caged animal needs her.

20

It's all my fault and no one knows

SCARLET

We pull into the shopping centre after leaving the cafe and decide to head to Kmart. They have the cheapest clothes, and I want to grab some travel-size containers for my toiletries and suitcases.

We start making our way towards Kmart, and suddenly I am stopped dead in my tracks. We walk past Myer, and the perfume section is right at the front of the store.

The scents of the colognes are making their way out the large open space, but one scent seems to travel faster than the rest. The smell makes my heart skip a beat and my knees go wobbly.

Guided by scent and nothing else, I walk blindly towards it like a zombie. It is woody but not musky. Strong but not overpowering. It has a masculine scent underneath the freshness.

To me, it smells like summer rain on a hot day in a field of flowers. I can't even remember what the cologne is called now, but I know the smell of it. I could pick it out of a sea of people. I am vaguely aware of Blake following a few steps behind me.

"Are you buying for your special someone?" the store attendant asks. I stare at her blankly like I don't understand the question. She repeats herself as if I didn't hear it.

"Are you looking for a present?" I ignore her completely now, not trying to be rude, but just focused on the scent and the shape of the familiar bottle on the shelf.

Somehow, without being fully in control, I pick the bottle up. I am turning it over and over in my hand. Then I bring it to my nose and breathe in the scent.

The store attendant grabs a little cardboard tag from the shelf.

"May I," she says, and she gestures to take the bottle from my hand. I lift my gaze from the bottle to look at her, but I say nothing as she takes it and sprays some on the tag.

"Nice choice," Blake says as he moves in closer to me and grabs the cardboard tab from the sales assistant's hand.

He passes it over to me to smell, but I don't need to take it. I already know the scent. I already know what it smells like under my nose, on his skin, on his clothes. I know the lingering smell of it in the air. I already know what this smell means to me. The part of my life it embodies. The chapter that is now closed, left gathering dust high up on a bookshelf.

I am still not in control of my actions or words. I am being pulled by strings. I am nothing but a puppet at the mercy of my master.

I see it happening in slow motion. An out-of-body experience. I am powerless to stop it or slow it down. There is no point in fighting it. I have already lost.

We walk out of Myer, not saying anything to each other. Blake doesn't ask any questions about why I bought a men's cologne. He just followed my lead as I took the box to the counter and paid. It dawns on me how strange it is that after all these years, I still remember the cologne he used to wear. Possibly even more strange, that in all the years since, I never smelt that scent again, until now.

I have no intention of ever giving this bottle to anyone, not even Blake. I actually have no clue what I am even going to do with it. I have to laugh to myself. If I don't laugh, I will start to cry.

"You ok?" Blake asks as I start to chuckle.

"It was what he always used to wear," I reply, looking up from the bag, meeting Blake's cool dark eyes.

"Planning this trip is bringing up a lot for you, isn't it," he states more than asks.

"I really didn't expect it to. If I am being honest, I thought I was doing ok. Thought that part of my life was behind me. I guess because we always used to talk about traveling together. We never got the chance, and a part of me feels really guilty about that."

"That's not your fault," Blake says, grabbing my hand, prying it from the bag with the cologne and holding it in his. I smile at him, and he releases my hand and slings his arm easily over my shoulder. It feels comfortable having him this close to me. I don't say anything else because, what could I say?

It was my fault. All my fault, and no one knew.

21

More than friends

SCARLET

The drive home back to Mandurah is quiet. I sit staring out the window, clutching the bag with the cologne. Blake never once lets my hand go. He doesn't ask any questions or try to get me to talk. Just holds onto my hand and lets me be.

We get home well after dinner time, and he walks me to the front door, giving me a kiss on the forehead before leaving to head home himself.

I say a quick hello to my mum and go straight to my room. I open up the bag and cardboard box that houses the cologne. I can smell the faint scent of it without opening the lid. Deciding that holding the open bottle up to my nose is not enough, I spray it all over my bed. All over my pillowcase and comforter and all over me. I am choking on it. But I don't care. What a way to go. I'd happily drown in this cologne if it brings even a fragment of him back to me. I collapse into the bed, drinking in the scent before drifting off to sleep.

I don't remember the first time Vin and I decided we were more than neighbours, more than friends. Honestly, no one ever said the words boyfriend and girlfriend. No one asked the other. It was kind of just implied, and we just seemed to become inseparable.

You didn't see one without the other. Everyone just kind of grew to know we were together, and that was it. I was fifteen, and it was coming up to our year ten formal dance. Vin had decided this was his last year of school and had an apprenticeship lined up at a local mechanic for the start of next year.

He had been doing work experience there one day a week through a school program and was a natural at it. The owner Clark loved Vin and had offered him casual work on a Saturday to help around the garage before he would start his apprenticeship in the new year.

Vin absolutely loved it. Not just because it kept him away from home more and away from Mike. I think for the first time, he had another male influence in his life that didn't just see him as a giant inconvenience or punching bag.

I never saw him happier than when he was learning about or working on cars.

It was a Saturday, and he was doing a morning shift at the garage. My mum was due to start work at twelve p.m. for the afternoon shift, so she was dropping me at the garage. Then Vin and I would go shopping once he finished work.

Mum had given me some money to buy a dress for the dance, and I wanted to go with Vin to try to find one. Vin was smiling from ear to ear and those eyes of his were electric when he finished up work and came out of the workshop into the little shop waiting area.

He had blue overalls on and was covered in grease. He had cut his hair shorter at this point; it sat on top of his head in a messy, wavy pile, short around the back and sides. He was still so tall. Taller than most guys his age.

"Come check this out Scar," he said as he grabbed my hand to lead me back towards the workshop he had just come from.

There was an old-looking blue car sitting in the middle of the workshop. He ran over to it with excitement and said,

"Look what I bought! She is not running yet, but Clark is going to help me fix her up."

He started rattling off a heap of things I didn't understand. Something about a turbo and a spoiler. I had no idea, but the look on his face was bliss. The way his eyes lit up when he spoke about the car.

After he had given me the tour of the car, he got changed, and we decided to head to the shops.

It wasn't a far walk to the shopping centre from Vin's work, so it didn't take us long. We had been to this shopping centre a million times before. We used to go there for fun on school holidays or weekends. We never really had a lot of money to burn, though.

Mike was on a service pension, and my mum, being a single parent, never had disposable cash for frivolous things.

Vin was earning a small wage from his work on Saturdays and after school. He was always very sensible with his own money, though. If Vin and I did ever do things like go to the movies or go out, he always paid for most of it for the both of us. But he very rarely spent money on himself. He said he was saving so he could get a place of his own and get away from Mike.

"Where do you want to go first?" he asked as we walked through the entrance doors and into the cool aircon of the shopping centre.

"Makeup!" I said. One of the girls in my class, Emily, always wore such nice makeup to school. School policy was that we weren't supposed to wear too much, but she always had on perfect foundation, lipstick, eyeshadow and mascara.

Me on the other hand, I didn't even own a tinted lip balm. I was just never one to really care too much about that type of stuff, mainly because my mum wasn't really one for it either. I never really saw her with her hair in anything other than a pony. She never wore lots of makeup, so it just wasn't a part of my upbringing, I guess.

My mind was made up, though. I was going to buy make-up. I wanted to be able to practice before the formal. Some of the girls were getting theirs professionally done on the night, but there was no way we could afford that.

We went into Myer, and I started looking around the makeup section. I had never really paid too much attention to this store before. It seemed too expensive for me. I didn't really know where to start. Vin started to sense that I was overwhelmed and grabbed my hand, leading me straight towards a lady near a makeup counter. It was so white and shiny that I could see my own reflection in it.

"Excuse me, could you help her find the right colours for her please?" I felt awkward and self-conscious but excited at the same time. Vin was so confident and sure of himself. I was glad he was there with me.

"Sure, come and sit in the chair and we can pick some colours that will suit you," the lady said with a warm smile.

I felt like a princess sitting in that chair while the lady worked on my face, brushing it gently with shimmering powders and creamy colours. I started to think, why don't I just come and do this on the day of the dance and get it for free? I started to quietly giggle at the thought, making my body jerk.

"What's funny?" Vin asked playfully, seeing my shoulders rise and fall slightly from holding in the laughter and the smirk across my face. He started smirking as well.

"Nothing," I replied, and I settled back down, knowing full well that the guilt would never let me do something like that. It felt way too dishonest.

The lady worked away quietly, and when she was finished, she held the mirror up to my face and showed me what I looked like. I barely recognised myself. My skin was *clear and dewy. My dark-blue eyes looked bigger and brighter. I had never really noticed before, but I had really long eyelashes. They looked twice as long with the mascara the lady had applied.*

I had full lips that she had coated with a light shade of pink that matched the hue of blush she had brushed on my cheeks.

"WOW," I gushed. "I, I, I," I couldn't find the right words to sum up what I felt. I could feel my cheeks getting hot with embarrassment. I don't even know why. I was happy, but I felt so incredibly awkward staring back at myself. It was a face I barely recognised. Vin looked down at me, his face lighting up with a smile that reached his eyes.

"You look beautiful Scar," he said so quietly that it was almost a whisper. Then he repeated a little louder, "You are always beautiful, though."

He grabbed my hand to help me off the stool as the lady started lining up the tools and products she had used on me for purchase. I only had enough to buy the foundation, mascara and lipstick, and that meant I would have to wear a dress I already owned. When I went to leave, Vin grabbed the blush and eyeshadow pallet and bought it for me.

We kept walking around Myer for a bit, me just really wanting to show off my makeup. Vin carried my bag with the purchases.

We laughed about our own little personal jokes. We used to make up stories of what our life would be like once we moved out and got a place of our own. I wanted to stay close to Mum, but Vin wanted to move as far away from Mike as possible.

We settled on traveling first. We always talked about seeing the world. The Eiffel Tower, the Louvre, the Great Wall of China and Niagara Falls, and so much more. It was an escape from reality for Vin to talk about places we could visit. We would sit on my bed some nights, cutting out old pictures from magazines and books, making vision boards of all the beautiful places we wanted to see.

We had done a few laps around Myer. Vin had brought some cologne. He brought it without even smelling it. He said it was one his friend had. He offered to buy me a dress, but I said no. I would borrow one from a friend if I couldn't find one of my own that I liked.

It was getting late, and the shops were starting to wind down. So, we decided to head home. My mum was still at work, and Vin never bothered to call Mike to come get us. Chances were he wouldn't answer anyway. There was a bus we normally caught, but it was still a thirty-minute wait away.

I could see Vin starting to get anxious about getting home so late. We never knew what mood Mike would be in. Especially on a Saturday night, if there was football on. If he would be mad or not because Vin didn't come home straight after work.

Mike was so hot and cold. Sometimes he acted like he was the most caring parent in the world. Other times he barely even noticed Vin was alive. Then there were the times he was enraged and looking for a fight, and every little thing would set him off.

He would lose his temper at the drop of a hat. Vin had started spending more and more time at my place over the years, and we had come to realise that there was a level gauge to Mike and his moods, sort of like a ratio of drunkenness to anger.

Sober = Grumpy, moody, not that great to be around. Will yell and name-call but not really get violent, just vocal.

Lightly buzzed = Awesome Mike, best dad in the world. Caring, funny and will agree to almost anything. Is drunk enough to not care about spending money on dumb things. This is his most functioning state. He will clean, cook, do house maintenance, you name it.

Like the time when we convinced him to give us a hundred dollars to spend at the candy store. We had learnt to take full advantage of this phase.

Buzzed = Verbally abusive but rarely violent. He will stay out of our way, and we will stay out of his. Usually, he will just sit in the backyard drinking or watching TV. Sometimes in this stage, he will muster the energy to do stuff around the house. He mostly ignores us in this phase.

Drunk = Angry, aggressive, violent, abusive, always looking for a reason to lash out. Stay out of his way at all costs.

Blind drunk = Angry, verbally abusive and will threaten, but usually too drunk to actually follow through. Although if he does find the energy to follow through, this is where he does his worst work. I had seen enough over the years to know to get well out of the way of this mood.

Gone drunk = Passed out.

Vin and I had come up with a bit of a code over the years. If Mike was in the Drunk phase, we would either feed him and get him lots of water fast, with the aim of getting him back to the Buzzed or Lightly buzzed.

Or we'd speed up the process by spiking his beer with stronger spirits or making him extra strong drinks. The aim was to get him to the Gone drunk phase. This plan sometimes backfired if we ended up in the Blind drunk phase, but Vin had a safe haven at my house to stay out of Mike's way if that happened.

When we got home from the shops, Vin wanted to shower. He had only changed clothes at work and still smelt of oil. Mum was not due home from work for another hour, so I decided to stay with Vin until she was home.

I wonder now if Mum was really that oblivious to what was going on under Mike's roof. I doubt she would have ever let me step foot in that house if she knew the truth.

Mike was sitting in the lounge room drinking and watching football. He looked up from the TV to stare at us. His eyes caught mine, and he seemed almost shocked for a quick moment. Then he went back to watching TV.

Vin went into the lounge to talk to him, and I waited in the hallway. Vin wanted to check his current state.

"We are at Buzzed," Vin said as he walked back out of the lounge room to meet me in the hallway.

"Good," I replied. "He didn't care that you were late?"

"Didn't even seem to notice."

Some nights he would stay in this phase and some nights he would skip this phase, so this was good news. I told Vin to go jump in the shower and I would wait for him in his room. I had been in Vin's room a million times, and in his house a million more. Mike had never been violent towards me. He barely paid me any attention.

Most of the time, having me there quelled his outbreaks a little bit. He stayed out of our way more when I was there rather than looking for a reason to fight. So, I was never too worried about being there.

Vin had only just jumped in the shower. I grabbed my phone and put my headphones on to drown out the blaring TV noise coming from down the hall and the sound of Mike yelling at the TV. He was watching football of some kind again.

I had my music up so loud that I didn't hear him come into the room. I didn't hear him shut the door behind him. I didn't hear him move across the carpet to the bed.

I was lying on my stomach looking out the window into the backyard, listening to music. I had it up so loud, I didn't even hear him when he leant over me, close enough to whisper in my ear.

The next thing I knew, he had flipped me over. He had both my hands locked together at the wrist with his one hand. He was staring straight into my eyes as they opened with shock and then blinked in confusion.

Once I finally caught up to what was happening, it was almost too late. It was like it was happening in fast-forward but somehow slow motion at the same time. He had one hand pinning my wrists down and the other fumbling for his pants, and then mine. I was screaming; at least I think I was screaming.

My headphones were still in. My music was so loud that I couldn't differentiate between my own screams, my music or the blaring TV coming from the lounge room. I struggled and wriggled and wormed to try to free myself. His hands were too big. He was a big guy. By this point, his full body weight was on top of me.

I closed my eyes as tight as they would shut. Fighting seemed pointless with how big and heavy Mike was on top of me. I was still screaming for Vin, but I had no idea if he could hear me. The bathroom was at the end of the hall, and if the shower was still running, would he be able to tell the difference between my screams and the TV?

I felt like I was being swallowed by the mattress. I was sure there would be a permanent indent of my body left there long after we moved. I felt like I was suffocating. Then suddenly he was off me and on the floor.

Vin was standing over him; he was fully dressed again. He must have taken clothes into the bathroom with him so he wouldn't need to walk down the hall in just a towel.

His hair was still wet, and fat clumps of water were dripping from his curls. Mike didn't try to move. He just started laughing. He looked over at me on the bed as I struggled to sit up, peeling myself out of the indent in the mattress. Vin backed away from Mike towards me, putting a barrier between me on the bed and Mike on the floor.

His chest was heaving. I could see everything in him tensing, ready to fight if Mike got up. A fight we both knew he would lose. He had only just managed to push Mike off me because of the element of surprise.

He looked ready to pounce, he was so wound up. Like a snake coiled up, ready to strike.

The world was spinning, and I felt numb inside. My whole body was throbbing and pulsing. I felt like I was going to vomit. I sat there unable to move. My music was still blaring in my ears, and my whole body was shaking in waves of shock, fear and panic at what I had barely just escaped or what was to come. I did not know.

I wanted to cry, but the tears wouldn't fall. I wanted to scream. but my lips wouldn't move. Mike got up and fumbled with his pants, which he had managed to unzip and slide down before Vin threw him off me. He chuckled as he walked out the room, winking at me as he left. Vin moved to shut the door behind him.

That was it. That was my undoing. I rolled off the bed and hit the floor, pushing myself to my hands and knees, and threw up on the carpet. I stayed on my hands and knees for a moment, heaving and dry retching as if to purge the feel of Mike pushing down on me, the smell of stale beer on his breath.

Vin kneeled down beside me. He gently swept my hair from my face as he put his other hand on my back, rubbing gentle circles. Then he softly took my headphones from my ears and put them on the floor.

"Are you ok?" he asked quietly. I turned my head to look at him, my eyes blurry and my throat burning from the screaming and vomiting.

I couldn't even form a reply. He pulled me into his arms like a small child, and I curled into him as if he could absorb the pain and fear I felt.

"You're safe now," he whispered in my ear. "I won't let him ever come near you again. We will pack and leave tonight, go anywhere you want. We never have to set foot in this house again." He stood up, holding me in his arms like I weighed nothing at all, and moved over to the bed.

"No, I can't leave my mum," was all I was able to say.

"Then I will take you home now. I will come over there, and you won't ever have to come here again."

"I don't want Mum to know this. She will call the police, and then what will happen to you?"

"I don't know! But maybe we should tell your mum, let her call the police."

"And tell them what? Nothing happened. I am fine, just shocked."

"Something could have happened, though. What if I hadn't gotten to you in time, what would he have done?" I didn't want to think about that question. Although I already knew the answer.

"I don't want to tell my mum, and I don't want to tell the police. I don't want to think about what would happen to you if Mike found out we involved the police. And what would the police do? He didn't actually do anything."

"I could tell them about my abuse, show them the scars. I have hospital records of the broken arm. Surely they could do something with all of that? I can't risk anything happening to you again." He was still holding me like a baby, now sitting on the bed while we went around and around.

"Please," I finally said. "I just want to go have a shower and forget this ever happened." Vin let out a big sigh. I could tell he was scared and frustrated. I had never seen him like this. He had never mentioned calling the police. Not after any of the many times I had patched him up.

Vin lifted me up and carried me down the hall to the shower. He locked the door behind us. I finally peeled myself from his arms and willed my jelly legs to hold my weight. Vin turned the shower on, and the room started to fill with steam.

I caught a glimpse of myself in the mirror. I still had the makeup on from earlier that day. However, I looked completely different to the fresh-faced girl who had looked back at me earlier. The clean dewy skin was now red and blotchy from screaming. The big blue eyes were red and bloodshot. The mascara that had previously made my lashes look long and thick was clumped around my eyes and running down my face.

Bright-red blood and swelling had replaced the plump pink that had been on my lips, where I had bitten down on them so hard that I pierced the skin. I could taste metal in my mouth, metal and bile.

My jeans button and zip were undone where Mike had managed to get to, and my top was completely scrunched up under my underarms from how hard I had been fighting. I stood there in shock, unable to move any further.

Vin stepped close to me. He took my hand in his.

"Want me to help?" he asked as he put both his hands on the edges of my shirt that was sitting just underneath my bra line, exposing my stomach. I was shaking hard, but I managed to nod my head.

Vin and I had been inseparable for three years now. We had kissed and hugged and had many secret sleepovers in the backyard or each other's rooms, sneaking back to our own beds before the morning. There had been lots of affection and touching, but we had never really taken it to that next level. We had not even seen each other naked yet. Underwear, bathers, yes, but naked, no.

At this moment, I wasn't thinking of anything other than how tired I felt. Vin lifted my shirt over my head. His eyes were glassy, and I could tell he was holding back tears.

He looked down at my unzipped jeans and pain lashed across his face. He grabbed the jeans' sides and shuffled them gently to the ground. He stood back up and took both my hands. Guided me closer to the shower.

"You ok?" he asked as I took the final step in and peeled off the remainder of my clothes.

I left my bra and knickers on the shower floor and grabbed the loofah and soap. I didn't answer him as I started frantically scrubbing at my skin. I scrubbed and scrubbed and scrubbed. I scrubbed until my skin felt like it was on fire, trying to get the feel of him off me. I scrubbed until the scalding hot water burnt the fresh layer of skin I had just exposed.

I scrubbed my face so hard under the scorching hot water that I was sure it would melt away. I scrubbed and scrubbed until my hands would not work anymore, and then I collapsed on the floor. Vin was sitting on the toilet with the lid down, trying to give me privacy. I could see his outline through the fogged-up glass. He had his elbows on his knees, and his head was in his hands.

I felt so tired all of a sudden, drained from a combination of what happened, the thought of what could have and what very nearly happened mixed with the hot water. It was like a massive adrenaline dump.

Every ounce of energy left my body, circling the drain, and I felt so weak and exhausted. I shut my eyes, and I wasn't in the shower anymore.

I was in a field. There were flowers all over, yellow flowers. My favourite. Everywhere I looked, there was luscious green grass. The sun was shining, and it was bright. I could feel warmth on my skin where the sun's rays touched me.

While it was warm and sunny, it was lightly raining. A sun shower. I could feel the trickles on me. The water dripped down my cheek and onto my chest. It smelt fresh; a warm, summery, woodsy freshness. I inhaled the scent. It was the most beautiful thing I had ever smelt.

I lay down in the grass and let the sun shine on my skin, the grass slightly damp underneath me, the warm sun on my shoulders and on my cheeks. I had never felt so safe, so happy, so content. A blissful feeling of calm washed over me and made me want to stay in that serene moment forever.

Then I heard it. "Scar, Scar, Scar." Nothing more than a whisper at first, growing louder. "Scar, wake up. Scar. Are you ok? SCAR."

I didn't want to leave the peaceful field, the sun shower and sunflowers. My eyes felt so damn heavy. It took every ounce of willpower to pry them open. Once they focused, I could see Vin in the shower with me, fully clothed. He had turned the water off. His hair was still damp from his own shower, but it was curling up in big chunks on his head. Messy and crazy, just the way I liked it. When he saw me open my eyes, he smiled at me. I could see him start to relax as I smiled back.

His shoulders dropped and his breath steadied. Piercing green eyes full of worry and pain stared back at me.

"The hot water was going cold," he said as he wrapped me up in a big towel and picked me up off the floor of the shower.

I didn't move, or talk. It felt like I didn't even breathe. He carried me back to his room and placed me on his bed.

"Do you want me to take you home?" he asked as he started to pull out one of his tees for me to chuck on.

"No, I don't want Mum to see me like this. She will know something is wrong straight away. I will message her and tell her I am staying at a friend's house."

While we had been in each other's beds and rooms what felt like a million times, my mum didn't like the idea of us sleeping over. Which is why we would always wait till after my mum was asleep, and then Vin would usually sneak in. I am sure she had a feeling, but she never said anything. If she knew I was here, there would have been nothing stopping her from coming over, and I couldn't let her see me like this.

I couldn't risk her calling the police. Vin was still legally considered a minor. If Mike went away, what would happen to Vin? Foster care? Would he be homeless? He had no other family he could go to. He was an only child, and Mike's parents had cut Mike off a long time ago. From what Vin told me, they didn't even know Vin existed. Vin's mum had died giving birth to him, and Vin said Mike never talked about her family. Mike had left the service to raise him. He had been an alcoholic for as long as Vin could remember. Part of me still wonders if Mike would have been different if Vin's mum hadn't passed and Mike hadn't been thrown into the deep end with a baby and no family support. Guess it's too late for thoughts like that now, and any sympathy I ever could have had for Mike went flying out the window the very first time I felt those bleeding welts on Vin's arms under my fingertips.

Vin took a deep breath, like he was disagreeing with me not wanting to go home, but I could tell he wasn't going to argue. I chucked on his tee and crawled under his covers. I heard him get up and bolt his door shut. He had put the bolt on himself a couple of months ago as a precaution for if Mike got crazy. I had never seen him use it, though. In hindsight, I guess I should have locked it any time I was there by myself. Well, that night Vin locked it.

He lay down next to me and pulled me in close, tangling his fingers in mine. I could still smell the freshness, the sweet smell of summer rain from my dream, and I breathed it in. I was safe now. As I drifted off into a deep sleep, one I thought I may never wake up from, I said, "I like your new cologne."

Later that night, I woke up as he shifted off the bed. I heard him get up and change out of his clothes and into something to sleep in, most likely. I heard him unlock the bolt on the door and exit the room, then come back in. I heard him cleaning up, coming and going from the room like a ghost. Just little creaks, shifts and bumps. I heard slightly louder clangs and hustling around, and then, when everything went quiet again, I heard him come back into the room and the bolt lock again.

I felt the bed sink from his weight as he sat down next to me. He put something on my cut lip where I had bitten down and pierced my skin. It was cold and soothing. His fingers were featherlight as he ran them over my swollen lips, like he was afraid his skin would burn me if he left it in one spot for too long. He swept my hair back off my face, and I could hear him whimper. Was he crying? He sniffed, and I could feel his arm move to wipe away a tear.

He spoke so softly that I almost couldn't make out what he was saying.

"I would never forgive myself if Mike ever hurt you Scar, I am so, so sorry, I should have never left you alone in my room while he was here drinking. I am so sorry I let that happen to you." He kept apologising, saying the words over and over again, like a song lulling me back to sleep.

I wanted to open my eyes. I wanted to tell him it wasn't his fault, that I didn't blame him. I wanted to hug him and say that he saved me, that if he hadn't shown up when he did it could have, would have, been a lot worse. I wanted to thank him. Tell him how much I loved him. How much better he deserved than what he had been living with.

But I couldn't. I couldn't open my eyes. I couldn't bear to see guilt and pain in those beautiful eyes of his again, and my body and mind were so exhausted from fighting. It felt like I was paralysed.

So, I just lay there, pretending to be asleep until it was the truth. Letting him think that it was all his fault. Letting him carry the burden like weights.

I threw out the makeup the next day. But every time he wore that cologne, it reminded me of what could have been. It made me feel safe. It reminded me of how he had protected me and the peace and calm he bought me after such an awful thing.

It was my fault. I blamed myself for being stupid enough to think that I could play dress-up and wear makeup around someone as deranged as Mike. For never telling someone *what Vin was dealing with. For never telling my mum or asking for help when we had the chance. I know Vin blamed himself as well. He had brought me the makeup. He had left me in his room to go shower when he knew Mike was home and had been drinking.*

In hindsight, we should have called the police. We were young and scared. We were afraid of what would happen. Afraid we would be separated. Mike or my mum might have moved away, and we would have been powerless to stop it. We were afraid of the unknown. Better the devil you know, right?

I pushed that night deep down in my memory bank. It had things piled so high on top of it that I rarely ever thought about what happened.

In moments like these, when I do relive it, my whole body starts to ache at the what ifs. Why we didn't go for help. How our lives could have been so much different if we just told my mum. Told anyone.

I wake up from my dream covered in sweat and tears, tangled in my sheets. His scent hits me again, and I nuzzle into the pillow to breathe it in deeper. I imagine him wrapping his long arms around me, pulling me into his chest. The way he used to hook his foot over my leg, trapping me to him. Like he couldn't get close enough. Squeezing my pillow, I fall back asleep.

22

It's complicated

To say I am excited would be an understatement, a colossal understatement. I have packed and repacked about five times, each time taking out a few garments only to add them back in on the next repack.

Blake, on the other hand, basically emptied the entire contents of one drawer into a suitcase and then zipped it up without giving it any further thought.

Our trip is finally here! I'm still not convinced that I've packed the right things. Do I have enough jumpers? Although it will be mostly warm weather over there. Temperatures in Vegas can be one hundred degrees Fahrenheit; I'm still trying to work out the difference between Fahrenheit and Celsius.

When Blake and I first looked at the weather for the US to help us shop and pack, I saw numbers like sixty and one hundred and almost died. How can it be that hot? Surely that's a mistake; people wouldn't be able to live. Blake laughed at me, explaining the difference. A short moment of brain lapse. Even then, though, a hundred degrees Fahrenheit is still thirty-eight degrees Celsius, according to Google. Absolutely not jumper weather!

I had to laugh at myself. I open the Contiki webpage again, relooking at the other people we will meet on the trip. They encouraged us to make a Contiki profile and check who else is going on our tour. You can connect and send messages to people before you leave to help make friendships. I saw some couples and a few groups of girls and guys with a couple of solo travellers. There was no 'It's complicated' section. No box to tick for a broken female traveling with a best friend (who is also somewhat broken but far better at hiding it) while pretending to be in a relationship. So, we just ticked single. We talked it over and thought that being so far away from anyone we know will be a good chance for us to live a little. Although we still have our plan of getting married in Vegas, that is going to be after the Contiki tour. Away from everyone, with just the two of us. So, to the people on the tour, we will just be friends.

Once we are married, Blake's parents will allow us to move in together, and they will get off his back. Well, so he believes. He is convinced he'll have more freedom and less pressure. Who am I to disagree with him on his own parents?

To me, marriage isn't a big deal. My mum never married, and the only man I will ever love is long gone. So, I am happy to follow Blake's lead on that one. I love being around Blake, and I know living with him won't be an issue. I check my phone, again. We have plenty of time. I am impatient and restless. The fact that I am actually doing this still shocks me. How did I get here from where I was? How do I deserve this? I suddenly feel guilty that I'm going to be free and see the world while others…. Well, others will never get the chance.

I look down at my phone again.

"It's all good Scarlet, just breathe," Blake says from behind me in the living room. He drove over this morning, and my mum is going to drive us to the airport.

I told my mum about our trip a few months ago. She was excited and supportive. A little nervous for me, but she gave me some cash she had saved to help me with spending money. Blake, on the other hand, waited till three days before our trip before he told his parents.

He told his mum and dad he had organized a leave with university and that he was going for over a month, then he'd be back. He told them he had all the money saved and didn't need their help. They were absolutely gobsmacked but too in shock to argue.

By the time they had processed the shock, he was already on his way to my place for my mum to take us to the airport.

"I'm ok, just a bit nervous," I reply, trying to swallow the guilt that has risen in my throat.

"You guys ready?" Mum asks, coming into the lounge room with the keys in her hand. I sigh, and Blake gives my shoulders a gentle squeeze.

We grab our bags, nodding, and follow Mum out to the garage to load everything into the car. First step taken, only twenty-five hours to go. I say to myself, you deserve this, even though I don't believe it. Not for one second.

23

Ice breakers

"Are you wearing men's cologne?" I feel heat rise to my cheeks as I process the words. I purse my lips together, turning around to see the asker of such a question, still deciding if I'll own up or lie.

After landing in LA, we made it to our hostel unscathed. The flight, while exciting and guilt-inducing at the same time, went mostly as expected. We did nothing but sleep the first night, and today is the day we meet up with the Contiki crew. These are the people we will be spending the next twenty-one days with.

We are waiting in the hostel lobby for everyone to arrive. I recognise a few people from their profile pictures; all of us uploaded pictures to our Contiki profiles.

I can't place the guy's name or remember exactly where he is from. But I know the accent straight away, as it mirrors my own. Australian.

"How do you know it's men's cologne?" I finally answer.

"I wear the same one, Chanel Bleu, right?" he says with a cocky smile. There is something interesting about him. Maybe his arrogance. It pours off him like liquid gold. He is what you would call traditionally attractive.

I don't know if that's the right term; he's one of those guys that everyone thinks is good looking. Not my type.

He isn't tall with green eyes, curly caramel hair, quiet and reserved but also confident and kind, anything but cocky.

This guy is perfectly proportioned and balanced. Blue eyes, sandy blond hair, strong jaw and manly features. Big white smile with perfect teeth. He looks like he fell straight out of a Kelvin Klein photoshoot.

I return a shy smile, turning away, frantically watching the stairs for Blake to come down from the room and save me.

"First trip?" he asks.

"How can you tell?"

"You look nervous as hell."

"I am nervous," I say with a laugh.

"Well, we can be nervous together then." He gives me a little nudge with his shoulders. I jerk away and stiffen at the contact. This guy doesn't look like he has felt an ounce of nerves in his entire life. But I also know you can't judge a book by its cover. So, I give him the benefit of the doubt.

"Just relax, it will be fun," he says as he nudges me again. I take a shallow breath and start screaming for Blake in my head. Where the hell is he? We are sharing a room with separate beds. Our room doesn't have an ensuite, so we have to use the communal toilets and showers. I basically packed an entire suitcase and allowed myself an hour for the shower.

When I went back to the room, all dressed and ready, Blake moseyed out wearing nothing but a towel and a pair of clean boxers. I told him we had to be in the lobby in ten minutes, and he replied that he only needed two.

Now here we are. Four minutes until we are due to leave with no sign of Blake. And Channing Tatum, who I just met five seconds ago, clearly has no respect for personal space.

"I'm Dean by the way," he says. Hmm, that tracks, I think.

"Scarlet," I reply. Our conversation halts as I finally see Blake come down the stairs into the lobby.

Then the tour guide arrives. She introduces herself as Leslie. She is short and has a full head of the wildest curls billowing down around her shoulders. She calls everyone in close and starts a roll call.

Then she insists we go around the room and introduce ourselves. Say our name and where we are from. Oh, here we go, I think to myself.

Nothing worse than an ice-breaker game. Why does every single instructor, guide, teacher or leader think that grown adults need ice breakers to make conversation?

I start to push to the back of the group, hoping I can sneak to the toilet and miss the whole thing. Blake notices me moving and brings me back to the group. He doesn't share my complete distaste for these games.

"This is what this trip is about Scarlet, getting out of our comfort zones. We can do this." I take a deep breath and let him pull me back to the group, where, with a shaky voice, I tell them my name and where I am from.

24

Bull or unicorn

SCARLET

"Ok, everyone, grab your things, we are about to start the tour!" Leslie is leading our group outside to where a top-deck bus is waiting.

We are scheduled to do a Hollywood star house-spotting tour before stopping at Venice Beach for lunch. Then a further tour around the city on the bus.

They have given us little maps with big yellow stars marked next to a name so we can see which A-lister lives in which extravagant house. I don't really care who lives where, but I have to admit, seeing the enormous houses will be pretty cool. The majority of the other girls in the group seem really excited by this part of the day as well.

Blake sits down next to me. "So," he says with a laugh. "Where are you from?" He's mimicking a lot of the conversations happening around the bus.

"Oh, nowhere you would have heard of," I reply, matching his sarcasm.

The bus takes off, and it doesn't take long for Blake to start up a conversation with the girls sitting behind us. He is really embracing this out-of-your-comfort zone stuff. I, on the other hand, feel entirely terrified.

They are a couple of friends from Canada. Around our age. I can hear Blake answering all the standard questions. Where he's from, how old he is. That he is studying.

99

He is so good at talking to other people. His mask is so firmly in place, sounding so upbeat and happy about his life, when I know in reality, he feels extremely trapped by everything. I half listen to the girls answering the same line of questioning as he mimics the questions back to them.

There is a steady buzz of chatter throughout the day. The bus drives around winding streets with lush green gardens and houses the size of hotels, giant green hedges perfectly manicured and as tall as double-storey houses next to wrought-iron gates with giant M's or W's or H's bent into them.

People are changing from one side of the bus to the other. The tour guide explains where we are and whose house we are looking at with excitement.

"If you look to the left now, behind this gate is where Tom Cruise lives." The bus fills with oohs and aahs. Girls are taking selfies with the winding driveways up to the expansive houses. I'm sure they will all come out blurry, as the bus keeps moving down the street at a steady pace. It seems slightly stalkerish to me. Besides, why would I want a closeup of my face with cereal from breakfast in my teeth, with a glimpse of Britney Spears' front hedge and gate in the background?

However, the top deck of the bus is open, and the day is perfect. Warm and sunny. The bus comes to a stop in front of Venice Beach. The tour guide speaks over the microphone, telling us we have an hour at the beach and to meet back at this spot.

I look out over the top of the bus. Low waves are lapping up over the golden sand. People are wading into the shallows in tiny bikinis and shorts. Happy couples are taking photos in front of a graffiti-covered skate park. Muscle men are working out in a beachfront gym.

I scan the beach; it is beautiful. From the water to the golden sand right up to the palm trees swaying slightly in the breeze. Everyone starts to fade away.

The noise dies down, and the people all became a blur. It's like the plastic version has been taken out of my teenage memory bank and spat out as a real place.

I remember it was raining. A heavy downpour that died down to a sprinkle as the day went on. I was seventeen at the time.

I caught the bus home from school. Only I didn't get off at home. I got off at the park a few stops around the corner. There was a playground there that was designed like a yacht.

Plastic palm trees surrounded it in the white sand. The beach was my favourite place in the world. We rarely went there, as it was too far away and my mum worked so much.

But this park was walking distance to my house, and I often sat there pretending it was a real beach. Especially when I felt down. I would go there, lie in the sand under the plastic palm trees and imagine I could hear the waves crashing on the shore.

I would drift off and think about diving into crystal-blue water that would leave my skin salty. The sand under my feet would be warm and golden. The air that brushed my skin would be crisp and fresh.

I lay on that sand that particular day, trying to think practically, trying to run through different scenarios in my mind. I was almost positive I was making it out to be worse than it was.

Vin had been working at the garage all year. Most days, I would catch the bus to his work and wait while he finished up. Then he would drive me home. He had just gotten his license that year, and the car he and his boss had been work-ing on for the last couple of years in his spare time was up and running perfectly.

Some days, Vin would finish work early and come and get me from school, and some days he would work well into the night, then he would come straight to my mum's place when he finished.

That day I was supposed to go to his work. I knew he would know to come find me here as soon as he didn't see me get off the bus at his work.

I suppose I wanted him to come find me. I wanted to confront him about everything, but I was struggling with the words, and I wasn't sure I wanted to know the answer.

I heard the car before I saw it. He had done all kinds of things I had no idea about to it. It made so much noise. I could hear him coming down the street. I didn't turn to look for the car. Not even when I heard the tires crush over the gravel of the car park.

I heard the engine cut and the door hinges creak as he opened the door. Heard his feet crunch over the gravel as he started walking towards me. Heard the noise die as he moved from the car park to the grass.

Finally, the internal pull I felt to turn to him won over. I couldn't fight it any more. I turned my head to look over.

He had let his hair grow out, and it was in wavy clumps around his face, almost down to his shoulders. The sun had bleached it, and the caramel colour was turning a light golden honey on the ends.

He walked slowly but with purpose. Without saying anything, he sat down next to me in the sand. Then he flopped back and lay so our heads were touching.

He had his hands on his chest, and the last of the rain was drizzling down on us both as we lay under the plastic palm tree.

We didn't speak for a long time, we just lay there, staring at the sky. Somehow, he always knew when I needed conversation and when I needed quiet. He always knew when

I needed to laugh or when I just needed a hand to hold. I knew the same for him. He knew something was wrong now.

I am sure he could feel my frustration.

"That one looks like a crab," he said, breaking the silence while pointing at a cloud in the sky.

"That one looks like a unicorn," I said with a laugh.

He tilted his head sideways and laughed too. "Nooo it doesn't, it looks more like a bull."

"No way, there is its tail and its horn. It's a unicorn."

"Oh ok, I kinda see it," he said as he turned his head to look at me. I could feel his eyes burning my face as I looked up at the sky.

"What's up?" he asked. "I can tell something is bugging you. I've felt you be off for days." I played around with the words in my head, trying to make them make sense before I spoke them out loud. Finally I just blurted it out.

"Why haven't we had sex yet?" My hands flew over my mouth the moment the words left, trying to shove them back in. I didn't mean for it to come out so brash. I couldn't think of how else to ask. When I spoke to my girlfriend at school about it, she had said 'He probably isn't that into you. Sees you as a sister type thing.' I felt like it was me. He didn't want me.

Vin sat up, and like we were one, my body followed. He tilted his head back to look up at the sky again, but he didn't speak.

The girls at my school talked about sex like it was an Olympic sport. Girls were sleeping with boys at parties. Rumours were flying around school like confetti. Amy lost her virginity to Mark but Mark likes Kate, Kate won't sleep with Mark. Jo and Clair hooked up at a party and so on and so on.

All of them, except me. My friends all just assumed that Vin and I had been sleeping together since day one, but the truth was we had barely moved past making out over clothes. My friends would ask questions, and I had no input to offer. No experience, no nothing. I had only confided in Mikeala, and her input had not filled me with confidence.

I loved Vin, and I knew he loved me too. But I wanted him badly; it was so much more for me. Did he not want me in that way?

"Well," I pushed after his silence, knocking my confidence even lower. I had now lost any coyness about the subject and had moved straight to anger. To me, Vin was everything, and I thought he felt the same about me. But my conversations at school these last few months had left so much doubt swirling in my head. Why had he never made a move for more?

"Do you not find me attractive? Are you sleeping with someone else? Do you just see me as a sister or friend? What is it Vin? Tell me!"

"Scar," he said quietly.

"WHAT VIN?"

"Do you know what you mean to me?" He said it with such calm seriousness that it knocked the anger right out of me. I didn't know what to say, so I said nothing. I just sat there, staring out at the sky. Dark clouds parted to show a lighter sky, sun rays striking through. The start of a rainbow was forming in the distance. Beautiful shades of purples, blues and greens.

After a moment of silence, he continued talking. "Scar," he said as he looked away again. "I cannot get the image of your face from that night out of my head."

"What are you talking about Vin?" I pushed, feeling the frustration in me rise again.

"You weren't even white. Your skin was almost green, pale, sickly green. You threw up from the trauma of it all." Suddenly it clicked. What he was talking about.

The night his dad tried to rape me in his very bed.

"You had bruises up your arms for a week, your lip was torn to shreds from your own teeth. Goddamn it Scar, one of your nails was completely ripped off."

I said nothing. I remembered it all. Vividly. But I also remembered the feeling of sheer relief seeing Vin standing between Mike and me. I remembered how safe I felt being scooped up into his arms and carried away. I remembered the feeling of his gentle hands soothing me, putting out the fire on my skin.

I remembered the smell of summer and flowers and the feeling of rain. I remembered being hugged to sleep, safe and warm. I didn't say any of this, though. I watched Vin as the pain washed over his face.

"Scar, you had nightmares for weeks. You would yell 'get off me' in your sleep and then wake up screaming in terror. Your body still stiffens every time you set foot in my house to this day."

I did not remember the nightmares, and I didn't know that I stiffened every time I went to his house. I really thought I was completely over what had happened. I didn't feel like it had affected me that badly.

I had made up some bull story to Mum about my lip, something about a soccer game we had played at school. I wore long-sleeved shirts and jumpers and never mentioned a word of what happened to anyone. Guess Vin saw the real side of how that affected me.

That was the first time we had ever really talked about that night. We often talked about his abuse. He never hid his feelings from me.

I was always slightly more reserved. I never really expressed how seeing Vin hurt broke me. I always felt like it wasn't happening to me, so I had no right to feel traumatized by it. Despite Vin trying, I never wanted to talk about that night or what had happened.

He continued speaking, just staring out at nothing. "After seeing what he did to you, what he almost did to you, how he hurt you. What his intentions were. How could I, how could I ever make you feel safe enough to want to do that with me? Especially in that house, that same bed."

He was shaking his head. I was shocked at what I was hearing. I knew that Vin blamed himself for what happened to me because I heard him that night. I knew that he felt responsible, even though it wasn't his fault.

How on earth he could think that I would link having sex with him to that, I just didn't know.

"Vin," I said. I wiped a tear off his cheek while fighting back my own. "That is not the same thing." He closed his eyes and rested his head on my shoulder. "I know you Vin, you wouldn't hurt anyone like that, especially me. I would never be afraid of you."

I put my hand on the top of Vin's head and twirled a curl around my finger. I could feel him relax under my hand. He loved it when I played with his hair.

"Vin," I said.

"Yeah," he replied.

"You know what happened to me was not your fault. You don't have to feel guilty about it."

He stared out at nothing for the longest time. Then he spoke again, softly. "I just... I dunno, in my mind, I know the difference, but I just couldn't bring myself to ever try to be close to you like that after the pain I saw you in. I was so scared it would bring back too much for you, and I couldn't bear to see you hurt like that again." He seemed so conflicted. Like he was trying to make sense of it all in his own mind. "I've wanted to, many times. Trust me. You are gorgeous to me, and how you would ever think I would ever be with someone else I have no clue. I'm yours Scar! Only yours forever." He took a deep breath and turned his body to face me.

He cupped my face in both his hands and kissed me softly on the forehead. I leaned into it, relaxing. "Every time I get close to you like that I panic. I just picture you, lying on the bed, bruised, scared and sick. and I just can't bring myself to take the next step." He stopped talking and I nodded, understanding what he was saying. "What brought this on anyway?" And just like that, he changed the subject. Flicked a switch and turned it all off. His tears had stopped now, and he lifted his head off my shoulder and stared back out at the park in front of us.

"The girls at school," I said.

"I see."

"There is a party this weekend, and pretty much every girl at school is talking about the party and who they are hooking up with. I feel like I am the only virgin in school." I looked across at Vin to make sure he was following along. Then I continued talking. He was still looking out at the sky, but I could tell he was listening. He kept nodding slightly every now and then. "People just assume we have done it a million times. I feel kinda awkward that I actually have no idea what any of them are talking about."

Vin turned to look at me, a look of concern painted on his face.

"Scar, you don't have to do anything you don't want to just because others expect you to or because they are."

"And if I want to?" I said, a tad too fast.

"Well, do you?" he replied.

"Yes."

"Ok."

"Ok what?" I spat out. He chuckled. He could tell I was uncomfortable. The conversation didn't seem to fluster him as much as it did me.

He stood up and reached a hand down to me. I took it, and he pulled me up into his arms.

"Scar, I would give you the moon if I could, whatever you want, how you want it… If I have the means, it's yours. And if I don't have the means, you better believe I will work my ass off to get it for you." He was talking about giving me the world, a life, but I was talking about sex. He was already everything and more to me.

"When?" I said as soon as he stopped talking.

"Girl, I would lay you in the sand right now, now that I know that's what you really want."

I looked up at him, engulfed in his hug.

"Maybe not in the sand." I replied. He laughed and hugged me tighter.

"Just say the word."

"Ok."

"I don't know what I am more offended about Scar, the fact you thought that I don't find you attractive or that you thought I would be cheating on you," he said as we walked back towards his car.

"Well, we have never actually made it official with words, so would it be cheating?" I asked.

"There is no one else for me Scar. To me this is as official as it gets. But if you need words, a ring, paper. I can do all that too." I smiled up at him, and he pressed his forehead to mine. "Scarlet James."

"Yes."

"Will you be my girlfriend?"

I started chuckling but stood up on my tippy-toes to kiss him. His arms tightened around me as he picked me up off the ground. My feet dangled in the air as he kissed me back.

I pulled my lips back slightly. Just enough for the word "Yes" to slip past.

He placed my feet back on the ground and opened my car door. I liked hearing him ask, but honestly, I didn't need

*the tag. I didn't need to hear him ask me to be his girlfriend.
I didn't need a ring or to be his wife. I just needed him.*

Blake sits down next to me in the warm sand.

"How awesome is this, Scarlet?" he says, shuffling his feet to dig them a little deeper in the sand. He has a massive smile across his face, where the dark stubble has thickened out the last couple of years since I first met him.

"It sure is," I reply, flopping back on the sand to stare up at the sky. There is not a cloud in the sky. Not a single shape to be made.

25

He's just not him

SCARLET

"So are you going tonight?" he asks me, upbeat and full of energy. The tour has finished, and small groups of people have started to bunch together.

The Contiki guide announced as the top-deck tour came to a close that tonight they have organised a pub crawl. It will start at the hostel lobby at seven p.m. We are going to head to a BBQ dinner at a local grill and then move on to an array of bars and clubs.

I have never been on a pub crawl before; I very rarely go out.

I worked full time the last few years, and when I wasn't at the salon, I was working at McDonald's to save for this trip. A couple of times, Blake and I told his parents he was at mine and we would sneak out to a bar.

His parents relaxed their strict curfews slightly over the years, but he always had to be home before ten p.m. on a weekday and midnight on a weekend. Sometimes we would go out closer to his university and visit a gay bar out of town, but they never really got going till well after we already had to leave to head home. I wanted Blake to be able to one hundred percent take the 'THINK' out of the 'I think I am gay.'

I don't really like to drink alcohol, especially after seeing the evil it created in Mike. Blake doesn't really like it that much either. So, when Dean asks me if I am going with the group tonight, I raise my shoulders in a shrug. Part of me screams 'Hellll yesss I am!' But part of me is terrified.

"Come on," he says. "This is the point of a Contiki tour, getting drunk and partying, letting your hair down." I know he is, in some way, right.

I know Blake will be keen to go out. He is far more comfortable in big groups of people than me, and I know he wants to let his hair down a bit, more than what he feels safe to do at home.

Dean, while somewhat cocky, seems nice enough. "Sure, what else am I going to do?" I say with a smile.

After spending all day with these people on the tour, I was feeling more comfortable around most of them and was even getting a little excited to be going on the pub crawl.

Blake and I get ready separately, me taking my usual hoard to the toilets and him just putting on a fresh pair of clothes and deodorant five minutes before we are due to leave.

We head down to the lobby at around quarter to seven p.m. and wait for the rest of the group to arrive. They come down in dribs and drabs in groups they formed through-out the day.

There is a couple traveling together, also from Australia, but Melbourne, I think they said. A group of three girls who are best friends from Miami. Dean and his friend Micheal, who are also from Australia. A group of three girls from Canada. Then quite a few other solo travellers. They seem to have paired off. Some with guys, some with other girls. Everyone is young and beautiful and free. Spirits are high, and you can feel the energy in the air.

Blake and I trail behind the group as we walk down the street. We have somehow fallen into two files as we walk to the grill. Our first stop.

When they show us through to our seats, Blake pulls mine out for me, and we sit next to each other. We eat ribs, chicken wings, steak, salad and chips. There are jugs of beer being constantly refilled, but I am quite done after half a beer.

Luckily Blake doesn't seem to share the macho antics of some of the other guys, who seem to make it a giant competition of who can drink the most.

The night goes by fast. By the third stop, I am well and truly done. I have stopped drinking, instead opting for a soda water with lime to avoid any peer pressure. In all honesty, I am still feeling the buzz from the beer at the first bar.

I am standing at the back of the bar with Blake as the rest of the group dance, flirt and chat with each other.

Having Blake near me puts me at ease in this jungle of drunk people. But I can't help but feel like I am holding him back. Like if I wasn't here, he would be dancing and drinking with the rest of them.

We start making jokes about who we think likes whom and who might be hooking up before the night's end.

We manage to stay together as a group. The tour guide leads us from bar to bar, and it amazes me that we haven't lost anyone despite how drunk some of them are.

By the time we make it to our last bar, even though I've been having fun, I am well and truly ready for bed. It's way past midnight, maybe two a.m.

We are at a nightclub called 'The Viper Room.' It's loud, and there are flashing lights and drinks being spilled. People are dancing and grinding on each other.

I feel a bit like I am at a zoo watching wild animals interact. Buff baboons banging their chests to impress the females. Peacocks doing mating dances in colourful flowing dresses to attract their mates.

I'm not sure how to dance, but I try to give it a go. My feet are sore, and I honestly just want to go home and crawl into bed. But Blake is having fun, and I don't want to be the first to say I'm done.

I'm dancing in a group with four other girls while a few of the guys lean on the bar, drinking.

I'm copying the girls' moves to make sure I fit in. Swing your hips from side to side, throw your arms around a bit. I must have been doing something right because Dean comes over to our group. He has stayed pretty close to me all night, trying to initiate conversation and making small attempts to touch my back whenever I walked past. It always made me flinch, but he never seemed to sense it. Guess I'm not all that surprised to see him come over. Especially since he asked me how Blake and I are connected, and I swear I saw relief wash over his face when I said we are just great friends.

He starts to move in from the side. A few of the other guys come over and start dancing as well. The majority of the girls start dancing with a guy, grabbing each other close, hands running all over each other's bodies. I keep dancing.

Dean is behind me now. He places his hands on my hips and moves closer to me. He is so close now that I can feel him against my back and butt. I am uncomfortable, but I am in a packed nightclub. What can possibly happen? I try to breathe.

I keep dancing and push the fear deep down. I try to let myself relax a little bit. Dean's hands move high and low over my hips and around my stomach. I can feel my body go cold as his hands wander over my stomach, over parts of my body I have always kept hidden, and for good reason. I am starting to feel claustrophobic. The walls are closing in around me.

I look over and see Blake. He is chatting to a guy on the other side of the dance floor. Panic is rising up inside of me.

Blake and I are affectionate but not intimate. I feel comfortable with his hand in mine or his arm draped over my shoulder. Safe even. This is something entirely different. I know the intentions behind every grab, every rub, even though Dean isn't being forceful or aggressive.

I feel sick.

Dean's hand drops for a moment, and I use the opportunity to leave the dance floor. I walk or almost ran over to the bar; I'm hot and I need some air. I want to go interrupt Blake and say let's leave, but I don't want to ruin his fun.

He has a beer in his hand and is chatting and laughing, flirting. I lean on the bar, trying to slow my mind and catch my breath.

Dean follows me off the dance floor and comes up beside me. He puts one hand on my back and leans in close to ask if I want a drink.

I flinch a little at the contact, but not enough for him to notice or to drop his hand. I turn around to try to remove myself from his hand, but he moves back and to the side to come up behind me. As I turn, I come face to face with him.

He must see this as a hint to make a move when I'm really trying to move out from under him and create some space. Now I'm locked in between the bar and him.

It happens so fast, I barely have time to register what is happening. Before I know it, he leans down, his lips finding mine in a kiss. One hand moving up behind my head, holding me in place, the other on my hips. I try to pull back, but the bar is right there.

He is bigger than me and has a few drinks under his belt. My back feels wet and sticky against the bar, a combination of my own sweat and spilt alcohol. I am starting to really panic now.

My eyes open, looking for an escape, darting from Dean to the exit. I'm not kissing back, but Dean doesn't seem to notice. He is beyond drunk, and I feel his weight crushing into me. I have nowhere to move to. I try to pull my head back, but his hand holds it firmly in place, clasping my hair. His eyes are shut, and he seems completely unaware of the level of discomfort or panic I am in.

It feels like an eternity, but in reality, it is probably mere seconds. Then Dean snaps back. Two hands claps down on his shoulders from behind. Then Blake moves to the side of us, one hand still on Dean's shoulders.

Dean instantly steps back and turns to half face Blake. He doesn't seem annoyed, and I don't think he intended to be as aggressive as it felt to me.

"Hey mate, I promised Scarlet earlier that I wouldn't leave without her, but I am ready to go," he says to Dean. His one hand is still on Dean's shoulder to make sure he keeps his distance from me.

Dean turns further to face Blake. I get out from under his hand and quickly side-step to move away from him.

"I can make sure she gets home safe," Dean quickly replies. I take my opportunity to make my getaway.

"Oh that's ok Dean, I am actually ready to go anyway."

Before Dean can respond, Blake grabs my hand and we start walking out of the nightclub. I'm not sure if Blake knew how uncomfortable I actually was and came to rescue me, or if he really was just ready to go.

Either way, I don't care. I'm glad to be leaving and glad to be leaving with Blake. The whole thing just reiterates to me that Blake and I are doing the right thing. For me anyway. A tiny sliver of doubt has been treading its way into my system, watching how free and happy Blake has been on this trip. Am I holding him back from finding love, from being his true self?

We walk home talking about the night, stopping at a little pizza cafe still open on the way home.

"Hope I didn't ruin your night by saying I was leaving," Blake says as we grab our pizzas and start to walk home.

"No, I was ready to go by like bar three."

He chuckles. "You looked a bit uncomfortable with Dean, but did I read the room wrong?"

"Nope, I was. I mean, he's obviously gorgeous but…"

"But what?" he pries gently. Blake never really tries to push me to talk, which I like.

"It just felt wrong, It didn't feel good. It felt…like a sick feeling deep in my stomach."

"Maybe you're gay too," he says, laughing at his own joke.

"He's just not him Blake. He's just not him." Blake nods like he understands. He doesn't push me to say more.

"What about you? You looked like you were hitting it off with that one guy. I am sorry if I ruined that for you."

"You didn't. You're more important to me than a one-night stand, Scarlet."

"You're pretty important to me too Blake." He throws the empty water bottle and serviettes in the trash can as we walk past and then reaches down for my hand.

It feels comfortable, good. Not at all how it felt when Dean touched me, but also nothing like when Vin did either. A new comfort, one I genuinely feel I will be content living with for the rest of my life. That sliver of doubt dissolves completely.

26

Broken pieces of my heart and soul

We walk home the rest of the way in comfortable silence. I feel thoroughly exhausted and quite full after the pizza. I expect to be out like a light as soon as my head hits the pillow, especially as it's well after three a.m. But I lie in that creaky, hard single bed tossing and turning.

I keep replaying the night. The feel of Dean's breath on me and how it felt so wrong. It was hot and heavy and smelt like beer. It was not Vin's little sarcastic huffs at our jokes or his little grunts when he was frustrated. Dean's hands felt hard and rough, forceful, not at all like the gentle grazes or strokes Vin would use. How he would push my hair from my eyes while we lay watching TV. How it felt to be in his arms.

"Hey Scarlet, is that Vin?"

I was on the bus on the way home from school. Candice yelled out across the bus at me as she was pointing out the window.

I was seventeen and in my last year at school.

"Scarlet, look, it's Vin in the cop car." I ran and jumped over to the other side of the bus to look where she was point-

ing. I saw what she and a busload full of kids from my school were seeing. I looked out the window at the bus and down at the cop car. Vin was sitting in the back.

The lights were not flashing, but he was in the back seat hunched over, staring at the ground. He had his long legs spread wide, and his elbows were resting on his knees.

I couldn't see his face, but his posture told me he was defeated. I stared down at him, and like always, I knew he felt it. He turned his head to look sideways up at me.

His hair was hanging in his eyes, and they looked dark. I reached my hand out to touch him. My hand smashed against the window.

He smiled up at me as the cop car sped up and moved in front of the bus. I saw it turn left down towards our street. It dawned on me. The cops were taking Vin home.

Home to Mike! Home after obviously doing something bad enough to be in a cop car. Panic flooded my system. I rushed to the front of the bus.

The bus had to do a loop, stopping at five other stops before it would get to my stop just in front of our houses. If I got off now, I could run down the street after the cop car and be home faster. I wouldn't beat them, but I wouldn't be far behind.

I lunged at the doors, hearing the driver's shouts.

"Whoa, sit down. What are you doing?" His gruff voice shocked me back to reality.

"I need to get off," I said.

"You have to wait until the next stop."

"I need to get off now, you don't understand, STOP THE BUS!" I shouted in a flurry.

"The next stop is right up here." His voice was even and firm. It left no room for compromise. He wasn't going to stop.

By now we had long passed the left-hand turn the cop car had made.

"You can get off there, ok," he said, pointing at the stop up ahead. I sat down impatiently and tapped my feet, hoping that the tapping would make time move faster. It didn't work.

"Here you go," the driver said as he opened the doors. By now, it would actually take me far longer to run from this stop. It was far from the left-hand turn the cop car made. It was pointless to get off now; I was better off just staying on the bus until it looped back and stopped at my stop.

So, I stayed in the seat and carried on tapping my feet, counting down the stops. Four, three, two, one. It must have been another ten minutes before I got to my stop.

I pushed open the doors with frustration and anxiety. They jammed and squealed against my force, until their own gears kicked in and they flung wide open. Fast!

Faster than I was prepared for. I went flying out the door and down the couple of steps, landing hard on the sharp gravel road next to the bus. My backpack was flung up over my back, and something in there hit me in the back of the head. Something heavy, probably a book.

"Are you ok?" I heard the driver ask. The doors were still open, and he was looking down at me for an answer.

I knew I was hurt, but I didn't have time to check out the damage to my knees or hands where I had landed on the rough gravel road. I definitely didn't have time to chitchat to the driver about my injuries. Ignoring him completely, I jumped up and sprinted across the lawn to Vin's door.

My heart was pumping and my lungs were burning. My legs felt heavy, and I was panting hard from my heavy bag and the fall. I smashed into the door, expecting it to be open or unlocked.

It was both shut and locked. I hurriedly flung my backpack off my back so I could move a bit more freely, scrambling for the pot that I knew the spare key was under. The pot smashed as I threw it over to get to the key. I jumped up and started unlocking the door.

I had no idea what I was thinking. No idea what I could even do to help. I should have gone to my house and gotten my mum, although I knew she would still be at work. I wasn't thinking about any of that. I just needed to get to Vin.

I flung open the door and stumbled into the living room. Just in time to see Mike holding Vin against the wall by the neck. He had his fist cocked, ready to punch him. Vin already had blood coming out of his nose. He looked like he had already been hit more than once.

"STOP!" I screamed. Mike turned towards me. Dropping his hands from Vin, he walked straight towards me. Long, fast, heavy, strides. I could feel myself getting hot. Panic rising up in me.

Every hair on my body stood up. My chest felt heavy. I held my breath, bracing for what was to come. But…he stopped dead in front of me.

I had never seen Mike hit Vin in the face before. It left too much evidence, Vin said. A black eye meant he had to stay home. People asked questions.

However, a bruise on the arms could be covered with a long-sleeved shirt. A bruise on the back or ribs or legs could all be covered up, and life could continue as normal.

So I braced myself, expecting to be hit in the stomach, ribs or across the back of the head. It didn't come. I opened my eyes slowly, one at a time. I felt him brush past me, his hand skimming mine. He grabbed his beer off the hallway table as he walked off towards the lounge room. Vin had rushed up behind Mike, ready to pull him off me or distract him. Ready to turn his attention back to him. He didn't have to. It was over.

Vin stood in front of me, eyes wide, chest heaving. Blood was running from his nose. He moved forward and put his hands on either side of my face, gently moving my head from side to side, up and down, like he was looking for something.

Then he grabbed my hand gently, turning it over in his, seeing the gravel still embedded in it, the blood smeared around it, now starting to dry. He turned, not letting go of my hand, and started walking down the hall to the bathroom.

He sat me down on the edge of the bath, and I realised that I was bleeding from my knees as well. It must have happened when I fell out of the bus and landed on the rough gravel. I must have smeared blood across my face when I was pushing my hair out of my eyes while running.

I saw myself in the bathroom mirror, and it wasn't pretty. I guess the mess had saved me, and Vin. Mike had taken one look at me and moved on.

No wonder Vin had checked my head, looking for a cut, I imagine. I had blood smeared all across my forehead. I was flushed bright red from the panic, my screaming and how fast I had run to the house.

Vin wet a face cloth and gently wiped the blood from my face.

Then he kneeled on one knee in front of me and started to wipe the now drying blood from my knees. He had one hand holding my calf so my leg was slightly raised, and he used the other to wipe the blood and bits of gravel from my knees.

He rinsed the cloth and kneeled back down, only now he grabbed my hand. One at a time, he did the same thing. He didn't look at my face, just at my hands and knees.

He was just focusing on what he needed to do. He didn't once stop to see or acknowledge his own pain. I could see his eyes starting to bruise and swell slightly.

When he finished, he threw the cloth in the sink and grabbed my hand in his again. He was still kneeling on one knee in front of me. He had a hold of my hand, palm up in his. He used his thumb gently, running it across my palm. His hand was cool from the water he had just used. It felt soothing on my cuts and grazes.

He traced the lines on my palm with his thumb, ever so softly. He brushed over the little holes made by the stones in the rough road. He ran over the creases that palm readers use to tell you how long you will live for and how many great loves you will have.

I already knew the answer to that one.

He leaned his head down and kissed the palm of my hand, near my wrist. His lips were soft and warm, and it sent tingles up my arm. He looked up at me, and my heart broke looking at his face. The tears welling up in my eyes turned to full-on streams rolling down my face.

He was still kneeling, but even so, he was almost as tall as me sitting on the side of the bath. I was only just looking down at him and him up at me. He leaned up and kissed me on the lips. A closed-mouth kiss, soft and gentle. He wiped my tears with the back of his fingers, swiping them gently across my cheeks. Then he rested his forehead down on mine.

I could feel his breath on my face and see the rise and fall of his chest. I ran my hands over his arms. They were flexed and holding onto the bathtub on either side of me.

I ran my hands up the length of his arms, feeling the little lumps and bumps left from scars over the years. Like the time with the belt. Little cigarette and lighter burns.

I moved Vin's one arm and stood up. He followed me, grabbing the washcloth out of the basin. I rinsed it in the sink, and then I wiped his face. His hands found their way to my arms, running his fingers back and forth up my forearm slowly. After I had finished, I threw the cloth back in the basin.

He grabbed my hand and led me back down the hall to his bedroom. He waited at the door for me to enter first, following me through. Without letting go of my hand, he turned to shut the door, then he locked the bolt.

Something stopped him. He rubbed his free hand over his forehead and then through his hair, thinking hard about something.

"Scar..." he finally said. His voice was filled with so much pain. "You should not have come here. What if he hit you? Do you know how scared I was?"

"I know Vin, I'm sorry. I couldn't let him hurt you."

We stood there. Together. His back to the door and mine to the bed. Him towering over me, looking down with our hands in each other's.

"If he had hit you..." He huffed out a big breath and shook his head, like he was trying to shake the image away.

"I know Vin," I said. "I know because I feel the same way every single time I see you hurt. Every time he hits you or pushes you. Seeing you battered and bruised, it breaks my heart Vin. So, trust me! I know!"

"No Scar, it's not the same." He dropped his hand from mine and took a big stride over to the bed, flopping down, rubbing his face with his hands.

"You don't know how it feels because it's not your fault. It's mine." He sounded so defeated.

I stepped closer to him, and he instinctively placed his hands on my hips as he pulled me in between his legs. I rested my hands on his shoulders.

"You have a mum who loves you. A safe home. You would never have been in these situations if it wasn't for me. You would never have nearly been...raped." He choked on the word as he said it. " You would never have had to see pain or fear. You never would have had to worry you might get hit or hurt. If he hurt you, it would be my fault. You should leave. You should leave and never come back."

He looked heartbroken. His face was full of pain, and not just the physical kind. He still had his hands on my hips.

"Vin, I would go through all of that to be with you. I'm never leaving you. I love you," I said as I traced my fingers over the little swelling under his eyes. Dark lines were starting to show up.

Tears started running down my face involuntarily again. Vin looked up at me, and I leaned down to kiss him gently on the lips. He didn't kiss me back. His hands still gently resting on my hips.

"VIN, I am not leaving you! Do you understand me? There is nothing you can do to make me leave."

He looked up at me through his lashes. "You are too good for me Scar, you deserve better."

"That's not true Vin, and even if it was. I just don't care. I want you!"

I placed both my hands on his face and pulled him closer to me. I kissed him again. Harder this time, forcing him to kiss me back. His lips opened as they met mine. My hands moved to the back of his head, holding him close, curling my fingers through his hair. His hands finally gripped me a little firmer.

He pulled me closer to him, and I let my body mould to his. Kissing him harder. I felt him starting to relax, tension draining from his body. His hands moved around to my back, slowly tracing lower until they rested on my bum. He stood up and picked me up as he went. I wrapped my legs around his waist and my arms around his neck. He had one hand in a firm grip on my butt holding me up, one hand cupping my neck, kissing me as he turned me around.

I felt him move onto the bed, reaching an arm down to steady himself. He laid me down slowly, still holding the back of my head. Then he hovered over me, not wanting to put his full weight on me, his arms flexed on either side of me and knees down.

He started kissing me again. This time more slowly. Softly. I grabbed the bottom of his shirt and pulled it up over his head. I let my fingers drag along his abs as I went. Then I ran my hands through his wavy hair and down his arms. Arms that I had touched a million times before. Arms that had felt like home from the moment I felt them wrap around me.

He relaxed his arms and allowed his weight to press down onto me. My eyes shot open as a brief wave of panic washed over me. He sensed it straight away and jumped off me like I had given him an electric shock.

I sat up and grabbed his hand. He looked down at me from where he stood at the side of the bed.

"Sorry," he said as he let me pull him back down to the bed.

"Don't be," I said as I gently pushed his chest down so he was lying on his back.

"I want you Vin, I want all of you. I love you and I am never leaving." He gave me a smirk, his pain easing. I moved to straddle him. He placed both his hands on my hips, and I slid my shirt up over my head. He'd seen me in my underwear a million times.

It didn't make me nervous to be naked in front of him anymore, and suddenly I felt annoyed that we hadn't done this before. I felt angry that we let Mike keep us from being completely together. That I let the fear he created in both of us stop us.

I slowly started to move my hips over him, and I could feel his body ache for more. He moved his hands up to the back of my bra and unclipped it. His eyes sparkled a little brighter when he saw all of me.

His hands roamed my body in a way they never had before, gentle but hungry. I lay my body down on top of him, and he curled up to meet me, kissing me, and his hands finally found their way to my breasts.

The feeling all but made me melt. I pushed further into his big hands and moved my hips in a rhythmic motion, feeling him grow beneath me.

I broke our kiss and shuffled down to access his jeans. I slowly unbuttoned them and undid the zip, shuffling them down. He helped me with the last part, kicking his legs to free them till the jeans landed on the floor.

He sat up and started kissing me again while finding the buttons of my jeans. I slid them down past my bum and then sat back, allowing him to do the rest. He moved slowly, trailing his fingers down my legs as he went.

With my jeans gone, he grabbed me around my one calf and slowly kissed up my leg till he reached my inner thighs. My skin tingled, and goosebumps lay in the wake of where his lips had touched.

I lay back down on the bed, basking in the feeling of his hands moving over me as his lips found the most sensitive places where I'd never been kissed before.

He ran out of leg to kiss and looked up at me through his lashes and darkened eyes. I knew him, and without words, he was asking my permission to continue. I nodded my head, and he smiled.

His lips moved over my underwear. I could feel his hot breath, and it sent shivers up my spine. I moved my legs wider so he could get better access as he grabbed the thin elastic of my underwear and slid it down my legs.

We made love for the first time that night. And it was love. We were young, but I knew enough to know it was pure. He was my forever. My soul, my heart, and I was his. Nothing Mike ever did would be able to change that.

I am lying in bed, Blake quietly snoring in the bed across from me in our hostel. Tears are streaming down my face as I cry in silence. How wrong I had been thinking Mike could never tear us apart. He took everything from me, from Vin, from us.

27

It has to be enough

I'm startled awake. My eyes feel puffy and swollen. I don't know how long I lay there crying last night, but eventually tiredness won. I grab my phone, looking at the time. Nine a.m. We are supposed to head for a walking tour at ten. I really don't know how I am supposed to keep this schedule of out all night and then out all day.

I stretch my achy body. Dancing all night has made me sore everywhere. Blake is still asleep in his bed across the room. My heart still aches at my swirling thoughts. Before I know what I am doing, I have tiptoed across the room and am sliding under Blake's covers.

He stirs, rolling over to face me, but his eyes remain shut.

"You ok?" he asks as he opens his arms, allowing me to curl in closer and rest my head on him. He pulls me in closer, and I wrap my top arm over his waist. Blake is gorgeous. Naturally lean, dark tan skin. But more than that, he is kind and funny and has always been there for me.

When I don't answer, he opens his eyes to look down at me. It's not weird for us to be affectionate. We often cuddle while watching a movie on the couch or hold hands while walking. Hug hello and goodbye. But not like this in bed.

I look back up at Blake, wondering what it would feel like. Wondering if I could feel those things again. The things Vin made me feel. Or would it always feel like it did with Dean when it isn't Vin.

I tip my head up and forward and press my lips to Blake's. He doesn't pull away, but he doesn't open up to me. I pull my lips away and stare at him.

His eyes look confused, brows pinching slightly together. But he doesn't say anything.

So I lean back towards him, and this time when I press my lips to his, I open them, sliding my tongue out to find his lips and enter his mouth.

He moves into me, opening his lips and kissing me back. Our tongues gently caress, our lips moving in sync.

Our hands haven't moved from the spot they are in. His arm is still under my head, his other draped over my waist and mine over his.

I pull back, closing my eyes, a single tear sliding down my cheek. He brings his hand up to wipe it away.

"Find what you're looking for?" he asks, not in a condescending way. His tone is full of compassion. He understands what I am trying to do, trying to feel.

"Dean kissed me, and I felt nothing but terrified. I wanted to see if it would feel like that with everyone or if there was a chance I could be normal again," I say, pausing to let my thoughts catch up. "I sometimes feel so broken Blake, still after all these years. He is all I see, all I feel, all I breathe. You feel so comfortable to me, but he….he was home. I am happy but there is a part of me that will never be whole again. Some days I don't know how to keep moving forward without him."

"What did you feel when you kissed me?" he asks.

I play it over in my head, grasping at the feelings. At anything I felt within my body. It was nice, comfortable. It felt good to be that close to him. It didn't feel terrifying like it had with Dean, but I knew it wasn't the same. It would never be what I had with Vin. Blake sees the answer on my face.

"What did you feel?" I ask. Blake starts laughing.

"Scarlet, I'm gay, not dead, and you are beautiful."

"Are you saying you felt…" I pause, not wanting to say the word horny out loud. I didn't want the dynamic to change between Blake and me. Our relationship is perfect. Why am I messing with it?

"My body reacted at the thought of getting off, but it wasn't the same. Not the same electric feeling I have when I have been with guys. It just doesn't feel quite right." He pauses. "There is this small feeling of… I don't really even know how to explain it. It's like this feeling deep in your guts that just feels…off. You could bury it and ignore it if you really wanted to, but you know it's there. Does that make sense?"

"Weirdly enough Blake, I know exactly what you mean. Sorry I kissed you." He pulls me closer to his chest.

"What brought all this on?" he asks.

I sigh, allowing my body to sink into his warm comfort. I start telling him about the night Vin and I first made love. I tell him about the morning after, when we decided everything would change.

We woke up in each other's arms that morning. Vin with a severely swollen nose and two black eyes.

He looked down at me through half-closed lids while I lay on his chest. He bent his head down and kissed me on the forehead while I lay there.

"If you won't leave me, I will take us both. Away from Mike. We have to leave. It's the only way we will be safe," he whispered.

We used to talk about leaving all the time when we were younger, traveling or moving out together, Vin moving away from Mike. We once planned that Vin would save his money to get a place of his own.

The older we got, the less we spoke about leaving. We spoke about it less and less, until one day, we stopped altogether.

"You love your job, I am still in school." I paused for a moment and then kept talking. "You have a roof over your head and food on the table. We have each other. And my mum." When I finished, I realised how selfish I sounded. I knew it was solely about my mum. I didn't want to move away from her, but I didn't want to tell her what was going on either.

I had all those things. A mum who loved me. A safe house, food cooked for me. Someone who washed my clothes and filled the cupboards with food. Told me they loved me. Helped make my lunches and give me money when I needed it. Listened to me when I needed help or advice.

Vin, Vin had none of that. Vin had me, and that was it.

He sat up, and my body followed. He turned towards me so he was facing me, holding both my hands in his.

"I know, but I can't stay here anymore Scar."

"Vin, I…I don't know. You know I would follow you to hell and back. But my mum." I continued to explain my reasoning to him. He listened intently and didn't try to interrupt.

We knew what Mike was capable of. We knew his moods and what made him tick. The outside world, we didn't know. We had my mum here. Friends, jobs, school. I didn't know what it would take to survive on our own. We couldn't afford to rent a house on Vin's wages alone, and I wanted to finish school.

Vin listened to me ramble on. He nodded at everything I said as I went along.

He didn't agree. I could tell without him speaking a single word. The slight grunts and huffs of frustration that he didn't even realise he was making. He didn't try to argue with me, he just listened. When I was finished, he held my hands.

"Scar," he said, staring at me with such intensity I thought I would melt. "I have loved you from the moment you came into my backyard and ran your fingers over my torn-up arms. I didn't want to love you as much as I did because I knew

I would never be good for you. I mean, look at my role model. I can't stand to see you hurt. Seeing how much everything Mike does to me affects you, it's killed me. The thought of him hurting you destroys me."

His eyes started to well up, and I didn't know if it was because they were swollen or if he was crying. He carried on.

"I love you Scar. I can take care of you. I promise. Let me take care of you." He was almost begging now. "I have tried to shield you from how bad it actually gets here because I know how much it hurts you. But I basically look after myself anyway. Especially lately. It's me that shops and cooks and pays the bills. I don't know when or how it shifted so much, but it seemed the older I got, the more useless he became." He continued. Pleading. "I know I can take care of you, cos I already do all that for him. And why? So he can punch me in the face over nothing. He didn't even let me explain why I was in the cop car. My car was yellow-carded. Something with the exhaust. I just need to take it to the garage for them to change some things and it will be fine. The police wouldn't let me drive it home. I have to get it towed to the garage. They offered to drop me home, as it was Friday afternoon and I couldn't get hold of a tow truck company. I'm not in trouble; you don't even get a fine. I just have to pay for it to be reinspected before they will renew the registration."

I realised I had been holding my breath the entire time while he was speaking, fighting back my own tears with a mix of emotions. Fear, anger, love. I didn't know what feeling to trust. The one thing I did know, the one thing I did trust, was Vin.

I started to realise how selfish I was being. He dealt with so much. So much more than what I saw. Why? So he could stay with me. If it had not been for me, I have no doubt he would have taken off years ago. I couldn't let him live like this anymore.

So we agreed then and there. I would finish high school, and he would finish his second year of his apprenticeship. Then we would leave. It was only a few more months. I would have graduated my final year, at least giving me more of a chance to find a job. And Vin would have time to talk to his boss to see if he could get recommendations for a transfer.

I didn't want to leave my mum, but I wanted to follow Vin more. A part of me thought if I told Mum the truth she would follow us, eventually. She would help, and we would all start over. Away from Mike. A fresh start. I just couldn't tell her yet. She would try to talk me out of it or come up with other ideas. Or my biggest fear, she would try to do something about Mike, and we couldn't risk him finding out.

We spent the nights after that locked in my room. Spent hours on my laptop googling places all around Australia. We looked for places that were near the beach.

"What about this place?" Vin said as he turned the laptop towards me.

Vin must have googled 'the best coastal towns in Western Australia.' A heap of little pictures came up on the screen, images of beaches with the town names underneath them.

"All the way to Western Australia," I commented.

"Yep, why not? It's the furthest away we can get without leaving the country. Plus the beaches look amazing," he said.

We were sitting in my room on my bed with crossed legs. We had the laptop and our notebook. Vin had now moved the laptop into my lap. He jumped around to sit behind me, his long legs spread open and wrapped around mine, engulfing me in a bear hug. His arms found their way to the laptop.

His head rested on my shoulder, hair tickling my neck. It felt right having him this close. It felt like home. I clicked on the button for the picture Vin had been talking about and started to scroll down.

*"How do you even pronounce it?" I asked, not really ex-
pecting Vin to know either.*

*"Man-doo-rah, Man-dur-ra." We both started to rattle off
pronunciations and were chuckling.*

*"How are we going to live in a place you can't even pro-
nounce?" I asked as I elbowed Vin's side playfully to stop him
whispering the name in my ear.*

*"That's the point," Vin said. "How can Mike ever find us
if he can't even pronounce the name?"*

*"You're assuming he will look," I replied. Vin said nothing,
and we both sat staring at the laptop for a moment, looking
at the screen, pictures of beaches, of an estuary with dolphins
jumping out to greet some people on a boat. Blue skies and
clear water.*

"Mandurah, huh," I finally said.

*"Mandurah," Vin repeated, low and soft in my ear. A smile
crept across my face as he slowly started to kiss my neck and
earlobes. He moved the laptop over to the side of the bed we
were not occupying. He then moved his hands to find mine,
holding them.*

*Our fingers entwined for a moment before he broke free
so he could find my face. I tilted my head back so he had
better access to my neck. I slowly started to turn around
until I was facing him, wrapping my legs around his waist.*

"Ok," I said. "Let's do it!"

Blake leans down and places a kiss on my forehead.
"You were planning to move to our town with him?" he
asks. I nod, admitting that the life I am living now with
Blake was what I had planned with Vin. The town, the
travelling. All of it.

"I am sorry you never got the chance to move with him,
to travel. To have that life you deserved with him. I don't
know what happened to him, and I know you don't want
to talk about it, but just know that I am here Scarlet. I will

always be here. You deserve to let yourself be happy. It might not be with him, but you can still be happy. I can make you happy."

I close my eyes, letting his words sink in. Letting the comfort of his embrace ease my guilt. I don't believe that I deserve to be happy. I don't believe that I deserve to be here, living this life that Vin can't. But I do believe Blake when he says he will always be there. I believe him when he says he can make me happy. Maybe a successful marriage didn't need sex. It needs two best friends. Trust and laughter. It has to be enough.

28

Best-laid plans

SCARLET

The heat is scorching. I can feel it warming my body as if it's coming from the inside as well as the outside. The only slight reprieve comes from the ice-cold cocktail that I take sips from as I twirl the frosty glass in my hand. It has a big piece of pineapple sitting on the rim of the glass, and a big pineapple leaf next to it that I have been using as a stirrer. It is strong, leaving bursts of sweetness on my tongue after every sip.

Blake is sitting next to me drinking a beer, a Corona with a wedge of lemon. Supposedly it enhances the flavour. I read somewhere that it was just to keep the flies away. Well, that's not needed here. It's too hot for even the flies.

We arrived in Las Vegas as the second stop on our Contiki tour, then came straight to Monte Carlo. We heard it had a lazy river and floaty donut things that you can lie in and float around in with a drink. We are actually staying at a much, much cheaper hotel just off the main strip. However, our hotel clerk told us that you can go to any hotel pool you wanted.

Still, we snuck in here with our own towels and tried to make it look like we belonged. We ducked our heads and avoided eye contact as we slid through the gate and passed the staff. No one seemed to really even notice us or care. We still felt like we were breaking some sort of rule.

We sat down on some deck chairs near the lazy river and ordered a drink straight away.

"Let's get in," Blake says after we finished our first round. I knew this was inevitable. I mean, what did I think was going to happen at a goddamn resort pool? I laugh to myself, thinking what an idiot I am.

Up until this point, I have managed to conceal my stomach by avoiding watering holes with people or by wearing one-piece bathers. No one has ever questioned it. But here, everyone is in the tiniest of bikinis. I would stand out like a sore thumb in my one-piece or a full-length top.

So, on a whim, I had bought and packed a bikini and decided I would not care what people think. I'd be brave and bold and step out of my comfort zone. I'd live again. That's what this trip was supposed to be about. Letting go of the past and starting new. For both of us.

But now I am regretting it all.

I knew this point would come. The point where I would get in the pool in my bikini, stomach on full display. Everyone would stare and wonder. Blake would ask. I know him. There is no way he won't ask.

I should have shown him beforehand. Should have come up with a good story. Although I know Blake will understand if I say I don't want to talk about it. I know he will find some way to make light of the situation and make me laugh.

My past is my past, and I cannot change it. It has made me who I am and all the rest of that self-help bull. What better way to do it with people I will most likely never see again?

Blake however, I will see again. We plan to move in together when we get home. Hell, we plan to get married over here. Fake or not.

However, I want this trip to be different. I want to move forward. To stop living in the past. In fear, in guilt. But saying that and doing it are entirely different things.

As I sit on the deck chair in my bikini with a white long-sleeved kimono covering my body, I feel the heat start to boil away inside me.

Not just the heat from the scorching hot sun, but the internal heat of embarrassment, shame, guilt. The kind that makes your cheeks flush red and your tummy do backflips.

I know that the time has come, and I have no real way out of this. Blake is already taking his singlet off, hunting for the stand to go and get us some tubes to float on.

"There it is," he says. "I will go get us some." With that, he walks off, not noticing me stalling, or the fact that I look like I am about to pass out. I stand up and look around, wondering if people are watching.

Nope, they aren't. It's all in your own head, I tell myself. I take a deep breath, close my eyes tight and let my kimono drop to the deck chair. Blake is already on his way back to me with two big tubes for the lazy river.

"Come on," he says as he walks straight past me towards the steps to the entry of the river. He puts both the tubes in the water and then jumps in. He gives no indication of whether the water is cold or not, nor does he seem to care who is watching. He has truly embraced this trip already. He steadies my tube while I follow suit. The water is cold, and I swear I can see steam coming off my body as it puts out the internal fire.

I lie on my back, letting my butt sink into the hole in the middle of the tube, floating with just the bottom of my legs, feet and butt in the water. My body temperature starts to adjust, and I let my hands swirl around next to the tube.

Blake is next to me, holding on to the handle of my tube so that we stay linked together. He has jumped on front first and has his back up towards the sun. We let the current from the pool jets float us along the river, Blake manoeuvring us in between people in the congested areas.

Groups of people have broken off and are standing together drinking or chatting. Couples are resting on the edge of the water, making out, while others are floating around linked together like us.

I see Blake's eyes skim down to my stomach. I see him notice the scar, but he says nothing. That's not like Blake, I think to myself. I can feel the heat of panic rise inside me again despite the cool water.

Blake notices how uncomfortable I have suddenly become. I suppose I could have hidden it better. Could have laid facedown like him, but why delay the inevitable? There will be lots of pools and beaches on this trip. I barely managed to avoid it in LA.

I don't want to be sitting on the sidelines for the rest of my life. Better to get it over with now. I start really regretting the fact that I have not told him earlier.

"Breathe," Blake says. I start chuckling.

"I'm trying," I reply. I don't know why I am so shaken. I mean, what am I expecting? Someone to run up and be like OMG look at that hideous scar? And then they'll magically know how I got it and all my deep dark secrets would start dropping out of the sky on paper for everyone to read?

"This part of the past you never want to talk about," he finally says, tilting his head down towards my stomach and the large, mean-looking raised scar that runs across it.

"It's a long depressing story," I reply.

"I got the time, you know," he says.

"You don't want to know."

"Ok, let me guess, you rescued a child from a shark and got bitten, but you survived and they awarded you with a medal and wrote stories about your heroics. Now you are a living legend in your hometown," he jokes.

"It was a crocodile, not a shark, and they have actually written a book about it. We are in talks for the movie deal,"

I reply in my most serious voice, countering his sarcastic playfulness.

We both start laughing hysterically, and Blake splashes water up at me into my face.

"You are funny, you know that?" he says.

"You bring it out in me," I reply.

Blake's mood changes as he locks eyes with me. His face suddenly turns more serious.

"What's wrong?" I ask.

"I dunno, I just… I haven't felt this free in a long time, that's all. You've always made me feel like I can be myself, no pressure or judgement."

"Strangely enough, I know exactly what you mean."

"Being so far away, away from my parents and the church, and being here with you. It just feels like I can finally breathe properly."

"Same."

We let a comfortable silence fall over us as we float around, Blake holding my tube so we stay locked together.

"You know, I meant what I said," Blake says, breaking the silence.

"About what?"

"About having the time to listen."

I nod. Maybe one day, I think to myself. But not today.

We have to be back at our hotel by six p.m. We are all meeting for a show and dinner. So we spend the rest of the day relaxing by the pool and swimming. We get back to our hotel at around five p.m. and head to our room. We are sharing a studio. It has two king singles across from each other and our own bathroom with a little kitchenette.

"Are you getting dressed up tonight?" Blake asks. It's not like him to care so much about outfits, but I suppose we are in Vegas. If there ever was a chance to get really dressed up, this would be it.

"I dunno, I bought a few dresses but..." I trail off.

I open my suitcase and start randomly pulling things out to try on. We are going to Cirque du Soleil tonight, but it is so goddamn hot in Vegas that I am actually considering staying in bathers.

"That one's nice," Blake says as I pull out a black body-con dress. The dress is short, tight and low with shoe-string straps. My mum saw it at the shops and bought it for me for the trip as a little gift. She said that every woman needs a little black dress. I packed it, not wanting to disappoint her, but I knew I could not bring myself to try it on, and the thought of actually wearing it makes bile rise in my throat.

"Hm, maybe."

"I bet you look stunning in it," Blake says as he holds it up.

"MAYBE," I say again, this time more forcefully. I snatch the dress from his hands, throwing it back into my open suitcase.

"Ok, ok. I will leave you to it," he says as he walks off into the shower. By the time he gets out of the bathroom, already wearing black chinos and a cream cotton button-down, I have decided on jeans and a dressy singlet.

Blake tells me that he is going to go to the bar to meet a few of the other guys who are ready early.

Once he is out of the room, I jump in the shower and start getting ready. I stare at myself in the bathroom mirror. I feel good, even though I know I am probably going to die from heatstroke in jeans. I feel comfortable. I grab my purse and head down to meet everyone.

Stepping out of the elevator and walking through to the lobby bar, I can see some of the other girls. Everyone is dressed up to the nines. Jessica has slipped into a low-cut blush mini dress. She looks stunning.

Rebecca is wearing a loose-fitting, very short dress that I know instantly is Camilla. It has bright colours, patterns and metal studs. She looks effortlessly sexy.

I do a quick scan of the other girls. Not one of them is in jeans. They all have beautiful dresses and high heels, looking flawless. Even all the guys look more dressed up than me at this point.

Quickly, before anyone can spot me, I duck back into the elevator and head to the room. I rummage through my suitcase and grab the black bodycon dress. Holding it up, I just stare at it. It's like it knew that I was going to wear it all along.

I grab the dress and head back into the bathroom to change. As I start to slip the tight-fitting dress over my body, a veil slips down with it. I am overrun, to the point that by the time I have the dress on, I feel like I can no longer breathe. It has nothing to do with the tightness of the dress. It is the guilt and heartbreak that are suffocating me. The part of my life I left behind, in the past. The sadness for the life I was supposed to have that was ripped from my fingers. The life of the boy I loved. The boy I lost. I am now staring at myself in the full-length mirror. I barely recognise the girl staring back at me.

I didn't think I had ever seen his eyes so bright. Little specks of gold splattered throughout them. Like someone had flicked a gold paint brush over a bright-green canvas while it lay sparkling in the sun.

He looked at me with that gorgeous sideways smirk of his. He was sitting on the little stool that they put in the change rooms for your handbag, his long legs spread wide so that they were not up around his chest. He put his big hands on my hips and pulled me in between his legs. His hands moved up the black material over my hips around to the curve of my back.

Then he turned me around so that I was facing the mirror and he was behind me. He rose slowly, moving his hands up to my shoulders. His head was now looking over my shoulder, and he forced me to look at myself in the mirror, standing barefoot in this slinky black bodycon dress. Tight over my hips, following the curves of my body. It had loose mesh flowy sleeves over shoestring straps. Low slung to show cleavage. Tight-fitting, hugging my body to finish mid-thigh.

"You look incredible, Scar," he said as his long hair brushed my shoulders. He was leaning down to kiss my neck.

"It's too much?" He wrapped an arm around my waist, pulling me back into his chest.

"Scar, look…. Are you seeing what I am seeing? You look so beautiful."

"Do you think people will think it's too much though?" I asked again.

"I think people can fuck off."

I spat out a laugh so hard I almost choked. I unwrapped his arm from around me and stepped back further, giving me more room to get a better look at myself. I stood high on my tippy-toes as if to get a feel for what it would look like once I had heels on.

"How do you feel?" His tone became more serious. He flopped back down onto the stool, his elbows resting on his knees, head resting in his hands as he stared up at me with those eyes. I looked back at him. Then back at the mirror.

I had seen the dress in the store window and had not been able to stop thinking about it. It cost way more than what I wanted to spend, but I loved it.

I closed my eyes and just stood there for a moment. Then I let my hands run up from the bottom of the skirt over my hips up to under my arms. The dress was snug and comfortable. The fabric was soft and buttery. I felt a smile creep across my lips. I spun around in a small circle and stared directly at him with a smile.

"I feel amazing," I finally said. His face broke into a huge smile, and his eyes became even brighter, if that was possible.

"Good, because you look amazing. This is definitely the dress you should wear to the end-of-year formal."

"I don't know Vin. You don't think it's too much for a school formal? Too low cut, too tight?" He chuckled.

"Scar, we just saw Kate Abrams at the Boost juice stand wearing less than that fifteen minutes ago." I started laughing as well, taking the dress off my shoulders and sliding it down my body. I wriggled out of the tight-fitting dress till it slid to the floor.

"I guess I am just nervous. We didn't make it to our year-ten dance, remember?" A pursed-lip smile slid across his face. He handed me my denim shorts and tee, and I started to get dressed in my usual clothes.

"I will get it and just see how I feel on the day," I said, handing the dress to him so he could hang it on the hanger for me. He was nodding his head with a cheeky smile.

The formal was a couple of weeks away and would see out the end of the year. The year I graduated from high school. The point that marked when Vin and I would leave. A few more weeks, and we would be on our way to a new life. We had saved our money and had it all planned out.

We were not going to tell Mike. When school broke, we were just going to take our suitcases with the bare minimum, jump in Vin's car and head west. We were planning to drive across the Nullarbor. We'd take our time and camp along the way, staying at caravan parks and cheap motels until we made it to Mandurah in the south of Western Australia.

We were going to leave a note for my mum explaining everything. Telling her about Mike and the abuse and where we were headed. I didn't have the heart to tell her to her face. I knew she would try to talk me out of it, and we had to leave. I had to leave. For Vin's sake.

I hoped Mum would understand. That she would come over, follow us. Or at least understand and visit.

Vin and I had kept so busy since the police drop-off incident. We didn't give Mike a chance to do any more damage. Vin worked as much as he could, doing cash jobs after hours as well as working full time. I was busy with school and picking up every extra shift I could get at the restaurant I worked at to save money.

When we were not working, we would go to a cafe with free Wi-Fi and continue to plan our trip. We would research places to stay and things we wanted to see on the way, printing and cutting and glueing them into a scrap book we were making for the trip.

That was the first time Mike had ever repeatedly punched Vin in the face like that. It had taken a solid month for Vin's face to heal, and he had hidden out at home saying he was sick. I think Mike knew it had raised questions with Vin's boss and my mum, so maybe Mike was laying low.

Vin was almost seventeen and had grown even taller seemingly overnight. He was taller than Mike now. He still had not completely filled out his long limbs though.

Now we had mere weeks before school ended, and we'd be free to start the next chapter of our lives. Vin was not allowed to go to the school formal, as they had a students-only policy.

He didn't seem to mind though. He seemed more excited than me, helping me pick a dress and offering to drive me and two of my girlfriends that had decided to go together.

We were going to meet at Ashley's house, as she had a great garden for photos. Then Vin was going to drive us to the event. He said he was happy to come back and get us, all we had to do was call. Secretly, I thought my friends were more excited to see Vin than they were to go to the formal or to see me. I didn't blame them.

Now the day was fast approaching, and the closer it got, the more nervous I became. About everything. The end of school, the start of life on our own. Actually making it to a formal after bailing on our year-ten dance due to the trauma of what happened a few nights before.

All the emotions and thoughts playing around in my head. What to wear to this damn formal was the least of my worries.

In all honesty, I was regretting the choice to stay and see the year out, and some days, I wanted to get in his car and just go. The anxiety and anticipation were killing me.

We had a plan, and we knew if we wanted to make a real go of this, we had to stick to it. But even the best-laid plans can all go up in flames.

I suck in deep breaths of air, reminding myself that I am safe and those memories are in the past. I run my hands down the dress to smooth it out, and I refocus on myself in the mirror.

"I can do this," I say to myself. I grab my bag and head back out the door, down in the elevator for the second time. Only this time, I make it to the bar and to Cirque du Soleil.

29

Guilty conscience

The weather is perfect. We sail out on the little boat from the Canadian side of Niagara Falls. I have been waiting for this part of the trip. I have no clue why, but when Vin and I would talk about where we wanted to go, this place was always at the top of my list. It was always at the top of his list too.

I am bouncing with joy and excitement. The boat goes right up close to the waterfall, and I can feel the power of it. The spray of the water as it comes down and hits the body of water. The roaring sound. It's magical.

I close my eyes and soak it all in. I can't believe I am actually here. I can feel the spray hitting my face. People have full-on waterproof ponchos to stop themselves from getting wet, but I am basking in it. Blake and I huddle together, taken in by the beauty of it all.

The boat starts its trip back to the dock, and I wipe the water from my eyes. I am hit with an electric shock, volts coursing through me. I blink, trying to focus.

Blake senses me stiffen next to him and instinctively wraps an arm around me.

"You ok?" he asks. I turn my head, almost like a magnetic pull. It feels so strong. Something in me is screaming.

"Vin!" I frantically search the crowd on the embankment, where I swear I just saw his face. It's so far away,

I can't make out anyone directly, but I am convinced I saw him. The boat moves closer to the dock. "He's here," is all I manage to choke out.

"Who?" Blake replies.

"Vin, he's here. I just saw him. I swear it and I…I… I can't explain it. I…I can just feel him. It was him."

"Scarlet, what do you mean, he's here? How?"

Blake looks genuinely confused. I suppose that makes sense. I haven't really told him much detail about Vin. I haven't told him about our ending and where he is now or was. He knows bits and pieces, but not the whole truth. Not all of it.

"I know this was a place you guys wanted to visit together, maybe that's what you are feeling."

"No, we wanted to do this entire trip together, we always planned to travel, but that's not it. It's the weirdest feeling, I can't explain it. I just… I swear, I just saw him over there. I mean, he…he. I—" I cut myself off, well aware that I am starting to sound crazy. Vin is not here. That is impossible. Or is it. I could have sworn I saw him, his height towering over the majority of the crowd, his piercing green eyes almost glowing in the sun. I mean the distance is significant, but it was him. My stomach is doing backflips, and I feel dizzy. Goosebumps pebble my arms, and the hair on my neck is still raised.

Blake pulls me in closer to him. I look back and up, trying to focus on the falls. The boat is moving away from the spray. I focus on the feeling of finally being here and experiencing this. What I felt under the falls. We were as close as anyone was going to get to being right underneath it.

Well, besides that crazy lady who went over the falls with her cat in a barrel. I read about that on the walk through the tunnel. I start laughing hysterically. I lean my head on Blake's shoulder and he gives me a squeeze, resting his head on top of mine.

"You ok?" he asks.

"I'm fine," I say through my fits of laughter. "Might be losing my mind a little, but I'm going to be fine." Blake chuckles, but he keeps his arm tight around me, allowing me to lean into him.

While I wish I could be seeing this place with Vin, I am glad to be here, and I'm glad to be here with Blake.

It couldn't have been Vin. It's just my guilty conscience in overdrive because we are visiting a place I know he really wanted to see. It has to be that. Right?

30

Born from the devil, raised in the flames

VIN

I know she is here. Don't ask me to explain it cos it doesn't even make sense to me. I just know. I can feel it. A magnetic pull, stronger than gravity.

Now don't get me wrong. I didn't go looking for her. I didn't follow her here. This is pure coincidence or fate, if you believe in that shit.

One minute I was standing on the embankment, leaning on the fence, watching the hypnotic water rush over the edge. Then the feeling washed over me. That familiar warmth, like being coated in pure sunshine. Then I heard her laugh. Loud, hysterical laughter. My head was on a swivel trying to find her, following the direction of that laugh that seemed to be coming from everywhere and nowhere at the same time.

I know I should have just walked away. That sinking feeling in my stomach, what now? What was I going to do if I saw her? Would I be able to walk away? AGAIN! I mean, the first time was a little easier, a forced separation. I told myself it was better for her. To let her go. Let her be happy.

She deserved better than what I was able to give her, and I knew deep down she would wait. There was a part of me that worried she would hate me for hurting her. But I knew her. I knew in my gut if I said the words, she would wait for me forever. That wasn't fair. She deserved happiness and sunshine and heaven.

Me! I was born from the devil and raised in his flames. I would never be able to give her what she deserved. So, I shut her out. I told myself over and over it was for her. For the best. She would be able to move on and be happy.

Hearing her laugh now, she does sound happy. I did the right thing, and I should turn around and walk away. Instead, I am madly rushing towards the addictive sound of her laugh. Pushing people out of the way as I go. They all start to blur together. I am tall and big, so it isn't hard to part the crowds, and I don't care who I step on to get to her.

Then…there she is. The laugh connects with the body, like a lightning bolt that has me unable to move further. She looks beautiful. She was always beautiful though. But my memories did her absolutely no justice.

She has her hair shorter than I remember, but it's wavy, loose waves rustling at her shoulders. Tangled in the breeze.

I always loved her hair when she left it wavy, but she was forever straightening it. It's the same colour, dark brown. She is wearing jeans with an army-green tee and black jacket. Laughing and smiling.

For a minute, I feel whole again. Feel like I can breathe again. Everything seems clearer and brighter. I am not sure how I have even been breathing without her.

Then I see him!

He is only slightly taller than her, dark tan skin and black hair. His arm is draped around her shoulders, like it is the most natural thing in the world. Her beautiful head is resting on his shoulder.

A loving embrace. More than friends. The breath catches in my throat and I swallow hard, trying to force it down.

I feel myself getting hot with anger at the sight of someone else touching her.

I have to calm myself down. This is what I wanted. What the fuck did I think she was doing for the last few years?

I mean, what was I expecting? I wanted her to move on. Wanted her to be happy. Here she is, happy and moving on. Yet all I can think about is how badly I want to pound that guy's face into the pavement, and I am not a violent guy. Well, not normally. Guess the last few years have changed me. Right now, I cannot think of anything I want to do more than break that arm he has over her and beat him to death with it.

I have to get it together. Seeing her now would do nothing. She has moved on, and that was exactly what I wanted.

I will myself to move. I am suddenly grateful for the fact that she is on a boat. But a boat sailing back to the dock I am now right above.

I look down at my feet and will them to move in the opposite direction. One foot in front of the other, until I am taking giant strides away from her. Away from him. Away from that beautiful laugh.

Somewhere between the tourist centre and my hotel, I break into a full run. Chest heavy, breathing hard. I barge through the hotel doors and completely bypass the lift, heading straight for the stairs. I take them three at a time and am at my room before I know it. I shove my things into my bag before launching straight back down those stairs.

I can't stay here. Not in the same place as her. Not without tearing the town apart trying to find her again. I don't care if I already paid for three nights. I don't care that this is my first taste of freedom in years. I don't care that I have wanted to see this place my entire life. I have to get out of here. Get as far away from her as possible.

I can't trust myself to be this close to her. I'd ruin everything for her. Everything I have already sacrificed and let go of so she could move on and be happy. My willpower is not that strong. I'm not that selfless. I have to keep moving. Far, far away. I don't let myself stop, not until I am safely out of that damn country.

Three days later on a beach in Bali, Indonesia, I finally let myself stop. Now what the fuck am I supposed to do?

31

Like floating in the ocean

Knock knock knock. "Come in!" I call as I fumble with the zip on my final choice of outfit.

"Are you ready?" Blake is leaning on the doorway, holding back a laugh at the dress I have chosen. I have been in the dressing room for the last half an hour, trying on a hoard of different outfits for our wedding in Vegas. The room is huge and lined with racks upon racks of dresses, all in size categories. I have tried on every style from sleek and fitted to lace to full-on death by tulle. I landed on a sixties-inspired puffy dress that was probably once white. It looks like it has been worn and washed so many times that it's now an off-white grey colour.

Blake is wearing a suit that is about three sizes too big and the shiniest black and white shoes of all time. I can pretty much see my reflection in them.

We are back in Vegas for round two. Cos once is never enough.

We have visited Graceland in Memphis. Immersed ourselves in the culture in New Orleans. Soaked up the sun at Miami Beach and rode way too many rides at the theme parks in Orlando. Cruised around the Statue of Liberty in the city that never sleeps. Felt the spray of Niagara Falls on our skin. Now we're back in Las Vegas.

Over the last thirty days, Blake and I have become even more inseparable, if that's even possible. I have seen a completely different side to Blake on this trip, and I am sure he saw a different side to me too.

Maybe it's being away from his family, the church, my mum. Away from work, study and any expectations. We were always so busy back home.

But this… This trip, we were able to be carefree. The walls we both built up were dissolved by salt water, fresh air and no responsibilities.

Although Blake always did make me feel so at ease, this trip has been different. Having no one else as a buffer but each other, we have opened up in a way that the reality of our normal daily grind didn't allow.

I have finally felt more myself than I have in years. Basically since that day. The day everything changed. The day I lost Vin. I have told Blake more about my past on this trip than I have in the entirety of our friendship.

Blake never judged or tried to offer a solution or his opinion. He would just listen. It didn't seem to bother him when I talked about Vin or opened up about my true feelings for him. He seemed to get it.

No one and nothing would ever replace Vin. When I lost him, I lost a part of myself as well. A part that will never truly be whole without him.

The last few years, Blake has slowly helped me heal. Like little dots of glue putting me back together. And now, we have a deeper, stronger connection. Something I never expected or thought I wanted.

So here we are, about to be married by Elvis in Las Vegas.

Blake walks over. "You look hilariously gorgeous," he says as he leans in and kisses my cheek.

"You look like Al Capone," I say as I lean into his kiss. Blake takes my hand and turns to lead me out of the dressing room and back out to the little chapel. I pull back on his hand as we walk towards the door.

"Everything ok?" he asks as he loosens his grip on my hand.

"Are we doing the right thing Blake?"

"Are you having second thoughts? Scarlet, it's what I want, but I would never force you into this. We don't have to do this, and we don't have to do it now."

"I mean, it was what I wanted. I have felt good about it, right up till…" I pause. Blake looks at me, his dark-brown eyes soothing my swirling mind. I have been trying so hard to forget the feeling I felt at the falls. How it felt like he was right there. How I thought I saw Vin.

I brushed it off like I was crazy, and even though I knew Blake would have been ok to talk about it, I never brought it up after that. Only now I am about to be married. I can't stop thinking about him, and I have this sinking feeling that I am about to make a huge mistake.

"I love you Scarlet," Blake whispers to me, leaning in close. "It may not be what people expect, and it may not be traditional, but I know we can be happy." He grabs my hand in his again. "But if this isn't what you want, we leave now and never talk of it again. I am dying for In and Out Burger anyway."

I chuckle because, well, I am also starving and it feels so foreign to have someone say those words to me again. Even more foreign is the fact that I feel the same. It's not crazy, tear-each-other's-clothes-off, can't-breathe-without-you love. It feels more like peace. Like floating in the ocean or watching the sunset. A deep feeling of calm. It may never be what people traditionally expect love to be, but it is love all the same. And I have to admit. I like it.

"Let's go get married Blake," I say, squeezing his hand in mine. "This is what I want. I am happy." And I mean it.

32

Darkness, complete & utter darkness

SCARLET

Knock knock. Knock knock. The door opened, and Vin came into my room, his tall wide frame, bright-green eyes and wavy caramel hair filling the doorway.

I was dressed in my little black bodycon dress and some heels I had brought to match. I had done my hair myself. It was long and dark, and I had left my natural wave and added some curls with the straightener.

"I'm ready."

He stood in the doorway smirking at me. I felt like a deer in headlights. Then he let out a little chuckle.

"Stop being so nervous Scar, everything will be ok."

His bright eyes and his sideways smirk made me relax. He stepped closer to me and cupped my head between his hands, then leaned down to kiss my forehead.

"Tonight will be amazing, and first thing tomorrow, we will start our new lives together," he said. I wanted to believe his words so badly. I believed nothing could stop our foolproof plan. Nothing!

I was naive and should have known better. Looking back, I wish we had left the very first night we decided to go. I wish we had told my mum years ago. Wish we were already gone.

"You look great Scar, what are you so worried about?" Vin asked as he pulled his hands away from my face and looked down at me through thick lashes.

"Thanks," I replied. "I suppose I just feel a bit awkward, that's all. Once I get there, I will be fine." He nodded in agreement.

"Well, say the word and I will be there in a heartbeat to get you, you know that right?" he said while holding my hands in his.

"Yep, I know," I replied as I walked to the buffet to grab my clutch and phone.

Mum was working the afternoon shift, but she was going to get off on a break and meet us at Ashley's house to be there for photos.

I did one last check in the mirror. "Ok, I think I'm ready to go." We started walking out the door and across the lawn to Vin's car, which was parked in his driveway.

"The letter," I said, stopping at Vin's car. "It's in your bedroom. I didn't want to risk Mum finding it."

"Ok, let's run in and grab it. Mike is out anyway."

He grabbed my hand, and we started up towards his house. Vin unlocked the door and we went inside. I rushed ahead to his room and grabbed the letter out of Vin's bedside table draw, a draw that was now pretty much empty, as our stuff was packed.

"Heeeellllllloooooo Vin, ohhhhhh heelllllooooo, where are you?"

I froze. Vin walked up behind me and placed his hands on my shoulders.

"It's fine, Scar. He sounds almost at the point where he will pass out. I will go make him another drink, and then we will get the hell out of here," Vin said, trying to calm my nerves.

Mike had been at a local football game all day with his buddies. Obviously the beers had been flowing. He sounded in his Drunk phase, and we both knew it. Yep, the loud, obnoxious and abusive drunk stage. To come home and straight away start yelling for Vin usually meant one thing and one thing only.

He was looking for a fight.

I grabbed Vin's arm as he went to walk out the door.

"Let's just sneak out the window, he will think we have already left," I suggested.

"My car is in the driveway Scar, he will know we are home, and he will hear the car start up."

"He will just think we are at mine, and then who cares if he hears the car start? We will be gone. Just stay out after you drop me until you're sure he's passed out or out of this mood," I pleaded.

"It will only make it worse for later."

"Hello shithead, where the hell are ya?" Mike continued to yell. We could hear him stumbling through to the kitchen. Vin went to walk away and I clutched his arm harder, not wanting him to go, pulling him back slightly.

"Who cares about later Vin? We will be gone. Let's grab our bags now, and we just won't come back. We can leave straight from the school."

"It will make it worse if he comes looking for me Scar," Vin said. "Let me go out there and smooth things over. I will make him a drink and we will leave straight away," he pleaded. I knew he was right. It would make it so much worse if Mike came looking for Vin. He would only get angrier and angrier the more he yelled with no reply.

I really wanted us to just sneak out the window and run. Hopefully Mike was too drunk to chase after us. But if he did it would be far worse. Especially for Vin.

"Ok," I agreed. "But Vin, please be careful." I knew something was not right as Vin left the room. I slowly loosened my grip on his arm as it slid out of my hand. He walked out the door and into the hallway.

Everything felt wrong. Things had settled down lately. Things had been slightly better. Why tonight? Pin pricks moved over my body, and I suddenly felt sick. I just knew something was going to happen. Or was I just being paranoid because we had so much to lose now? We were so close.

I stood by the door and listened, trying to slow my own breathing and thumping heartbeat so I could hear better. I heard Vin walk down the hallway into the kitchen.

"Hey there old boy," Vin said, upbeat and playful, trying to lighten the mood. "How was the footy?" he asked. I could hear Vin opening the fridge to get a drink out for Mike.

Then I heard a thud and nothing else. I froze in a panic, too scared to leave the room for my own safety but too scared for Vin's to stay put. I waited for the next noise so I could get a sense of what was happening.

"What the hell do ya think you're doing touching my beer boy?" Mike was yelling, and I could hear Vin gasp as if he had been pushed or hit or taken by surprise.

I should have let Vin handle it, but my instinct to protect him kicked in. I bolted out the bedroom and down the hallway, shaky in my heels.

I ran into the kitchen to see Vin's head pressed against the fridge door. He still had the beer in his hand. Mike's hand was pressed firmly against Vin's head, holding him to the fridge, pushing him harder and harder against it. I could see Vin was not struggling to break free. I followed his lead and tried to stay calm. I walked up and grabbed the beer out of Vin's hand. He glanced at me through a squished face.

I opened it and held it out to Mike. "It was for you Mike," I said with a forced smile. "How was the game?" I asked as I handed him the beer. He snatched it with such force that beer sloshed out the top of the can and went over his hand and onto the floor. But it worked; he let go of Vin's head.

Vin straightened up but made himself slouch over a bit, as if to make himself look smaller than Mike. I could see he did not want to aggravate his dad any further. He said nothing.

We glanced sideways at each other as Mike took a huge gulp of the beer. I could see Vin was saying thank you with his eyes. He gave me a slight nod and a half smile.

Now normally in this situation, we would just make a super strong drink for Mike, then leave him in front of the TV to enter the next phase of drunkenness. However, tonight was different. We panicked. We had too much to lose. Mike had come home in a fighting mood, and we knew he needed more. We needed to distract him if we wanted to leave anytime soon. Especially without incident.

"Do you want me to get you something to eat?" I asked, trying to think of a way I could keep him occupied for a little while so we could leave without him noticing. Mike was gulping his beer now, and Vin just stood still as a statue.

He knew he had already pissed Mike off somehow. He didn't want to further aggravate him. Especially not in this mood. Not tonight, please not tonight, I just kept thinking. Let this be it. Please.

"Yeah sure," he said while looking me up and down. "Why you dressed like such a slut?" he spat out at me, still eyeballing me up and down. I could see Vin clench his jaw at the name-calling, but he knew better than to react. Sticks and stones, right?

I stepped closer to the fridge, making sure to stand sideways to it and not turn my back on Mike.

"It's my end-of-school formal tonight. Me and some girlfriends are going together," I said. I opened the fridge and pulled out some leftover lasagne to heat up for Mike. I also grabbed the ginger ale while I was there, thinking I could make him a strong whisky and dry. It might just get him onto the harder stuff while we were gone so he would be passed out when we got home.

I knew Vin knew exactly what I was doing. He moved over to the cupboard where the tumblers were and grabbed one. I cut a slice of lasagna and put it in the microwave. The whole time, Mike was just watching us with squinted eyes, his body slightly swaying from side to side as he sat at the kitchen table.

He was close to Blind drunk. Vin and I both knew it. This is what we needed. On the one hand, I did not want to sober him up with food. On the other, we needed him to be distracted, otherwise we would never get out of here.

"You should not be wearing that. You're asking for it," Mike said as he slapped me hard on the ass.

It hurt like hell, but I could not let him see it. I could not react in any way. Not when we were this close. I could see Vin's muscles tightening in his arms, his jaw clenching harder. He was trying to remain calm while making Mike's drink.

I knew it killed him to watch and do nothing. The only time I had ever seen Vin react or fight back was when Mike had tried to rape me. What could he do? If he reacted, it would make it worse. I knew that because I felt the same every time I saw Mike hurt Vin.

I felt like such a coward, although having me around quelled the fire most of the time. I had definitely seen my fair share of beatings. All I could do was stand back and watch, cower in a corner and then help Vin pick up the pieces and put him back together.

Vin stepped in between me and Mike and placed the drink down on the table. Then grabbed the plate of food from the microwave and placed it in front of Mike.

"Get out the way boy, I am talking to Scarlet!" Mike yelled as he pushed Vin sideways with an open arm. Vin complied and moved, but it gave me a chance to take a step back so I was out of arm's reach of Mike.

"You gonna let her go out like that?" Mike spat at Vin. "You should be telling her to change, she will give everyone the wrong idea," he babbled on. "The last thing I want is all the neighbourhood talking about what a slut your girlfriend is." He was slurring his words.

I don't know why he suddenly cared about what the neighbourhood thought. It was not like he was an active member of the community. Regardless of how ridiculous his claims were, I decided it would be best if I went along with it. I'd tell him I was headed home to change. He would have no clue I didn't.

"Come on then Vin, let's go back over to my house and I'll change," I said calmly, thinking it would give us the chance we needed to escape.

I turned around and started to walk back down the hall to Vin's bedroom to grab my clutch with my house key. Vin started moving to follow me.

As he walked past the table, Mike reached out and grabbed his arm, hard.

"Where do you think you're going boy? She doesn't need you to change her outfit," Mike said with venom in his words. I turned and looked at Vin, panic written all over my face. He just nodded at me like it was all ok.

I felt glued to the spot. I didn't want to piss Mike off more by not going, but I couldn't leave Vin. Mike was in such an aggressive mood. How would Vin get out of here? I slowly turned and started walking towards Vin's bedroom. I could hear Mike slurring his words, talking about something.

Vin was not replying or retaliating, but that seemed to make Mike even angrier. The alcohol was not working fast enough. I left the door open and waited for a minute, hoping Vin would get free and join me. I could hear Mike getting more forceful and baiting Vin for answers. I had to get back out there.

There was no way I could leave Vin. I rummaged through our bags we had waiting under Vin's bed so we wouldn't risk my mum seeing them. Surely I had something I could chuck on to not piss Mike off. I found a long maxi dress. It was a tan colour and had short sleeves with buttons up the front. No cleavage, flowery. Surely this was a safe bet.

Mike was tormenting Vin now. "You deaf boy, or just dumb? Answer me boy." Vin made a comment. I couldn't hear what he said.

No Vin, I thought, just stay silent. Nothing you say will help.

"You think I am stupid boy?" Mike was yelling. I heard his chair scrape along the tiles as he pushed it out to stand up in a hurry.

I panicked, throwing the maxi to the floor before rushing back down the hallway. I saw Mike push the table into Vin, who was sitting across from him at the little round table.

"No, I know you are not stupid," Vin replied.

"Then don't you lie to me."

"I am sorry," Vin replied as he remained seated but shuffled his chair backwards to make room for the table that was digging into him.

I had no idea what they were talking about, and I had no clue what came over me. I felt angry and frustrated. I got defensive. It was stupid. Stupid stupid stupid. I knew it as soon as the words left my mouth.

"Just leave him alone!" I yelled as I raced into the kitchen. I should have kept my mouth shut, and I knew Vin was thinking the exact same thing.

Why Scarlet? Why did I open my mouth? We should have just made a run for it the moment Mike came through those doors.

Mike took one big stride towards me and backhanded me across the face. It happened so fast I didn't even see it coming. The force had me stumbling to the side, and my eyes went dark for a second. I felt my lip swell instantly, and I could taste blood in my mouth where my teeth had cut the inside of my lip.

"Shut your mouth you stupid slut." He was spitting and slurring his words, and he moved closer to me. I tried to steady myself as I stepped backwards into the hall. He raised his hand to strike again, only this time Vin grabbed hold of his arm and yanked him backwards.

Mike spun on his heel and punched Vin hard in the face. Vin stumbled backwards but didn't go down. Then…then he swung back. For the first time ever. He hit Mike. Hard. Right on the jaw. Mike stumbled backward in shock.

"THATS ENOUGH!" Vin said firmly. "We are leaving NOW! Scar, go and get the bags," Vin said. I stood there shocked, not really comprehending what was happening, still spinning from the blow to my face. "Scarlet, go," he repeated in a pleading voice. I turned and ran to the bedroom to grab the bags that Vin and I had already packed.

We each had a suitcase and a backpack. I flew down the hall, stumbling in my shoes. I kicked them off as I swung into Vin's room. I could hear things breaking in the hallway. There was huffing and grunting. I could hear it in the background as I was rushing, and I knew that they were fighting, Mike throwing and Vin fighting back for the first time ever.

I didn't know what to do, but I knew we had to get out of there. I grabbed the bags and ran, praying Vin could hold him off long enough for me to throw the bags in the car and start the engine.

I grabbed Vin's keys and raced down the hall, past the lounge room and out the front door. I was dragging the two suitcases and had a backpack slung over each shoulder, not caring what I smashed on the way to the car. I popped the trunk, crammed both the suitcases in and chucked the backpacks on the back seat.

I started the engine and left both the driver and passenger doors open so we could just jump in. I ran back inside and could hear them still fighting.

I ran down the hall, back to the kitchen. By this point, Mike was on top of Vin, punching him in the face while Vin's legs flailed.

All I could see was blood.

"STOP!" I screamed through ringing in my ears from my own blood pumping so hard and the sting of the backhand.

Mike kept punching Vin. I wasn't thinking. I had no plan. I ran and jumped on Mike's back. I started aimlessly hitting, scratching and pulling, trying to get him off Vin.

Then Mike stopped hitting Vin and turned his attention to me. He spun around and knocked me off. I hit the ground hard; the wind was knocked out of me.

Slowly and shakily, Vin stood up. I could see through hazy eyes that Mike's face was bleeding badly. It looked like most of the blood on Vin was from Mike's cuts, a big gash on the eyebrow and another on the upper lip.

Vin didn't say anything as he slowly got to his feet. He didn't look hurt, but the way he was stumbling told me that he was.

Vin took a small step forward, almost as if testing that his legs still worked. Mike took another step forward and kicked me hard in the stomach as I was trying to stand back up.

I felt like I was going to vomit instantly, and pain was radiating through me. My vision was covered in black spots, and I had no idea where Vin was. All I could see was Mike's feet.

I knew he was going to kick me again. I had to move. I didn't see Vin lunge towards the knife I had used to cut the lasagne. I didn't see his hand grip the handle. I didn't see him move towards us.

I grabbed the edge of the table and pulled myself up, only I overshot in my hurry to move, dizzy from the second blow, *filled with pain and fear. I stumbled forward more than I thought.*

Mike went to kick, and Vin went to drive the knife into Mike's back. But as Mike moved forward to kick, I moved up and forward as well. Mike's kick missed, as did Vin's knife.

White-hot pain seared through my stomach, shooting up and down and everywhere in between, like a firework had been set off in my stomach. The breath huffed from me.

I looked up to see his face looking down at me. He dropped the knife instantly, and shock spread across his features. He fell to the ground, like his knees just suddenly gave out and turned into jelly. His eyes were wide with shock, horror and panic.

I looked down at the handle now protruding from my stomach. Mike turned back around and headed straight for Vin, who was sitting frozen on the floor, a mix of my and Mike's blood staining his hands.

I don't know what I was thinking. I am actually one hundred percent sure I wasn't thinking at that stage. I had left my body. The only thing in me was my need to protect Vin.

I grabbed the knife with both hands and pulled it from me. I drove it into Mike's back as he took another stride towards Vin. Only I didn't let go.

I kept pulling it out and driving it back in. Over and over and over until all of a sudden, it stopped.

I don't know if I stopped on my own or if Vin stopped me. I was paralysed. I could not focus on anything. My blood was pumping so hard I could hear it in my head.

My skin felt hot and sticky, and bright flashes were dancing in front of my eyes. Then everything just went black. Darkness. Complete and utter darkness.

33

My life, my heart, my saviour

VIN

She looked so beautiful. Long hair left wavy. Tight black dress and big smile. She always looked beautiful to me, from the very first moment I saw her to the first time we actually talked, when she snuck into my yard and we sat on my trampoline watching the stars.

The concern on her face, the way she delicately ran her fingers over my arms, then held my hand. I couldn't remember a time I had ever been touched so gently. A time when someone had cared that I was hurt.

She was my saving grace. My lifeline. I don't remember the first time my dad hit me. But I do have some good memories with him. I like to think he wasn't always so bad.

I wonder if my mum was the piece holding him together. If the trauma of losing her broke him. Or if he was always just an asshole.

There were times when he would throw a ball with me or kick the football. Times I would help him mow the lawn. He loved that damn lawn. Times he would show up for school assemblies or allow me to play after-school sport.

It seemed to get worse the older I got. By the time Scarlet came into my life when I was eleven, it was bad enough that it was expected.

My anger, frustration, the out-of-control feelings I lived with constantly, the sadness, the pain. Somehow Scar made it all better.

When I was with her, I didn't care what had just happened or what would most likely happen again. I didn't care that my dad... I couldn't even bear to call him that anymore. I didn't care that Mike cared more about his lawn, beer and football than me. She eased the pain. Quelled the frustration.

Being with her felt like that first little ray of sunshine coming out from behind the clouds on an overcast day, warming your skin and brightening everything it touches.

I never wanted her to be hurt because of me. I was selfish and I couldn't let her go. I needed her! And not just her. Her mum was so kind to me; the mother figure I never had.

She fed me on days when he couldn't be bothered. Helped with homework when he was too drunk. She didn't know it, but she gave me a safe haven when he was drinking and angry.

I understood when Scar said she didn't want to leave her mum, and a large part of me didn't want to leave her either. If Scar wouldn't leave without me, then we had to go together. I had to get her away from him. That time had finally come. We were packed and ready. Scar really wanted to go to her dance. She hadn't said as much, but I knew she was sad to be leaving her friends.

I knew her heart was breaking leaving her mum and the life she had here. Her life wasn't bad. I was the only bad part of it. And now I was making her leave it all.

I felt guilty, but I knew she wouldn't stay without me. I knew it would break her heart more if I left without her, and I couldn't stand to be the one to break her heart.

So she was going to go to her dance. Have her last party with her friends. First thing in the morning, we would leave.

She was standing in front of me looking like she was sent from heaven. She looked nervous, but she always felt uncomfortable dressing up. She was at home in shorts, a tee and sneakers. Messy hair and a cap as she sat in my dirty work garage telling me stories and making me laugh while I worked.

We walked out of her house to my car. "My letter," she said. I knew she had written her mum a letter detailing where we were going and what we were doing. Explaining everything.

She and her mum were close, and I knew she didn't want to leave it in her house. Mike never went in my room, so it was safe at my place. He had no clue what we were doing half the time.

We walked up the path to my door. I unlocked it and motioned her in, following as she went to my room. Then we heard it.

Mike was home. He sounded Drunk. Angry, aggressive, abusive. I was worried, but I didn't want Scar to worry. I placed my hands on her shoulders, trying to calm her down.

She started pleading for us to bail out my window. I had visions of her sneaking in and out at night. It made me smile. It would be easy. The fly screen was already off to allow us to sneak in and out.

I should have listened to her. But I had this horrible vision of him catching us sneaking out and it making everything so much worse. I had successfully quelled his moods every now and then by giving him stronger drinks and getting him to pass out.

I thought this would be one of those times. I'd go and calm him down, we'd leave. Plan back on track. All would be good. We'd get our happy ending and Mike! Well, he could die in a ditch for all I cared.

I went out to the kitchen. God, he was in a state. I grabbed a beer out the fridge for him, only this seemed to enrage him. He slammed the fridge shut, and I barely got my hand out in time before it closed with a thud. I went to pass the beer to him, but he grabbed me by the back of the head, grabbing a big chunk of my hair and pushing me down to the fridge door. He pushed my head against the fridge. I didn't dare move, didn't fight back. I tried to slow my breathing and stay as calm as possible.

At seventeen, I was big compared to most guys my age, but Mike was bigger. Stronger. Scar came stumbling into the kitchen. She looked at me, and panic washed over her beautiful face.

I had long ago quit feeling embarrassed at her seeing me in this humbled state. She had seen me in worse positions than this. She grabbed the beer from my hand and opened it, handing it to Mike. I gave her a smirk and little nod to say thanks.

Mike let me go, and I stood back up, trying to make myself smaller so I wouldn't piss him off more. Scar was smart, and I knew she knew her way around Mike.

She offered him food, and I saw her grab the ginger ale out the fridge. I took it from her and made my way to the cupboards to start making him a stronger drink.

We just needed to distract him long enough to leave and get him on the hard stuff. He would be long passed out by the time we got home. Come morning, he'd either be asleep or in his Buzzed phase, which was fine.

Only it didn't work. He was in a fighting mood and trying to bait us. I could tell. He never usually involved Scar, not until that one time and never again since. Mostly he ignored her completely.

Sometimes he would see her, and it would quell his mood a bit. He didn't like being a dick in front of her because it left a witness. There was always a risk she would tell her mum.

Sometimes, though, he was too drunk and too angry to care. She had well and truly seen enough over the years. She had patched me up more times than I could count.

This felt different. Very different. I was starting to panic, but I had to stay calm. For Scar. If she saw me panic, she would panic, and I needed her level-headed. I needed her to get the hell out of here.

I didn't want to scare her. He slapped her ass, hard. I saw the pain and shock on her face. I went to react instinctively. I never gave a shit what he did to me.

It would be over faster if I just went with it. Didn't fight back. But seeing her get caught in his crosshairs destroyed me. I clenched my jaw, holding myself back.

Stay calm, I thought, stay calm. He started spitting some shit about her being dressed slutty. I was so angry that I wasn't even listening to the trash he was talking. I wanted to punch him right in his drunk, smug face.

Not in front of Scar. Stay calm. I couldn't risk her getting hurt. He crapped on about her going to change, and she forced a smile and said she would.

She was calm and smart, and she used it as a way for us both to bail. But when I started to follow her, Mike grabbed me and made me sit across from him at the table.

It was ok. Scarlet was out of harm's way. I took a deep breath. Mike started back up with his crap. He made me sick, and I started regretting my decision to stay this long. To ever let Scar near him.

What was I thinking? He was going on about me and Scar, asking if I had slept with her, although he was using far cruder words. He kept calling her a slut, and the things he was asking made me want to jump across the table and smash his face in.

My only hope was that Scar was smart enough to get the hell out of the house. But I had a sinking feeling that she wouldn't leave me.

Mike was yelling at me now, baiting me for answers I didn't want to give him. He got mad and shoved the table into me. It hit me just below the ribs and pushed me back in the chair.

It hurt, but I didn't react. I was used to it. Scar came running into the kitchen. She hadn't changed, and she was yelling, her little hands in tight fists by her side, anger pouring off her. I pushed my chair back to stand, and Mike took a big stride towards her. He hit her across the face. I didn't see it coming, but I sure as hell wouldn't let it happen again. I saw red. Her head jarred to the side, and I saw her lip split straight away.

I moved towards Mike, and before he could hit her again, I grabbed his arm and spun him around. I punched him as hard as I could.

When I connected, his head splayed back. I felt his jaw crunch, but he didn't go down. My hand hurt like hell, but I'd be damned if I was gonna sit there and do nothing while he hit Scarlet. I knew I could never beat Mike in a fight, not even in his drunkest state. He was huge and a trained soldier. But I would die before I let him hit her again. I may not have been able to save myself, but I could buy her enough time to get to safety.

I told her to run, to get our bags and go. I knew I wouldn't be following her. Something in me knew I wasn't gonna make it out of this. Not after hitting Mike like that. He was a grown man. A trained soldier. I was a seventeen-year-old loser who never had the guts to stand up to him before. I was gonna fight to protect her. To my last breath. I had to. If nothing else, I'd keep him occupied and she could run. I prayed she would get in the car and leave. Call for help even. I never expected her to do what she did.

Mike moved towards me, and I swung again, this time bending my arm to use my elbow, as my hand was sore. I connected with his brow, and it split right then and there.

A big nasty wound. Blood running down his face. A tiny light of hope went on deep inside me. Maybe I would be ok.

He kept coming towards me, only now my hand and elbow hurt. I hunched low and charged, hoping to tackle him to the ground. The top of my head caught his lip, and it opened up as well. Blood started rushing all over me.

The light got a little bigger. Only then it went out altogether. He was far bigger and stronger than me and was trained in close combat. Drunk or not. It was muscle memory.

He threw me to the ground like I weighed nothing, and before I knew it, he was on top of me, throwing punches. I put my elbows up over my face to shield as much as I could, but he knew what he was doing. Every time my hands went up, he went to my ribs or stomach. When they went down, he went to my face.

It was a losing battle. It didn't feel like he was ever going to stop, and I had stopped trying to fight back. Hopefully Scarlet was long gone. It felt like a lifetime since she ran out the kitchen. I was happy to die on the floor right there if she was safe.

Then I felt it. Mike moved off me, and I heard a thump. I moved to get up. My ribs and stomach had taken the majority of the blows, and I felt like I couldn't breathe. Everything hurt. I rolled to the side, and I saw her.

She was lying on the floor. I willed myself to get to my feet, even though nothing in my body wanted to comply. You can't die yet, I told myself. You can't let him hurt her. Why didn't she run? Why the fuck did she come back? He took a step towards her, and we locked eyes.

I'm so sorry, I thought. And I knew she knew. Mike stepped forward and kicked her in the stomach. She recoiled around his foot. She let out a scream that had my heart shatter into a million pieces.

I saw the knife on the bench. I pushed myself up and lunged for it, grabbing it and gripping it tight. I wanted him dead. I wanted him to feel this pain. I wanted him to stop. For it all to stop.

I lunged forward. He had his back to me, focused on Scarlet. She was trying to get up, clinging to the kitchen table, pulling her body up. She wasn't looking at me. She was staring straight at him.

My body hurt so badly, and it was a struggle to even grip the knife. I moved forward and willed every ounce of strength I had left to drive the knife right into his back, down low. Slightly to the side just under the rib.

Only he went to kick her again as I moved forward. I thrust my arm forward and up, right at the same time Scarlet found the strength to pull herself up. She used too much force and stumbled right to where Mike was standing. Right as he missed her and stumbled forward out of my reach. But my hand connected with something.

I looked down, and she was staring up at me. Big blue eyes, bloodshot from screaming and crying. Her face marked from where Mike had hit her.

A whimper tumbled from her lips, and her mouth opened and shut again. My eyes widened, and suddenly I couldn't control my limbs. My hands dropped to my side. My knees went weak. I collapsed down in a lump on the floor, like a deflated blow-up castle. Like everything in me had turned to rubber.

Mike turned around and saw me collapsed on the floor. He stepped towards me with a feral grin coated in blood. Good, I thought. Let him kill me. I was still in shock at what I had done.

In my bid to save her, I had hurt her. I deserved to die. My breathing was shallow and raspy. I didn't even brace for what was to come. Didn't even shut my eyes. Then suddenly, Mike went down like a tonne of bricks. He fell face first next to me. Scarlet was on top of him, screaming. She had blood everywhere, and she was stabbing him over and over and over.

I forced myself back to what was unfolding in front of me. I jumped up and grabbed her. When she felt my arms around her, she relaxed.

She dropped the knife and turned to me. I hugged her close. I didn't even go to check on Mike. I knew he was dead. He wasn't moving. Blood was everywhere. He lay in a lump on the floor.

I could feel her arms around me start to lose their strength. They dropped to her sides. She looked up at me. Her eyes were so dark. Her skin was pale, her breathing shallow.

What have I done? I had a sudden urge to vomit, but I had to pull it together. For her. She needed me. I would not let her die here. I would not be the one who killed her.

I sat her on a chair and grabbed some tea towels. I pushed them against the wound on her belly and told her to hold them.

I grabbed my phone from my pocket and went to dial 000. A thought stopped me. She looked so out of it, propped up in the chair clutching her stomach.

I had done that. I stabbed her. and instead of helping herself, she saved me. There was no way I could let her go down for this. No way she could take the fall. I tried to think clearly, but everything was so foggy. I wiped the handle of the knife and then picked it up. Held it like she had. Two hands. I already had Mike's blood all over me from the fight.

I chucked it back on the floor. Then I called the police. Told them I had stabbed her and killed my dad.

Then I wrapped Scar in a blanket. Scooped her up and carried her to the couch and waited. It didn't take them long. I had hurt her. I didn't know how badly. She didn't look good, and I had no clue what else to do. Did she want my comfort? I wanted nothing more than to wrap her in my arms. To hold her. Tell her I was sorry.

I couldn't stop pacing the room.

She didn't say anything. Neither did I.

I was holding back tears, but I deserved everything that was coming to me. Whatever they were going to do to me. I deserved worse.

My beautiful Scar. My life, my whole heart. My saviour. I had hurt her. May have killed her. She was slumped over on the couch, not moving, gripping the towels on her belly like they were a lifeline. She didn't look at me. She barely even moved. Not when the police came rushing through the door. Not when they threw me to the floor and handcuffed me. Not when they dragged me out the door. And I didn't blame her.

34

Nothing but darkness

The rest happened in flashes. Flashes of lights. Bursts of noises. I saw glimpses of things happening around me. Vin had put something on my stomach and put my hands over it. He was talking, but I couldn't understand anything he was saying.

Then he grabbed the knife. He started wiping it down with something. Then it all went dark again. Black.

Then I was sitting on the couch. I was still shaking, and I could not focus on anything. It was like I had left my body and was watching from above.

Unable to make any decisions. I was freezing cold. I could see Vin. He was pacing the lounge room. Then black. Darkness again.

Then police were rushing through the door and inside the room. Everything seemed to move in slow motion, and I was still floating above my body.

I don't know who called them. How much time had passed.

A police woman sat down next to me, and I saw two men in uniform taking Vin out of the house. Paramedics came. They started asking me questions, but it was like they were speaking a foreign language.

I don't think I answered a thing. I don't think I even spoke a word. I couldn't talk, I couldn't move. All I could do was watch as the scene unfolded below me. The paramedics laid me on a bed and started cutting my dress apart.

They put things over my stomach and attached me to all kinds of cords. Then they pushed me into the ambulance. I was so cold, alone and confused.

"Where is he?" The words snuck out through ice-cold lips that trembled as they parted.

"You are safe now, just relax. You are safe," was the only reply I got and the first words I understood as I emerged from my daze.

I was safe.

The paramedics put an IV in and must have given me something to make me sleep, because then it all went dark again for what felt like an eternity.

I woke up groggy and sore. I had no idea where I was. The room was white and silent, besides a slight hum of machines working away in the background. I was freezing cold.

I had a gown on, with an itchy blanket that did nothing to quell the chill that had crept deep into my bones. I found the nurse button and pressed it continuously until someone came into the room.

"You are awake," the nurse said with a pleasant smile.

"Where is he?" I asked, my voice raspy, my throat burning with each swallow.

"You are safe here hun," the nurse replied. "Your mom has just ducked out for a coffee; she has been by your side the whole time. She will be back shortly."

"Where is he?" I repeated. Louder this time, trying to shake the rasp from my voice.

"It's ok, just breathe. You are safe here. He is with the police," she replied matter-of-factly. What was she talking about, and why could I not find my words properly?

I was starting to panic. I could feel the room closing in on me. It was becoming harder to breathe, little patches dancing across my lids again.

"You're ok, just breathe," the nurse kept saying. She had a hand on my arm now and was trying to force me to lie down. I didn't even realise I was trying to get up, not until I felt the pressure from her gentle but firm grip.

"Where is he? Where is he?" I could not focus on anything, I just wanted Vin. I needed Vin. The nurse was yelling something now, but I could not hear anything besides the pumping of my own heart. It felt like it was trying to rip free from my chest.

The nurse was holding me down tight to the bed. I felt trapped. Fighting for air. No matter how much I tried to suck it in, it felt dry and shallow. More people rushed into the room. A different nurse helped hold me down on the bed while I wrestled against their painful grips.

I fought harder against the nurses and could hear nothing but the blood thumping through my veins. A man came in wearing scrubs. He grabbed my arms. He had a needle, and he jammed it into the little rubber thing that was attached to my cannula. It felt cold, and I could feel the liquid snaking its way through my veins. Then it all went black. Again.

35

The lie he told became my truth

"Scarlet, Scarlet, Scarlet, are you there?" She looked at me with kind eyes. I knew she was just trying to help, but I had nothing to say. I did not want to talk.

My room felt cold. Maybe the chill was coming from inside of me. No matter what I did these days, I could not stop the shivering that would come in waves and overtake my entire body.

Mum handed me a cup of warm tea and sat down on my bed across from me. I was reading the newspaper with the article written about Vin's sentence and our tragic tale.

'Teen injured and veteran killed in tragic case of domestic abuse.'

The article was full of shit. It implied Vin was the abuser. The story read that Mike and Vin had a physical altercation. That I was stabbed by Vin while trying to break them up. It brushed over the fact that Mike had attacked me. It said nothing about the years of abuse Vin had suffered. There was no mention of me stabbing Mike. The article said Vin had brutally killed him, stabbing him repeatedly.

It kept reiterating the fact that he had stabbed me. Vin must have told them a completely different version of events. I was so confused by what was happening and what had *happened. The police had tried to question me at the hospital, but they already had Vin's confession, and I was so out of it.*

I was in hospital for eight weeks, and no one really told me anything. By the time we got home, he had already confessed and was in jail awaiting trial.

Suddenly six months had passed. I barely left my room, let alone the house. Now the article covering his sentencing says he has been charged with manslaughter and been sentenced to six years in prison. The prison he was in was about an hour away from where we lived. I couldn't believe what I was reading.

Reading about the sentencing gave me a jolt that zapped me from the zombie-like trance I had been living in. It was a startling realisation. A 'what have I done' moment of pure electricity charging through my body.

"Mum, he didn't do what they are saying, I...I... I mmmean, hhhe did but he dddidnt," I stuttered. Nothing made sense to me. How could I explain it to anyone else?

This was one of the first times I had even talked about anything that had happened in the last six months. Seeing this article and reading about Vin, knowing he would be in prison for six years for something I did... I felt like the sky was falling down around me.

Everything up to this point had felt surreal. Like I was living underwater, barely able to come up for air to keep me alive. Now suddenly I was thrown back on land, the stark reality hitting me harder than a freight train, pulling me back to the actuality that I had been shutting out since that night.

Mum just looked at me. She took a deep breath but didn't say anything.

"What happened then, Scarlet? You have to talk to me about it at some point. You can't go on like this. Hidden under your covers. If not me, at least talk to someone. There are people who are trained to help with these things."

I held the warm cup, twirling it in my hands, and took a sip of the hot tea, thinking it would warm up my insides. Instead, it made me colder. It felt exactly the same as the drugs did entering my system that night. Like thick, ice-cold liquid entering my veins and moving through my body.

I squeezed my eyes shut, a small tear escaping from the pressure on each side. Every time I closed them, it took me back to the hospital. Back to the cold bed. Restrained and terrified. The itchy blanket and the pulling of the tape holding my cannula in place. Every time I moved, I felt the pressure of the restraints around my wrists. The feeling of strong hands pinning me to the bed as I fought. I heard the nurse telling me that I was safe. However, whenever I tried to scream or talk back to her, no sound came out of my mouth. I was like a fish on dry land, just moving my mouth with no noise, slowly and painfully suffocating.

Sometimes I felt like I was in quicksand. It was constantly trying to pull me back to that day, and I fought against the drag every second of every minute.

I was so tired, even though all I did was sleep, and I was about ready to surrender to the quicksand. It felt too strong. I wanted to let it swallow me whole.

"Are you starting to feel warmer?" Mum asked with a big smile, trying to change the subject and break the thick layer of ice I kept freezing between us. Her soft voice and worry-stricken face reminded me why I continued fighting the quicksand. Why I kept opening my mouth trying to suck in air even though it didn't feel like it reached my lungs.

I wanted to hug her. I wanted to curl up like a baby in her arms and cry. I wanted to scream the truth, to trust her with it all. But I couldn't. I could barely even admit the truth to myself.

The whole time in the hospital was a deranged fog. I knew that I had been in shock, and it made me have panic attacks. They needed me to rest after my surgery, and every time I woke up, I was apparently a completely unhinged mess. Screaming and trying to get up.

I understood why they had sedated me. It was weeks before I finally calmed down and felt clear-minded enough to process everything that had happened.

They had sent people in to talk to me. Psychologists, psychiatrists, police. I didn't want to talk to any of them. I wanted to talk to Vin.

No one was explaining anything to me, and it was making me insane with rage. So, I just shut down. I blocked it all out and shut down. The doctors recommended I be moved to the psychiatric ward for further treatment; to help cope with the grief and trauma once my physical wounds had healed. They told my mum I had post-traumatic stress disorder.

How could they think Vin would ever hurt me? Could they not see Vin's injuries? Why was my mum not standing up for him? She knew him. She knew Mike enough to know he was a drunk who yelled a lot.

She loved Vin and hated Mike. When I was finally released from the hospital, I asked my mum to take me to him. She said he wasn't allowed any visitors yet besides his lawyer. Every time I brought it up, she would change the subject and ask me about what happened.

I felt like she was keeping me from him, and I could not understand how she would think he would hurt me.

The whole thing was so confusing and frustrating. I felt so powerless. I felt like everyone was trying to shield me from the truth. In doing so, they made me conceal my own truth. I never meant to stay so silent. I never meant for Vin to take the fall. I had no clue what he had told the police or his lawyer, and I wasn't allowed to go to his hearing.

Now it was all too late. He was in prison, and it was my fault. I had killed his dad. My silence had dug a huge hole for both of us, which was now burying me alive.

The whole thing was my fault. If only I hadn't forgotten the letter. If only I hadn't opened my mouth. If I hadn't gotten in the way, if I hadn't completely lost it and stabbed Mike, if only I had kept my cool and spoken to the police earlier. I didn't know which way was up or down.

"Mum, he didn't do it," I said again. Mum just looked at me with confusion.

"Scarlet, his fingerprints were all over the knife. He had marks and bruises on his knuckles, and Mike's face was hit multiple times. You were stabbed, for Christ's sake Scarlet! You could have died."

I went to talk, but the words caught in my throat. I willed them out.

"Mike attacked me, Mum. He hit me and Vin protected me."

"Was it Mike that stabbed you?" Mum asked.

"I...I...I," I went to explain, but I didn't know how. I was already lying to her. Letting her believe it was Vin who killed Mike.

"No, it was Vin, but it was an accident. I got in the way, he was trying to protect me from Mike. He was going to kill me Mum, I swear."

"Honey," she held my free hand in hers, "has Vin ever hurt you before?"

"Mum, NO!" I couldn't believe she would think that. "Mum, you know him, you knew him from eleven years old. He never ever hurt me. It was Mike. Mike abused Vin for years. Mike attacked me. and Vin tried to protect me. Mum. you have to believe me," I pleaded, squeezing her hand.

She nodded and gave my hand a gentle squeeze back. "I do, I believe you. Why didn't you tell me sooner? About Mike."

"We were scared you would call the police and they would take Vin away. I can't be without him Mum, I can't live without him. We have to fix this." Tears were rolling down my face.

"Honey, there is nothing we can do now. He killed someone." The look on her face was gut-wrenching.

So I let her believe a truth everyone else believed. To protect myself. I was a coward. I couldn't stand to see the disappointment that would be on my mum's face if she knew I was the one who had killed Mike. I was a murderer.

Somehow, the lie Vin told became my truth, and I just went with it.

I deserved to be rotting in that prison, not Vin. I just had no idea how to change what had followed that horrible night. But I knew I had to do something. I had to try to fix this.

I just needed to see him first.

36

No visitors

SCARLET

Time felt like it was moving in slow motion, except everything around me was happening so fast. Like I was stuck in a whirlwind, everything spinning around me but moving forward slowly.

I didn't know how to fix what I had done, but I knew it started with seeing Vin.

Finally I worked up the courage. I had contacted the prison to find when visiting days were. And when I told Mum that I was going to visit Vin whether she liked it or not, she agreed to take me.

I needed to hear his voice, to see his face. To tell him I was sorry and that I would tell the truth. I needed to explain why I had stayed silent for so long. I needed him to know that I had not abandoned him and that I was going to do everything I could to set things straight.

I just needed to talk to him. To get it clear in my head. To get it clear with him. To tell him it wasn't his fault and I didn't blame him. Not one little bit. But did he blame me? Like I blamed myself? I needed to know.

We arrived at the prison on a Monday morning. I desperately tried to hide my trembling hands by sitting on them in the waiting room, feeling the cold plastic chair beneath my skin. I was nervous and afraid. I was afraid he would be mad, upset even. Upset that I didn't visit him earlier. Upset that I let him take the fall for what I did. Would he be angry I killed Mike? He was his dad, after all. I didn't know what I would be walking into, but I knew one thing. I had to see him.

Mum put a gentle hand on my leg.

"It's going to be ok Scarlet," she said softly. I knew she didn't think it was a great idea for me to see him. My legs must have been shaking involuntarily, and once I felt the stillness of her touch, I started to become very aware of them moving. I crossed my legs and took a few deep breaths.

"Scarlet James." I heard my name being called by the administrative officer at the front desk. Surprisingly, my legs worked without me even knowing what was happening. Before I knew it, I was standing in front of her desk, my eyes wide, my breath shallow, hands still shaky and sweaty.

I felt my mum's presence beside me as she did her best to calm my nerves.

"I'm afraid he has requested no visitors today," the officer said. The words sent me back a step.

This couldn't be right.

"He knows it's me?" I asked, my voice breaking far higher than I expected it to. "This must be some kind of mistake," I said as I turned to Mum. Panic washed over me.

"We will get it sorted," Mum reassured me as she placed a hand on my arm to steady me.

Mum took a step closer to the desk. "Can you please check again, make sure he is aware it is Scarlet James here for him?" The lady looked up at my mum through her eyebrows. I could see her roll her eyes as she said, "Sure thing, wait here."

She disappeared behind a door again, and this time we stood at the desk and waited. The room suddenly felt very still. Everyone in the waiting area seemed to fade away, leaving the deafening tick, tick, tick of the clock on the back wall.

The handle on the door started to rattle, and a light next to the door flashed green. The door made a buzzing sound as it unlocked. The lady walked back through it with the same sombre look on her face. She approached the counter and said two words with a frown and raised eyebrows. "NO VISITORS!"

I felt my legs start to go weak as heat rose up through me. I turned to Mum, and she opened her arms to hug me, but I was too mad, too frustrated, too confused.

"This lady isn't telling him it's me!" I yelled. "There is no way he wouldn't want to see me!" I carried on.

"There is nothing more I can do," the lady said in a frustrated tone before calling out the next name on the waiting list. "Mark Macintosh."

"Hang on a minute!" I yelled as I slammed both hands down on the high desk in front of me. "Vin is my family, and there is no way he wouldn't want to see me. You have to just let me see him." I think I was trying to convince myself of this fact more than the lady behind the desk. A small part of me believed he would be mad at me for killing his dad, and an even bigger part thought he hated me, resented me for letting him take the fall for what I had done.

The officer let out a big sigh. A big burly guy covered in tattoos from head to toe came up behind us and tapped his foot impatiently. Mark Mcintosh, I presumed. I could feel the tears in my eyes as I desperately tried to hold it together.

"Please," I pleaded as the tears started to overflow. "Please," I pleaded one last time.

"I am sorry hun," the lady said, her tone now more sympathetic. She could see how distressed I was getting. "All I can do is tell them they have visitors. If they don't wish to see anyone, we can't force them. May I suggest you try again next week?" A slight undertone of impatience was creeping back into her voice.

Well, I did try again the next week, and the week after that, and the week after that. I tried every week for a year, fifty-two weeks in total. Every week it was the same. He wasn't accepting visitors. Every week I was met with the same sympathetic eyes of the same officer at the counter. Every week she would give me a gentle smile as she handed me the sign-in sheet.

Then I would watch her punch some numbers into the keypad on the door, listen as it buzzed and flashed green. It would then click open to allow her through. Time would slow down while I waited for her to return, her eyes always looking down to avoid seeing the heartbreak in my own.

She would mutter the same words to me in softly spoken syllables that would leave me shattered each and every time. I would brace myself for the disappointment, but there was always a sliver of hope. A small light that would flick on inside me just praying 'what if?' What if today he is ready to see me?

"No visitors today hun," she would say, and I would release the breath I was holding. As I exhaled, the light would dim a little more, until one day it went out completely. "See you again next week?" she asked. I had come to learn the officer behind the desk's name was Margaret. She was fifty-three and had three daughters of her own.

"I don't think so Margaret," I said, heartbreak painted all over the words as they left my mouth. She gave me a half smile, and I just turned around and walked out the door. That was the last time I ever went to that prison. It was the last time I scribbled my name in the visitors' sheet. It was the last time I ever saw Margaret.

I let that last bit of hope that I would ever see Vin again die. I dragged my feet along the gravel car park as I walked towards Mum's car. She always came with me. Each week, she would schedule time out of her day and drive me to the prison. She had taken to waiting in the car for me while I went in. It just seemed faster, as we both obviously knew what was coming.

"He's not accepting visitors today," I said for the last time as I slid into the passenger seat.

37

Let her go

VIN

Time moved in slow motion after that day. I didn't care. I deserved it, a slow, painful death. I could barely remember what happened after I called the cops.

I remember being taken to the police station. They asked me a heap of questions, and I told them the same story I did on the phone. I asked them to let me know if Scar was ok.

I said I never meant for her to get so hurt. That I just got angry. They prodded me for every detail. With each word, I swallowed the truth. That she was the love of my life, and without her, life wasn't worth living. That she had saved me from hell on earth, day in and day out. That I would rather bathe in lava than hurt a single strand of hair on her beautiful head.

Yet that was exactly what I did. I stabbed her. I almost killed her, and in return, she saved us both from Mike.

I fought back tears. I couldn't tell them what she did. She was so innocent. In my eyes, she deserved to be free. Free of me and Mike. I didn't know what would happen to her if they knew she was the one who killed him.

Would it be considered self-defence? I knew nothing about the legal system, but what I did know was that she didn't deserve to be grilled over it. She didn't deserve to sit in a cold empty interrogation room. To be asked questions. To be looked at the way they looked at me.

To be left hungry and thirsty while others decided your fate. To have people judge her. To have her friends and mum think less of her. She deserved to be free. Innocent! I couldn't save her from Mike or even from myself. But I could save her from this.

I deserved this. And she deserved her freedom.

They asked if I wanted a lawyer, and I declined. I was sent one anyway, and I told him the same thing I told the cops.

I was put in a holding cell for a few days, and then I had to go to court, where I told the judge the exact same shit I had told everyone else. It was starting to become second nature. I didn't even have to think about the lie, it just fell out of my mouth. I had no need for bail; where would I even go? Who would pay for it? So, I didn't bother asking. The lawyer asked. Blabbed on about something we could do to try to request it. I didn't listen. It all went in one ear and out the other. I wasn't intentionally trying to be rude. It's just that my mind was made up. I deserved everything that was coming to me. Probably worse.

Due to my age and not having a criminal record, I was chucked in jail awaiting my proper sentencing trial. I was eventually given six years.

I barely even remember any of it. How long it took. The whole process. The sentencing or what they said. Apparently, though, I was lucky. If I had been over eighteen, it would have been more than double that time. The judge said something about showing remorse, my age and no former record.

Maybe they were lenient because I kept asking if she was ok, maybe because I couldn't seem to stop the tears from coming the entire time. Fucking stupid. I had barely cried a day in my life. Not through any of the years of hell. But one thought of hurting her, and I was a goddamn mess.

I didn't deserve any mercy. They should have given me double. I felt nothing for Mike. He deserved everything he got.

I was glad he was gone. I only wished I had been the one to do it. Not my beautiful Scar. She shouldn't have had to have a speck of blood on her hands.

I was happy to be there in her place. Whatever prison would throw at me, I was ready. Bring it.

After the sentencing, my lawyer told me that Scarlet was going to be ok and that I was being transferred to a prison about an hour away. I cared about nothing else but the fact that Scarlet was ok. Whatever my fate would be... Well, that was just karma.

I had been sitting in the dining hall when a guard came over to me. My lawyer had submitted some appeal that allowed me to be in a low-security ward due to my age, my lack of a prior criminal record and the fact that a psychiatrist had deemed me non-violent and said the outburst seemed out of character.

I had to have regular psychiatric sessions and attend anger management, but it meant I was with other young and non-violent inmates rather than in a higher-security section.

I couldn't have cared what happened to me, though. I deserved it all.

I had never paid much attention to the visiting days. I thought Scar and her mum would want nothing to do with me. Rightly so. I had no other family, and I didn't really expect any of my friends to come; I didn't have many anyway.

So, when the guard said I had a visitor, I was shocked. I started following him to the meeting hall thinking maybe it was one of my mates, my boss even. We had been close. Then the guard said it was someone named Scarlet.

I froze. There was no way she should want to see me. I had stabbed her. Put her in danger, almost killed her.

I turned and started walking back to the table. The guard followed me back, confused.

"Most guys are excited for visitors," he said. "Especially a lady."

"Well, I don't want any. Tell her to go."

"Ok," he said with a raised eyebrow.

My heart sank. Why would she come? Was she mad? Did she want to say a final goodbye? Maybe she still loved me. Or maybe she came to tell me what a piece of shit I was and that I deserved to rot in a blazing hell for all eternity.

Either way, I couldn't see her. Maybe I was a coward, but I couldn't look into those beautiful blue eyes of hers and not be heartbroken over what I had done to her. What she had done for me.

The sooner she moved on the better. She needed to get far away from me. Be free, be happy. She always did deserve better than what I could give her. But now! Well now she definitely did. It was clear. I would always be bringing her down.

She came each week. I lost count. Each week it got slightly harder and harder to say no. After months, I started to forget what she looked like. Forgot what she felt like in my arms.

My memory of her started to blur. I would wake up in hot sweats from dreams of her, her wavy long hair tangled around me as she lay in my arms. The smell of her, the way she would run her fingers over the scars on my arms, connecting them like a game of connect the dots. The way she would twirl my curls with her fingers. I would hear her laugh echoing around my cell at night.

Every week, like clockwork, the guard would tell me I had a visitor.

'Scarlet James for you Vin.'

My heart would skip a beat. My breath would catch, and I would have visions of walking out to the hall and seeing her sitting there, her dark wavy hair falling around her face, deep-blue eyes calming my soul, wide smile brightening my *life, soft hands easing my pain. I would almost involuntarily start walking, but then I would catch myself. No, you can't Vin. Let her go. She needs to move on.*

I still wasn't sure what she wanted. Was she mad at me? Did she hate me, blame me? Or did she forgive me? Still love me?

Either way, I couldn't give in. I was no good for her, and she needed to forget all about me. It was better this way.

But each week, I seemed to take a few more steps towards her. It got harder and harder. She was fading away from me, and it was getting harder and harder to see her in my mind.

I found myself starting to count the days waiting for that visiting day. I would wake up excited and have to calm myself and talk myself out of it.

Until one day I couldn't anymore. I needed to see her. She was now such a distant memory, and her smell and voice were fading from my mind. I needed her back. I needed to just see her smile. Something to cling to. To remind myself such beautiful things did exist. She was mine once. I waited impatiently in the dining hall for the guard to come in.

I saw him come into the room and start rounding up the guys for visitors. I stood ready to go. But he never came to me. He walked straight past me.

"Hey, she here today?" I asked as he passed.

"No one for you today Vin, sorry mate."

Well FUCK!

I slumped back down into the cold metal chair, rested my elbows on the table and let my head fall. The table felt like ice under my forehead.

Maybe she was sick, stuck in traffic, busy today!

I waited till the next week, to no avail. Nothing. My boss came instead. I tried to not let the disappointment show on my face. I was grateful for the visitor. He had come every now and then on the odd weeks. But she never came again.

It was what I wanted, after all, I suppose. My only hope was that she was happy. That she moved on and got everything she deserved. Pure love, happiness!

I let her go. For good. Or so I thought.

38

Love 4 eva

SCARLET

I was sitting in the waiting area at Sydney Airport staring at nothing in particular. Mum had suggested moving not long after I got home from the hospital. I finally agreed after I found the bags in the garage.

After that night, Vin's car and house had sat untouched, taped off for weeks. Finally a police officer knocked on our door and handed Mum the backpacks and suitcases out of Vin's car.

The police said that Mike didn't have a will, so everything would go to an estate and be sold off unless contested. But he believed these were mine.

Mum did not want me to see them, as she was worried what it would bring up, so she hid them in the garage. About a year after the last time I went to the prison, just over two and a half years after the tragic event, I found the bags in the garage.

I can't even remember why I was in there. I think I was looking for an old pedestal fan to put in my room. But then I saw the familiar backpack and pulled it out. I asked Mum about it, and she explained what had happened and why she hid them. She expressed how worried she had been about me.

I had refused to see anyone since I got home from the hospital. No friends when they called or tried to visit. I never left my room. I barely ate. I only ever left the house to go to the prison, and once I stopped that, I did nothing but rot in my room. I was a shell of who I used to be. Empty.

Mum tried to get me to talk to someone, anyone. But I refused.

I was having nightmares. I would wake up screaming and thrashing in bed. Mum suggested moving multiple times, but I just couldn't. I couldn't bear to leave his house, even though it had long been sold and renovated and looked barely recognisable now.

New people had moved in, and I often wondered if they knew what had happened there. Who was sleeping in the room Vin and I had slept in together? Cooking dinner in the very kitchen where I had stabbed and killed a man?

I pulled the bags out of garage and took them to my room. I cried as I went through the clothes we had chosen to take with us on what was supposed to be our new life. Then I opened the backpack and saw it. I had forgotten all about it. It was an A4 book with a picture of a beach on the front. It had big black letters across the front that read 'Scar and Vin.'

Straight away I was flooded with memories, memories of Vin and I sitting on my bed with magazines and printouts, cutting out pictures of beaches and houses and swimsuits we would wear. Little stories we had written about what our life would look like. Love hearts around our names with 'Love 4 Eva' written under it. I flicked through the pages, and there it was. 'Mandurah' written in big letters with pictures I had drawn of dolphins jumping out of the water. I looked at one of the pictures I had printed out of one of the beaches.

All our plans were written under it. Detailed directions for the four-day drive across the country. Places we would stop and sleep, places to eat and fuel up. Caravan parks we could stay at once we arrived. Suburbs we could look for rentals in. Job listings, a to-do list, which had notes scribbled out and rewritten and items ticked and highlighted as we must have gone through the motions. This felt like a lifetime ago now, and I had forgotten this book even existed.

I could hear Vin's voice as we chatted about our lives together. Could feel his long hair tickling my neck as he sat behind me with his arms around me. I could smell his scent as if he was right next to me, see his beautiful eyes light up and flicker with gold when he had an idea. I kept flicking through the book, relishing in the sweet memories that were supposed to be our lives together.

At the back of the book was an envelope containing all the cash we had saved. There was almost six thousand dollars in there. Crisp one-hundred-dollar bills in little piles with elastic bands around them.

I made my mind up then and there. I was going to honour the life we had planned, even if I was going without him. I would move to Mandurah.

I finally agreed with my mum. We should move. I told her I wanted to go to Mandurah in Western Australia. I didn't tell her why. I made up some story about seeing a flyer for it online.

She didn't question it. I think she was just happy that I finally had some life back in me.

Mum organised everything, and I gave her the money Vin and I had saved. She gave me a look, but she didn't ask about it. I think she didn't want to ruin any momentum for the move.

This only added to my guilt. My mum had sacrificed so much, and I couldn't even be honest with her. Worse, I had completely shut her out. The guilt crushed me, but the lies had already been told. I had no idea how to even begin to speak the truth now.

I couldn't stand to see the pain that would be on her face if she knew the truth about me. And what would it change now? Vin wouldn't even speak to me. I had taken a life, ruined the life of the boy I loved and flipped my mum's life upside down.

The best I could hope for was a fresh start.

"This will be good for us," Mum said, filled with hope. I smiled and nodded in agreement, praying that it would be the truth.

39

We got this

SCARLET

"Are you nervous to go home?" I ask. We are on the plane headed back to Australia from LA. It is the end of our trip; we are headed home as husband and wife.

I can see the worry in his eyes. They become darker when he is worried. If that is even possible. They look as black as night right now. He is restless beside me in the tiny airplane seat. Shifting from one side to the other, crossing and uncrossing his legs.

I have been watching him from the corner of my eye. He has been flicking through the same list of movies for the last half hour.

"I don't know. That was the point wasn't it?" he replies.

"Do you think they will be mad?" I ask, but I already know the answer based on what I know about his parents.

"Oh yeah, they are gonna be pissed, but not as pissed as they would be if I told them the real truth. They will get over this, they will come around… Eventually!"

He is shaking his head, and the colour is draining from his olive skin. Like just the thought of having to expose his real self to his parents makes him feel physically ill.

I am sympathetic. I can see his pain when he speaks about it. I can feel his energy shift from this outgoing, confident larrikin to a scared little child. Things that have been drilled into him over and over, telling him how he should feel, how he should act, who he should love. It just isn't him.

He struggles with it daily. I can tell. He is so ashamed of who he really is that he can't share it with the world, let alone his parents, who he wholeheartedly believes will be so dead against it.

"Are you?" he asks, placing a hand on top of mine.

"Yes and no. I mean, my mum loves you. Everyone already thinks we are gonna end up together anyway. So I'm not really nervous to tell people, but..." I pause, pursing my lips and letting out a bit of a sigh.

"What?" he asks, concerned.

"Well, I just feel like maybe we didn't think this all the way through. I mean, what happens when people come around to visit and see we sleep in separate rooms?"

He looks at me, and I can tell he is mulling it over. "What happens when you get an urge?" I continue.

"An urge?" he spits out, almost choking on the words in laughter. "What am I, a dog?" I too now start laughing, and we both fall back in our chairs in hysterics.

"You know what I mean," I say once the laughter has slowed and I can catch my breath.

"You're gay, you like men. What happens if you want to meet people, have sex with people?"

"I'll do what I've always done," he says, looking sideways at me. "I'll go out of town. No one else would have to know."

I've never really thought about it in that way before when he went out, which was very, very rare. I never questioned what he was doing or where he was going. He has been more carefree on this trip, and I saw him hook up with a couple of guys, but he always kept it very discreet and never really talks to me much about that part of his life.

But we are married now. What if people see him with someone else? What if people find out? I start to panic again. My stomach is sinking.

"What about you?" he asks.

"I could never imagine being with anyone but Vin," I reply.

"You say that now, but what about in five years, ten? You can't be celibate forever."

"Why can't I?" I say. He huffs.

"We aren't gonna have all the answers right now. And maybe we didn't think this through for the long term. But as of now, I'm pretty damn happy. It will get my parents off my back. I will get some freedom. I can move out of their house and get some space from them and their constant pressures."

"One step at a time huh," I say. We keep our hands in each other's as we flop back against the seats. I take a deep breath to calm my growing nerves.

"You thinking about him?" he finally asks, sensing my inability to completely relax.

"Do you think I am going crazy? Do you think it was really him?" I ask.

"What, at Niagara Falls?"

"Yeah, I could have sworn I saw him, felt him. It was the strangest feeling."

"I dunno, I mean, would he be out by now?"

"Yeah, I think so. I mean, I've kept track. Not on purpose. But it's hard not to. I think he would have been out earlier this year. If my math is right. But I have no idea how it all works. Is it to the day? Do they get early release for good behaviour like in the movies? Or extra time for, I dunno. Not following rules?"

I stop rambling, but my mind is spinning.

"Would he even be able to leave the country with a criminal record?" Blake asks.

"I dunno, probably not, I suppose."

The wretched guilt hits me again. Hard. I have not thought about the fact that Vin may never be able to travel. Because he took the blame for something I did. That should have been me.

Blake squeezes my hand.

"I must be going crazy," I say.

"This trip brought up a lot for you, Scarlet. But you have faced it all. You've opened up, and I feel like this will be good for you. We are moving forward. You deserve to be happy."

"Yep, me and you Blake. We got this."

"We got this," he repeats as he drapes an arm over my shoulders and pulls me close. I rest my head on his shoulder and take a deep breath. It always feels easier to breathe around Blake.

40

Another plane to another beach

VIN

What now? What now? What the fuck do I do now?

Her image keeps spinning around my mind on a fucking carousel. Her laugh echoes around me, and everything just reminds me of her.

The blue of the ocean waves reminds me of her eyes. There is a beach hut next to me renting surfboards that is painted green, which just reminds me of the shirt she was wearing.

The white wash of the waves lapping the shore remind me of the spray of the falls where I saw her. And every goddamn couple that walks by laughing and enjoying their holiday reminds me of the way his arm was draped around her. The way her head rested on his shoulder. The way she laughed into him. It all just reminded me that it wasn't me with her.

If I thought being locked in a cell being tortured by her memory was tough, this makes that seem like a fucking cake walk. I don't get that saying, it's stupid, everything is so fucking stupid.

I get up from the warm sand I'm sitting on, twisting an ice-cold bottle of Bintang in my hand. I'm holding it hard enough to almost crush it.

I hate alcohol, after what it did to Mike. I honestly don't know why I even bought it. A guy came up to me with an Esky offering one for basically one dollar, and I felt bad, so I took it. It tastes like shit. I tip it out in the sand as I stand up and walk toward the water.

I let the little waves lap up over my feet. Taking the fall for Scar had been a no-brainer. I'd do it again in a heartbeat. Not seeing her in prison was tough, but I knew it was the right call.

She was happy, she looked happy. She has moved on. It was the right call. Only now I can't seem to let it go. In prison I was trapped. All I had to do was say no visitors; someone else did the hard yards. I didn't have to say it to her face. I didn't have to physically walk away from her. I had no choice.

I do now. I have a choice. And I can't let it go. My heart won't stop pounding in the strangest rhythm. Palpitating. It's making me feel nauseous and dizzy.

There is a ringing in my ears, and I can't tell if it's the pounding of my own heart or the swirl of thoughts running rampant through my head.

The last few years have been a blur. I got a job in prison. Yep, who would have thought you have opportunities to study, to work, to even make a small amount of money in prison? I managed to finish my apprenticeship inside and get some experience working on government contracts through the prison. It kept me busy.

When I got out, my old boss Clark put me up. He had continued to visit through the years. He let me stay with him and even offered me a job back at his garage.

Trying to travel has been a nightmare. A lot of countries won't allow you entry with a record. It took a heap of work and help from lawyers to organise visas for where I wanted to go. But I eventually made it to Niagara Falls.

Then, as quickly as I had arrived, I left.

I stand sinking my feet into the warm sand, thinking about how badly I miss her, how badly I need her.

I would have suffered through anything to have her. All the hits, the verbal lashings, the broken bones. No amount of pain I suffered from Mike was worse than how it felt to hurt her. How it felt to be without her. I thought letting her go would be the best thing for her. And I hope I was right. But now I have to know. I have to find her. I have to see her again. I have to know if she is truly happy. If she has moved on. I tell myself if she did, if she is happy without me, I'll let her go. Again.

Maybe I am being selfish. I think a large part of me has to know if she has forgiven me. Maybe if she did, I can let go of my own guilt and move on myself. Maybe then I won't be so haunted by her memory.

Small waves lap up onto the shore. She was overseas, but for how long? Where does she live now? How will I find her? As I watch the waves roll in, listen to the calming sound of the ocean, the birds chirping, it clicks. I know where to find her. I know where she would have gone.

Aboard another plane to another beach.

41

Everything changes

SCARLET

"*S*carlet, you have a client asking for you."

I look up from my burger that I am madly shoving into my face. I only have ten minutes before my next client is due, and despite the fact that it's two p.m., this is the first chance I've had to eat all day.

"Who is it?" I ask, a piece of bread roll falling out my mouth. It is so full it can barely close. I hadn't realised how hungry I am.

"Just some guy, says he knows you." I gulp down my bite and take a swig of water to help it go down. We've been back from our trip for two months.

It's been a shock to the system coming back, that's for sure. Telling our parents was a whirlwind. We quickly found a small apartment to rent and wasted no time moving in together. My work had agreed to leave without pay while we were away, so I was lucky enough to walk back into my job.

Blake's parents are still absolutely livid. They feel betrayed that we didn't go about it the so-called 'proper way.' Not much they can do when he isn't living with them anymore and we have the marriage certificate in our hands.

They did make a few threats, like now that he is married and living with his wife, he has to pay his own way. They said they weren't going to pay for his university fees anymore. He was fine with this, as he really didn't want to continue anyway.

But when he told them he was pulling out, things escalated. They are still working it out, and Blake is doing a lot of soul-searching, trying to figure out what he actually wants to do with his life. In the meantime, he's decided to stick to finishing his degree until he makes up his mind.

I had to ring Births, Deaths and Marriages when we got home to find out the correct process to register our marriage. Apparently, even though our Vegas wedding and paperwork are legal here in Australia, no banks or institutions will accept the certificate for my name to change.

I need to apply for a change of name and then use that certificate to change my name on my ID and bank cards. Blake and I discussed it, and we decided I would keep my name and not bother with the change. The process sounded complicated, and I didn't have a huge desire to be Scarlet Abernathy anyway. I was happy to keep James, and Blake was happy with it too, much to his parents' disgust.

My mum, although upset she had missed the wedding, was happy and excited for me. I knew she would be. It made the fact that I kept such a big lie from her an even harder pill to swallow.

I am so used to keeping this secret now. I did not even tell Blake the full truth of what I did. He knows about Vin and that night, but I always stuck with the lies Vin told. I've kept my truth buried so far. I don't think I will ever be able to say it out loud.

Life has somewhat started to settle into a new routine. We are happy, finding our rhythm as 'husband and wife.'

I wipe my mouth with my napkin and gulp down a few more swigs of water.

"Ok, thanks Tay," I say as I jump up from my hairdresser's stool in our back room.

Taylor is our new apprentice, and her role at the moment mostly consists of answering the phones, making bookings and cleaning up after us. So it makes sense that she didn't ask this guy a heap of questions. She is still learning the ropes. It's probably my next appointment rocking up slightly early, which I'm not about to be mad at. It's when they meander on in twenty minutes late that I want to rage.

I walk out of the back room and through the basin room. As I enter the open floor, I see the front counter. Behind it stands a man I would recognise blindfolded. But I can see him clear as day now. He is exactly the same, only somehow so very different.

He was always tall, but now he has filled out those long limbs. His broad shoulders strain against his black tee. His hair is short, shaved close to the skin at the sides and back. I pull my eyes away, looking down at the floor.

"Hello Scar-let."

He fumbles over the syllables that form my name like he hasn't dared to speak them in years. Although he never called me Scarlet. I was always Scar to him. I could place that low, husky voice in a choir of people.

I am suddenly frozen. I have thought about what I would say to him if I ever got the chance a million times over. Only now he is right here, and I can't move.

I can't even look directly at him. It hurts. I am terrified. Terrified that the boy I knew and loved would be long gone. Would his eyes, that were once bright and full of love, be dark and cold from loneliness? Would his gentle touch be hardened by things he had to do to survive the last six years? I have no idea what prison is actually like.

I take a deep breath and will my feet to move. Just an inch. But he does all the work, taking a few long strides around the counter and stopping just feet from me.

He is so close, close enough that I can smell him. I could reach out and touch him if my body wasn't turned to stone. My heart is hammering in my chest. My body feels flooded with adrenaline. I look up to face the man that the voice belongs to, not knowing who he would be now.

I am swept away. I feel like a tsunami has hit me and I am being sucked downstream, flinging my arms and legs around, trying to grab hold of anything to steady myself, gasping for air while I pop up before being sucked back under.

I am so dizzy. I am about to let the water take me when strong hands grip the sides of my arms.

"Are you ok?" he asks me, pulling me out of the water and back to dry land.

I swallow hard and plant my feet, then take a shaky step forward, unsure if my legs even work. I stretch a hand out to touch him. Is he really here? Am I dreaming?

"Vvvvin…" I stutter. My fingers reach out to touch his chest, and I half expect him to disappear in a puff of smoke like a ghost. My fingers hit solid mass. I am one foot in front of him now. I feel tiny compared to him. He is so much taller than I remember. I barely recognise his body. Yet it still feels so familiar under my fingers. They burn being on his chest. He does not move, nor does he speak again. He just stands there. His big arms have dropped back down, hanging by his sides as he waits for me to adjust. I look up at him again. Pain, confusion, love, frustration in my eyes.

I am shocked when our eyes meet. Those same electric emerald-green eyes I remember so vividly. Bright with flecks of golden yellow dancing around in them.

His face has changed. I guess mine has too. We are not teenagers anymore. He has a five o'clock shadow on his face. He could barely grow underarm hair when I knew him.

Now he has stubble all over his jaw. I realise I still have my hand on his chest, resting flat now, palm to heart.

I am suddenly very aware that the entire salon is now staring, watching us standing there looking at each other without speaking. It slams me back to reality. The reality that I have not heard from him in six years. The reality that I stabbed and killed someone, his dad. I almost died, I was hospitalised in a psychiatric ward because I was more concerned about this man than myself. The reality that I spent a year of my life trying to visit him, trying to see him, speak to him. To tell the truth, fix what happened. The reality of all the minutes, hours, years I have spent thinking about him. Why wouldn't he speak to me? Why did he never let me visit? Why did he never read my letters? So much anger and frustration boils up inside of me.

Why now? After all the opportunities he had to respond to me. Why now?! Why after all these years would he come here? How did he find me, how did he know where I work? It was him I saw at Niagara Falls, wasn't it? Did Blake have something to do with this?

I feel so many things. All the frustration and pain and anger from those months on end of visiting him. All the tears I cried when I felt the rejection after being turned away. How hard I struggled in those months after. How lonely I felt. The sting of each letter returned unopened and unread.

I'm not in control, and my emotions bubble over. Before I can do anything to stop it, I slap him across the face. I turn around and walk straight through the basin room to the back, grab my bag and head out the back door. I am vaguely aware of everyone in the salon following me with their eyes as I go.

I don't care. I have to get out of here. I don't care about my clients, my job or my colleagues. None of it. I just need to get away from here. I need to breathe. After so many years of wishing to just have one more touch, to hear his voice, to see his face just one more time.

Now suddenly he is here and I am running away. I don't understand it, but I am so overwhelmed I just have to run. Everything is different now.

I had finally accepted my fate. I was moving on.

I am happy! I think? I am, aren't I? I mean, I was. Knowing he is here... It changes everything.

42

Hand to hand

I walk off the plane in Perth. I grab my bags from the carousel and walk towards the exit, then out the automatic doors into the main airport floor.

There are big crowds, lots of people waiting to greet those arriving home or visiting for the first time. I scan the crowd, my head towering over most of the people in here. I have no clue what I'm looking for.

She isn't even here. I know that, I saw her in another country a mere few days ago. Why the fuck am I here? What the fuck am I doing?! I have no clue.

I have no clue if she even lives here. She could be spending all her time traveling. Living in another country, a different state. God, she could be anywhere. Could have settled anywhere.

I'm a fool to think she moved to Mandurah, a fool to think she even remembered our time together and the life we planned. She probably has a life a million miles away from here.

This was such a stupid idea. I actually have no clue what I was thinking. By this point I am running on pure fumes. Delusional. I need to get a hold of myself.

I have thought about this town multiple times. Envisioned it in my head when I made up stories of what our life would be like if shit never hit the fan. If we actually made it into my car and across the country.

I am here now, so close. I have to see it. I have to just know what it's like. Is it how I pictured it? As beautiful as the pictures made it out to be? Would we have been happy here? Well shit, I am here now, might as well take the extra one-hour trip south and see the place, right?

I stop at an info desk. An older woman with grey hair and quirky red glasses greets me. I ask her what the best way to get to Mandurah is and she hands me a bus and train timetable. A quick bus ride to the train station and straight line on the train, and I would be there.

I make it down to Mandurah easy enough, but fuck, I haven't thought this plan all the way through. I have nowhere to stay, not a heap of cash, no job, I'm an ex-con and I have absolutely no clue if the girl I am chasing even lives here. Googling the place now, it seems so much bigger than I remembered it being when we first decided on it. The train station is fairly busy, and there are cabs waiting in a taxi line. That's great, but where the hell am I headed?

I sit down on a bench outside the station in the sun and do a bit more of a Google search of the town. There is a largeish shopping centre a ten-minute walk from the train station, so I decide to make my way there to form a plan.

It feels surreal to be here after all these years. I make my way to the food court of the shopping centre and sit down. I have ordered a chicken kebab and chips, but my hunger is non-existent. I am buzzing and anxious. I haven't been able to steady my raging heart since I heard her laugh at the falls.

The electricity seemed to pull me here without me having much of a say. Now I am here though, I need to calm the fuck down and figure out what I do next. Do I actually want to find her? Track her down? I spent so many years trying to fight the memory of her, convincing myself to let her go. I thought I had. I thought I was finally free of her chokehold on me. Free from prison, I had a plan to travel for a bit and then head back to my hometown. Work at the mechanic's and live a simple, stress-free life.

Shit, I'd better call my boss and tell him what the fuck is going on. He isn't expecting me back for a couple of months, but am I even going back now? He has been the one constant in my life for the last few years. A safe place to go away from Mike. Showing up to prison to visit. Giving me a place to stay and a job when I got out. Helping me sort out my passport and visas. I can't let him down. But I need to find her.

Ok, that's the plan. I will track her down. Make sure she is happy, hear her say she forgives me or face the reality if she hates me for what I did to her. Then I will head home and carry on with my life as planned.

Ok, step one, track her down. I slump back in my chair and start picking at the chips. A group of school-aged girls come noisily down the aisle and sit down at the table across from me. None of them notice me. They are laughing and chatting, taking selfies on their phones.

"Oh my God Claire, post that one, it's so good," one girl squeals.

"Yes, that's gonna be my new profile pic," the other says. I look up at them across my food. Profile pic, huh, I think to myself. I don't know why this has not occurred to me earlier. Maybe because I don't have any social media. I have an email address and that's it. I know about them, well, Facebook and Instagram anyway. I think there are a million more social networks around.

I grab my phone and google Facebook. Create an account. Would she even be on here? I go through the process and set up an account. It's easy enough. Only now it wants a profile pic and a bio. I laugh to myself. Ex-con who stabbed the love of his life. No current job, no home and no money. About to try tracking down the only person he has ever loved to find out if she hates me or forgives me. The girls at the table all turn to look at me, and I realise I have started to laugh out loud.

Ok, I'm pretty sure I can't use that as my bio. I decide to leave it blank for now. I add a pic I took of the clouds out the plane on my first flight out of town as my profile pic. Lame, I know, but this whole thing feels lame to me.

Am I really ready to face rejection? I feel I know it's coming. Even if I do find her. It's been years, and she was with someone else, for Christ's sake. I talk myself off the ledge and hit finalise on the set-up.

I head to the search tab, type in Scarlet James and hit search. The screen loads for a second, and then a heap of little squares with pics start popping up. I hit the 'See all' button and watch as they appear down my screen. They all have an 'Add friend' button underneath them. Some have locations under the photos with their city or state.

Well shit! That was all a little too easy. There she is. Her profile pic is a picture of her and the guy I swear she was with. They are standing in front of a graffiti wall at a beach. It's a close-up pic, and I recognise her instantly. Her deep-blue eyes, wavy dark hair wrapped around her shoulders.

She is hugging the guy. Dark hair, dark eyes, dark skin. I want to scream. No, I want to rip his arms from her body. I hover my finger over the profile. I have absolutely no clue how social media works. Will she know if I click her picture? Will she get an alert?

I jump back to Google and search 'Can someone tell if you view their profile on Facebook?' I read a bunch of stuff, but it all says no. She will only see if I try to add her as a friend or like a picture.

Ok, I can do this. I jump back to the app and tap the profile pic. It comes up with a larger profile pic and the 'Add friend' button but not much else.

There are only two photos under her posts. One is her profile pic and one is her updated cover photo: some rose bushes. She always did love roses. There is no other info. I stare at the screen, willing it to give me more information. Anything. I click on the profile pic, making it larger.

But there is no info to be gained from it. I can feel my heart shattering into smaller pieces with every second I stare at it.

I click out of it and click on the cover photo. The roses are all different colours. All in bloom. Beautiful reds, yellows, pinks and whites. I zoom in on one of the flowers. In the background is a blurred building. Old brown brick. I can't see the entire building, only a small section of the front doors. Old wooden ones with big brass handles. I am definitely not great with technology, but surely there has to be a way to find where this photo was taken.

I am this close, I can feel it. I am not going to lose her now. Part of me wants to slap myself for being so desperate, but a bigger part needs to find her. Now my mind is made up, I will do anything. I jump back to Google and type 'How to find where an image was taken.'

Google comes up with a few things, but one title stands out: Reverse Google image search. Ok, all I have to do is save the picture to my phone, jump on the Google image search and add the image.

I click back to Facebook and screenshot the pic of her and the guy. I jump back to Google and click the link to the image search site. I click the camera box and select the photo from my photos on my phone. When I hit search, it instantly comes up with Venice Beach LA.

Well I'll be damned. It worked. Although it's not helpful at all, as I am on the other side of the world. Has she just been there? Is she travelling around? We always used to talk about it. Is she living our dream?

I jump back to Facebook and save the picture of the roses. Jump back to Google image search and repeat the process with the new photo. I am not hopeful for this one. It may not even be an image she took. Could just be one she liked off the internet.

Heat courses through my body, rising all the way to my head. I can feel my heartrate doubling. Shit, shit, shit, shit, shit, shit, shit.

It's here, fuck me sideways. Mandurah. She's been here. I copy the name of the church by highlighting it, then I jump to maps and paste it in. It's a twelve-minute drive from here. Hand in Hand Church. A fucking church. What the hell? She is not religious. Well, she wasn't when I knew her. Guess a lot can change in six years.

Maybe she just liked the flowers. Maybe it isn't her photo. Either way, I am one step closer to finding her. I grab my bags and chuck my whole kebab and most of the chips I didn't eat into the trash. Skull my water and head to one of the exit doors.

I look at the map again to see what direction I need to head in. It shows me the time it would take to walk, drive and bus. I click the bus option, and it comes up with times and a bus number. I click the button to show me the closest stop and then head in that direction.

Twenty-five minutes later, I arrive outside the church. The flowers look exactly like the picture, and I can see the brown/red brick with the big wooden doors. I walk up, moving on autopilot, driven by nothing but my need to find her.

The church is shut, doors all locked up. Doesn't surprise me. It is late afternoon on a Wednesday. There are lots of people around, so I head in their general direction.

A short walk down the street has me finding a coffee shop. I head in and order an espresso and sit down at one of the little tables. Pulling my phone out again, I search for a place to crash. I haven't really slept much since leaving the falls. It feels like days ago. Probably has been. I lost track of time.

I find a motel a fifteen-minute walk away. I finish up my coffee and head there for the night.

Nothing else I can really do now. Although I can't sleep, I lie awake staring at her photo, wondering who the guy is, wondering if she is as happy as she seems. Wishing that it was me that was pulling her in close under my arm.

I give in and end up searching her mum's name as well, but nothing comes up. Eventually I must be overtaken by sleep, as I wake up in a hot sweat ten hours later.

43

Happy and in love, simple

VIN

I am sitting at the coffee shop near the church again. It's my only tie to her. I have enough adrenaline coursing through me to start a fire, but I order an espresso anyway. I ask the lady behind the counter if she knows when the church is open. She says she knows they open Sunday for service but was sure they also do a few open days and community events. But she isn't sure when.

She tells me to check their website. Why didn't I think of that? Churches have websites? Who knew. I chuck the church name into Google and find the site I need. There is a section for events. I scroll through it, not really finding anything coming up.

I move to the contact section and find the office opening hours are eight thirty to twelve thirty daily. It is currently seven a.m. I order a bagel and wait for it to be eight thirty. My skin is practically crawling by the time I'm standing in front of the big brown doors at precisely eight twenty-five waiting for them to open.

A middle-aged woman with a blonde bob opens the doors and greets me with a warm smile.

"I'm Marion Abernathy," she says, holding out her hand for me to shake. "How can I help you?"

I tower over her, but she doesn't seem timid. She has kind eyes and a stiff posture. I run my hand over my mouth; it suddenly feels very dry. I haven't really thought this through. Why am I here? What am I doing? How do I find her here? I don't want to seem like a complete stalker.

"Vincent Henderson," I say as I all but swallow her petite hand in my own giant one.

I don't think I have ever used my full name. Literally no one has ever called me by it. But I am in a church. Suddenly I feel incredibly self-conscious. I smooth my hands down my crumpled tee, feeling like a fish out of water next to this lady dressed in her crisp white cotton blouse and cream pants. She looks like she floated directly down from heaven, if such a place does exist.

Next to her, in my solid black oversized tee, black denim shorts with rips in them and black sneakers, I look like I've been thrown up directly from hell. And the way this heat keeps washing over me from the pit of my stomach, it feels like it too.

"Is there something I can help you with?" she asks kindly when my silence has become borderline awkward. She steps through to the entrance and grabs a pamphlet off the table to hand to me. I mindlessly take it from her, clearing my throat. I take a step around her to the pinboard hanging in the entrance area wall. It's covered in flyers advertising upcoming events, children's drawings and a heap of photos. One in particular catches my eye. I home in on it, taking a giant step around the woman to stand directly in front of it. It's him! The guy from the Facebook profile photo, the same guy I saw at the falls with her. The one holding my girl. Well, who used to be my girl.

It's the same dark tanned skin, dark hair and eyes. It's him all right, no mistaking it. Although in this photo, he has his arms around a different woman. A shorter, older woman. I turn my head to face Marion.

"This is you?" I say, pointing at the photo. It wasn't a question though. She takes a few quick steps to come up next to me.

"Yes, that's me and my son."

"Son," I repeat, shock coursing through me. I bite my bottom lip, trying to think what I can ask next.

The entrance room suddenly feels smaller than my prison cell did. I have never once felt claustrophobic, but right now, the walls feel like they are moving in from the sides and are about to sandwich me to death.

"Your son works here as well?" I ask, trying to make myself smaller so she doesn't find my questions threatening or feel like I'm interrogating her. She nods proudly, and a large smile crosses her face.

"We volunteer here, my husband Jeffery and son Blake," she says proudly.

His name is Blake. "Are they here now?" She gives me a puzzled look but doesn't step away from me. I realise my line of questioning is approaching creepy territory. She is an older woman, and I appear to be asking if she is alone. Me, a solid six-foot-four ex-con. can't make myself small enough to not seem threatening, even if I kneeled.

We are, however, in a church, and she doesn't seem afraid of me, so I stand by my question.

"My husband is a surgeon. He works a lot, so no, he isn't here, and Blake is taking some time off university to travel with his girlfriend," she replies calmly, not moving away from me.

Aaaannd there it is. Girlfriend. The word hits hard, harder than I've ever been hit. Somehow harder than any physical blow and harder than seeing her with him in real life. This feels official. Scar is his girlfriend, and they are traveling together right now. I need to find a better way to get the information I need without scaring this woman half to death. Or having the cops called on me.

I take a step back. I know enough for now. They live here in this town. It's clear. This woman, her husband and son all volunteer here. He will be back and she will be with him. My Scar. I found her!

"Our pastor is in the office if you would like to come in. I can show you around or talk to you about our programs. If there is something specific you are looking for, I can answer any questions," she says as she places a gentle, soft hand on my forearm, directing me away from the pinboard and towards the office. I can now see two other people sitting at a table talking.

I am starting to feel like a complete stalker. I think I have done enough for today. I need to process what info I have and figure out the best way to go about all this.

"I think I found everything I need," I say as I turn back around. Still holding the pamphlet in my hands, I walk back towards the door. "Thank you for your time," I say, giving her a nod as I walk out the doors.

I chuck the pamphlet into my back pocket and run my hands through my hair. I have kept it short while inside. It was just easier. I know Scar always loved it when I grew it out. She loved twirling her fingers through it. I was just a kid then, though. I am twenty-four now. Still young, but somehow everything I have been through has put years on me.

My hair feels messy, and I am suddenly feeling awfully conscious of the way I look. I know she isn't even here, but I want her to feel happy to see me again, not look at me like I am some wild beast. I walk back to the cafe and head inside. I approach the same lady I asked about the church earlier.

"Hey, do you know where I can get a haircut around here?" She is busy plating up a muffin for another customer, but she looks up and smiles at me.

"There are a few salons around here and a couple of barbers too. If you walk left from here, you will walk past a couple of malls that have salons. You will be able to take your pick."

"Thank you," I say as I walk out and head in the direction she told me. It doesn't take long to come across a strip mall. Further up, there seem to be more shops as well. I decide to keep walking and head in that direction. I find another strip of shops heading down towards a grassy area overlooking a waterway and decide to head down towards it.

Worst case, I don't find a salon. I can at least go for a walk through the town. There are a few shops. Clothes and other homewares, and sure enough, I walk right past a salon. I walk in and wait at the counter.

A brunette comes up to me. She looks young. Maybe seventeen.

"Hi, do you have an appointment?" she asks, looking down at the computer to look at the schedule.

"No, I was just walking by and thought I would check if someone has time," I say, running my hand through my hair again. It's the longest it's been in years, but it is nowhere near as long as I used to let it get.

"For yourself?" she asks. I nod.

"Let me just have a look." She looks down at the computer again and clicks the mouse a few times. "Just give me one sec."

"Sure." She walks away to one of the other ladies who has gloves on and is painting something on another woman's hair. They talk quietly for a second, then she comes back towards the counter.

"If you don't mind an apprentice doing it, I can do it for you now. I am a second year, so I am confident with men's cuts, and it will only be twenty dollars instead of the usual forty-five. Is that ok?" she asks, looking up at me. Her voice is slightly shaky, like she is nervous, and she avoids my eyes.

I have no idea if hairdressing is similar to being a mechanic, but I did my apprenticeship, so I am assuming she is in her second of three or four years. It doesn't matter. My hair grows fast; can't be worse than a prison cut. I spread my legs wider behind the counter to try to make myself a bit shorter, less intimidating.

"That's fine with me, as long as you're comfortable with it." She smiles up at me and takes my details to punch into the computer. Then she gestures for to me to follow her around to the main area.

"Would you like it washed?" she asks. I shake my head.

"No, it's fine." She motions for me to take a seat and hits the foot pedal to lower the seat right to the bottom. She places a cape around my neck.

"What would you like done?" she asks, looking at me in the mirror in front of us as she runs her fingers through the wavy mop on my head.

I laugh internally, wondering if I should tell her that for the last six years, I've been in prison, where I used to just have it shaved short. I can already see her small hands shaking, so I decide that probably isn't the best way forward.

"Just short. I am happy for you to just do what you want to practice as long as it's shorter."

"Really?" she says. It comes out in a bit of a squeal, like she is excited to have a free run.

"Sure," I say, nodding.

She grabs the clippers and starts fitting things to it. Then she seems to find her confidence and gets to work.

I avoid looking at her in the mirror so I don't make her more nervous. She makes quick work of it once she gets into it, shaving it almost skin short at the sides and back and then cutting it to blend in with a little bit more length on the top.

I glance up at her work every now and then. She looks like she is concentrating, so I don't bother talking. She finishes up and starts playing around with the little bit of length on the top.

"What do you think?" she asks, looking at it in the mirror. I nod and smile.

"Best cut I have had in years." She gets a big smile on her face like she is proud of her work. I decide not to add that it wasn't hard to beat. She has done a good job. It's different to anything I've ever had before, but I like it.

"I've been dying to practice this type of cut. I've been mostly doing kids' cuts, but the last couple of months we have been short-staffed, as one of our seniors is traveling. So I've been able to do more fun haircuts."

I freeze, looking up at her in the mirror, and our eyes meet. But I have no clue what to say.

"Are you sure you like it?" she asks, seeing my face change.

"It's great, you're very good at this. Thank you."

Surely it can't be. It does seem a tad too coincidental. Scar did always talk about being a hairdresser, but she wanted to finish school first. She lives in this town and is currently away traveling. No, it would be far too coincidental. I mean, how many people live in this town, how many people travel? It could be anyone. Just fucking ask. I push myself. You will regret it if you don't ask.

I go to speak but force it back down. My hair grows like wildflowers. I'll need another haircut in less than four weeks, especially if I want to keep it short. I'll just come back. Come back and see if she is here. Fuck, I am definitely starting to feel like a fucking stalker now. I pay the girl, thank her and head out the door.

I have no clue what I am supposed to do with my time now. But I jump on Google and type in the salon name as I walk. I am getting good at this Google shit. Their website comes up, and I move to the 'Meet our staff' section. Sure as fucking shit, there she is. Scarlet James. There is a picture of her with her name underneath it. Shit she is beautiful. Her hair is long in the photo, longer than it was when I saw her at the falls. It frames her face in neat waves. She wears less makeup than all the other girls. Just something on her eyelashes and a soft colour on her lips. She has a big smile on her face. Her bio says she has four years' experience and has worked here since she started her apprenticeship. She loves colour work and specialises in blondes. I have literally no idea what all that means, but holy shit.

Now all I have to do is figure out how I go about telling her I'm here. Do I just show up at her work? Add her as a friend on Facebook? Go to church? Just keep stalking her and stage a random bump in? Pretend it's fate that I just wound up here and didn't fly all the way across the world, stalk her on Facebook and reverse search her images to find out where she hangs out? My head is spinning.

I've already fucked up so much with her; I have to get this right. I've come this far now. I just need to see her. Then she can tell me that she is in love with Blake and that she is happy. It will confirm that I did the right thing, and I'll pack my bags and leave.

It's settled then. I'll just head back to the salon in a few weeks and see if she's there. If she is, I will tell her everything I did to find her, why I'm here, and beg her for forgiveness. Then she will tell me she forgives me, that she is happy and in love with Blake, and I will leave. Simple.

44

Time to go home

VIN

*J*ust do it! Dude, stop being a giant pussy, just go in there.

It's been just over four weeks, and I am standing outside and just to the side of the hair salon. I have done literally nothing but stew over how to do this for the last four weeks.

I still have no clue if she is even back in town or back at work, but I do need another haircut, so If I head in and she isn't there, I will just get a haircut and try again in four weeks.

And what if she is there? The thought scares me more than anything in this world. I am not sure I am prepared to actually see her again.

I poke my head around the wall to where I can see through the glass windows into the salon. I am very aware I look like a giant fucking weirdo, and if she sees me doing this it's all over. Someone is going to call the fucking cops on me soon.

Just walk in there, ok? Just do it. I can't get a proper view of everyone in there, so I just walk past the window towards the door. I brace myself as I grip the handle of the door to pull it open. I look up through the glass door, and my stomach drops. My breath catches in my throat, and my chest feels like it is about to explode from the pace my heart is setting.

She's there. She is standing behind a lady sitting in a chair and is working away, chatting, wrapping the woman's hair in shiny foil. She is completely oblivious to the fact that I am here, about to turn her fucking world upside down. A force pulls me back, and I drop my hand from the handle.

That's what I am about to do, turn her world upside down. She is happy. I saw her smile in her pics, the laugh while she nuzzled into her boyfriend. What the fuck am I doing? I'm going to ruin everything for her. She doesn't want me. I stabbed her, almost killed her, bought her nothing but pain, ignored her, pushed her away, and now I want to just fucking stroll on in there like I'm not the devil himself?

'Oh hey Scar, remember me? Haha I almost killed you. My dad tried to rape you and then attacked you. Wanna drop your seemingly nice churchy boyfriend and let me drag you back to hell?'

I'm a complete idiot. What the fuck have I been thinking? I have nothing to offer her.

I turn my back to her and the door and walk away, back down the way I came. I'll buy a pair of clippers and cut my own damn hair in the motel basin. Which is exactly what I do.

I plan to leave. Head back home and forget I was ever here, but I can never seem to pull the trigger.

Every time I have the flights added, I can't seem to confirm and book. I can't turn away from her. I can't help but walk past that salon every day. She never sees me. She is engrossed in her work.

I am all too aware of how ridiculous this is getting now. I have been here for three months. She has been mere metres away from me for two of them, and I can't bring myself to close the distance. I give myself a mental pep talk. Fucking get this over with or leave this town for good cos you are looking like an absolute stalker, and very soon it's going to become weird. It's already weird.

I shake my hands and exhale a couple of loud breaths like I am hyping myself up. I almost want to start slapping myself across the face, but I refrain from doing that, as then I definitely think someone will call the cops on me.

I use the adrenaline coursing through me to pull the door open. I greet the girl at the counter. It's a different one this time, but she is also very young. Scar isn't on the floor, but I know she is here. I know she works Tuesdays.

"Can I speak to Scarlet please?"

"Sure, I will just grab her." With that she walks off towards the back room. My hands are sweaty, and I rub them down my thighs on my shorts. I wait for what feels like a lifetime, but it's barely a full minute, forcing my feet to stay planted and not run back out the way I came.

She rounds the corner of the back room and walks through the little basin area. She spots me and comes to a standstill, her blue eyes trailing up my body to meet my gaze, then quickly falling to the ground. She doesn't look at me and she doesn't move. The colour drains from her face and she starts swaying slightly.

"Hello Scar-let." It comes out shaky. I went to say Scar, but that was always my pet name for her. It's different now. It's like I have forgotten how to talk. My tongue feels like a lead weight in my mouth.

She doesn't move. I am not sure what I was expecting. For her to run and jump into my arms and wrap her legs around me while I cling to her, breathing her in? Then she would kiss me and I would lose my hands in her hair. She would feel exactly the same. Like no time has passed between us.

Only she doesn't do that. She doesn't do anything; she looks like she is about to faint. The need to protect her that was always embedded in me kicks in, and as if on autopilot, it takes me two steps to be in front of her. I place my hands on her arms to steady her.

"Are you ok?" I ask. She slowly looks up at me. My name falls from her lips in a stutter, making my already pounding heart skip a beat.

When she doesn't move or speak again, I drop my hands, all too aware of everyone in the salon now staring at us. We are both frozen. Her hand reaches out and touches my chest. Her fingers feel like they are melting through my shirt and branding my skin. She places her palm flat to my chest. The feel of her hand, even over my clothes, has my heart slowing back down to its normal rhythm. Home! She feels like home, which is a feeling I have not had since the night I lost her.

Then she does something I never expected. I mean, I don't know what I expected. But it wasn't to be slapped across the face.

This girl saw me be beaten my entire childhood. I was so used to being hit that it stopped hurting. The physical and mental pain of the beatings did nothing to me anymore. It was expected.

The sting of her slap has my ears ringing. A pain unlike anything I've ever felt, because it came from her.

She turns to walk away as I hear gasps. One of the ladies moves further away from me while another moves closer to the front desk. I see her hover over the phone, waiting to pick it up and dial for help if I retaliate.

I would never. I would die before I hurt a hair on her head. Well, before I ever hurt her again. Because I did hurt her. I stabbed her. I almost killed her. I can feel my eyes well up. Fuck! I am about to cry in a room full of women I don't know. I take a few deep breaths.

"I...I...I... I am..." Breathe Vin, breathe. "I am sorry everyone, I'll go," I say as I turn and head out the front door. Scarlet is already long gone. She went out the back, and I heard a door slamming. I am assuming there is a back entrance.

Well fuck me. That didn't go as planned. Although, what the fuck was I expecting? What an idiot. I slump down on a bench just down the street from the salon and rub my hands over my face. The watering eyes have stopped, thank God.

"Ok, well, that's that!" I say to myself. Guess it's time for me to go home.

45

He's back

I don't remember driving home. I was so dizzy. I marched straight inside to find Blake in the kitchen cooking dinner.

"You're home early, dinner isn't quite ready yet," he says.

"Did you speak to him? Did you tell him where I work? Did you know he was here?"

I am firing questions at him left, right and centre, and he can barely keep up with the line of fire.

"Whoa, whoa, whoa, just slow down Scarlet," he says, placing his hands on my shoulders. I can see the confusion in his eyes.

"What are you talking about?" he asks as he slips my work bag off my shoulders and places it on the floor. He hands me a cold glass of water and walks me to the kitchen table. He pulls out a chair for me to sit down on and follows suit to sit next to me.

"What happened?" he asks again.

"Vin!" I say.

"Vin," he repeats. "Vin what," he pries further.

"He's here, he was at my work." Blake looks at me with even more confusion.

"Vin was at your work." He just keeps repeating what I am saying, and it is infuriating. I can't seem to string a sentence together to fully explain.

"Vin is out of prison and he was at your work this afternoon?" Blake asks slowly, as if we are playing a game of charades.

"Yes!" I shout, like we just won the game and I am angry it took him so long even though I was making no sense. Blake goes quiet, until he realises his dinner is burning. He jumps up and runs to the stove to turn it down and stir it.

It smells good. The smell of food and the ice-cold water are relaxing me a little bit.

"Go have a hot shower, and when you get out, dinner will be ready and we will talk," he says to me, trying to calm me down even more. I don't argue. The shower will give me time to process and sort my feelings anyway. So I get up and mope to the bedroom, peeling off layers of clothes and just dropping them on the floor as I go.

When I get out of the shower, my hunger has completely gone and I have calmed down. I can't believe that I slapped Vin. I don't know what I was thinking. I wanted nothing more in this world than to see that boy, well man now, again. I would have sold a body part just to hear his voice one more time. He was here. Right in front of me, close enough to touch. And I slapped him. What came over me?

How could I do that to him, after everything he has been through? All the times he has been hit. How could I stoop so low to be someone who would raise a hand to his beautiful face? I feel sick to my stomach.

I am panicking now. What if I ruined my chance to talk to him? How do I even know where he is now? I have no way of contacting him. What now? He could be lost forever. I just blew my only chance to talk to him after all these years. To apologise, to set it right. It's all I have wanted for years. To tell him I never forgot him, never moved on, never stopped loving him. I head to my room and crawl under my bed to grab the box with the letters. I start flicking through them all, trying to remember what I wrote and when; what was happening in my life at the particular time. I take the box out to the kitchen, where Blake is waiting at the table with dinner.

"You hungry?" he asks.

"Not really, sorry."

"It's ok, we can have it for lunch tomorrow." He stands up and starts cleaning up. He eyes the box with the letters in my arms, but he doesn't ask. I walk over to the rug in the lounge room and sit down on the floor. Blake comes and sits next to me. I open up the box again.

"What happened?" he finally asks, breaking the silence.

"I slapped him."

"You what?!"

"I was just so overcome with emotion, I don't know what came over me. I just kept thinking of all the times I tried to reach out to him and he rejected each and every attempt. To show up now. Why? It just brought up so much pain and frustration. Why would he ignore my every attempt to see and speak to him over six years to come here now? It makes no sense. How did he even know where to find me. Was it him at the falls?"

Blake is silent for a minute, just letting me get it all out. He grabs my hand in his, and it calms me down.

"You owe it to yourself to find out, Scarlet," he says.

"It's too late now anyway, I don't even know where he is or how to contact him." Tears prick at my eyes. I blink and one escapes, tumbling down my cheek.

"There was a time when you knew each other better than anyone else. Just think where you would go," Blake suggests. I sit there for the longest time. The beach keeps coming to the front of my mind. But what beach? Our town is almost an island, surrounded by water. Beach on one side and estuary on the other, kilometre after kilometre of coastline. He could be anywhere.

I start thinking, does he have a car? Is he staying close to the town centre so he can walk everywhere?

"He may have left town already. If he came here for me. I slapped him. It kinda sends a pretty clear message to leave. He's probably already on the way to the airport by now."

"Let's assume that it was him you saw at the falls?"

"Ok," I reply, not really following his train of thought here.

"Well, that means he has travelled halfway across the world to come here."

"It could be a coincidence. We always planned on moving here, before everything went sideways."

"Maybe, but maybe not. He would not have come all this way, possibly in the hopes of finding you, to turn around and run after one mishap."

"MISHAP! I slapped him. He's probably running in the opposite direction as fast as he can."

"Ok, new tactic… Let's say he hasn't left. If he was feeling shitty, his reunion with you didn't go to plan, he's in a new town. Where would he go?"

I try to calm my breathing and mull over Blake's words. Where would he go, if he was new to town and feeling down?

"The beach, definitely. We loved the beach, but we didn't live close to one. It was the main reason we chose this town."

"Ok, good. So what beach?"

"Million-dollar question."

I close my eyes and squeeze Blake's hand, mentally running through every beach within a close proximity to my work.

"We can drive up and down the coastline till we find him," Blake offers.

"No, I have to do this alone." Blake nods. I can see the worry in his face, but he moves closer to me. Wrapping me in a hug, he kisses me on the forehead.

"You got this Scarlet. I'm here if you need me."

The tears are rolling now, and I wipe them away with the back of my hand.

"I'm serious Scarlet, no matter what. You will always have me. I love you, you know that, right?"

"Thanks Blake, I love you too."

I am torn. I love Blake dearly; he is my husband and best friend. I know he feels the same about me. We are so happy together. But he isn't Vin, and I am not a man. I am sure Blake knows that if I walk out that door and find Vin, our lives and relationship will most likely never be the same again. He also knows that he can't hold me back from this. He has to let me go.

And so, he does. Even if it breaks both our hearts a little.

I slip my hand from his embrace, moving my forehead back from his warm familiar lips as I turn towards the door and head out to find Vin.

46

Slipping through my fingers

BLAKE

I'm minding my own business, vibing to country music while cooking a curry when the door flies open with a bang. Scarlet comes storming in like a hurricane, screaming at me.

She looks like a crazy person. Breathing heavily, she is rambling something like, 'Did I know, did I tell him?' I try to calm her down enough to understand what in the hell is going on. I've never seen her like this.

Finally she speaks a normal sentence and I repeat it, piecing it all together. Far out! Vin is here, he is in town, at her work. Holy shit!

I compose myself. The animal in me that has been kept in a cage its entire life starts to roar. We can't lose her. We only just got free.

I can't be a twenty-five-year-old divorced gay man. Shit shit shit. It won't go back in that cage, no matter how hard I pull at its leash. It just roars at me. It's had more freedom in the last few months than it's had in years and it wants out, all the way, all the time, forever.

It's been great having Scarlet as my beard. No one questions what I do. It's nice being freely able to explore my sexuality more and more without the fear because hey. I'm technically married.

I am not going back. I can't fucking lose her. The animal wants to grab her and throw her in her bedroom and say, 'Too bad, he can fuck right back off to where he came from cos he isn't having you.' But that's just not me. I use all my strength to yank the animal back into submission. Scarlet is my best friend. Far out, I love her. More than anything. But she isn't a guy and I am gay, one hundred percent gay. I'm good at masking it, but I will never be able to give Scarlet what she needs. Not fully. I am not her lost boy, the love of her life.

I can't hold her back from this. He is right here, in town. She needs to see him, even if it is just for closure. Part of me hopes that's all this is. Closure. He says he forgives her, she says she forgives him, and they go their separate ways. We go back to our blissful fake marriage and he goes, I dunno, to wherever he wants to go.

A larger part of me though, the part that loves fully and openly, the part that is unselfish and giving, wants this to be all she has dreamed of. He misses her and loves her and never moved on. Just like I know she hasn't. She ends up with her happy ending, and I, well, I go wherever divorced gay twenty-five-year-old men go; probably hell if you ask my parents. Shit, my parents. If I thought telling them I got married in Vegas was bad, telling them I am getting a divorce is going to destroy them and our relationship. My gut drops, nausea washing over me. But I choke the bile down.

I tell her to go. She has to know for sure. She has to go, and I'll be damned if I am gonna hold her back. I offer to go with her, but she says she needs to do this on her own, and I respect her space.

I feel her slip from my embrace and most likely my life as she grabs her keys and walks out the door.

47

The man
I once knew

Our main part of town is small enough, surrounded by water. Beach on one side, estuary on the other.

I head back towards my work, thinking I'll drive along the coastline within walking distance to my work and then fan out further.

I'm not speeding or rushed. Quite the opposite, actually. I am driving so slowly I could be given a ticket for obstructing traffic. I stop for longer at the stop signs and take corners far too cautiously. I'm nervous. It's making my stomach do backflips, and my skin feels hot and sticky.

I'm nervous that I won't be able to find him. Nervous that I will. Either way, I have no clue what I'll do. If I don't find him, I guess I'll wait, try again? For how long? It's already six p.m. now, and I can see the sky starting to show signs of a setting sun.

If I find him, what will I do? What will I say? What will he say? How will it feel to see him, touch him, talk to him again? The closer I get to the coastal drive, the more nervous I become. The butterflies in my stomach flap and dance around, and with each stretch of road and each turn, I get a little bit closer to finding the answers to my questions.

I slowly accelerate around a corner, a steady stream of commuters behind me. Each and every one of them is eager to pass me, taking a long sideways glance at who is taking far too long at the stop signs and going far too slowly around the roundabouts.

I skip the marina, as I know it will be busy, and if Vin is the same man I once knew, he will avoid the crowds and opt for a more low-key place. I come up to the car park of the beach I have in mind. Beyond the large car park is a grassy area and playground.

I pull in to park, both hands clutching the steering wheel hard while I slow my breathing. I get out of the car. You can't see down onto this beach unless you head up and stand right at the steps that lead down.

I slowly walk to the top of the car park and look down over the rocks that form a groyne, breaking up the beach points. The white sand and the blue water laps against the shore.

I can't believe what I am seeing. A large figure slumped over on the sand near the shore in the distance. His big shoulders hang over his body, and he has taken his shoes off.

His feet are buried in the sand. Knees bent and up close to his chest, his arms resting on his knees. He is looking out over the water towards the sinking sun, which is now throwing beautiful shades of pinks, oranges and reds out across the blue sky.

I steady my breathing and walk down the steps, keeping a tight hold on the railing to stop my jelly legs from giving way. I walk across the white sand. It feels like dragging my feet through mud.

I say nothing as I sit down in the sand next to him, mimicking his position, only a much smaller version. He doesn't look over at me, but rather keeps staring out towards the sky. For the longest time, we just sit there like that, not saying a word or moving, watching the sky turn from orange to pink and eventually to grey.

"That's a car right there," he says, not turning to face me but nodding his head up towards the sky. I can see the exact cloud he is talking about. It looks like one of those really vintage models. Large skinny wheels, open top, curved narrow bonnet.

"I see it," I say back to him as we fall into silence once again.

48

The autobiography of my life

SCARLET

"I'm sorry I slapped you," I say, breaking the silence. "That was horrible. I should have never done that. I was just so shocked, and the emotion got the better of me."

"I am sorry I shocked you," he says through furrowed brows, looking sideways at me.

"How did you know where I work?" I ask, skating around the actual questions I wanted to ask. Like do you forgive me, do you still love me like I love you? He chuckles.

"It's quite a story, to be honest."

"Tell me."

He starts talking, explaining how he saw me at the falls, how he came here on a whim. But then he searched my Facebook and reverse searched my image. How he found the church and met Blake's mum. How he just so happened to find my work, and how he came back and saw me but was too terrified to actually come in for months and months. How he was too frozen in fear to actually take the next step.

I was processing what he was saying. I was mad. I spent years of my life coping with losing Vin and the guilt I felt.

A year trying to visit him weekly, only to be rejected each time. I have spent years writing him letters about my life and how I feel about him. How sorry I am and how I still loved him with everything I had, only to have each one returned unopened.

Yet he has been out for how long? He just decided to up and move on and travel, and now he has been here for months just watching me while I live with half a heart.

I try to swallow my anger and stay calm. I try to remember the boy I knew. The boy that I loved. I can feel myself losing it. I need to reel it back in before I say something I will regret forever. I inhale deeply and shut my eyes, focusing on the Vin I used to know. The Vin who would have died for me that day. The Vin who sacrificed his own life to keep my secret.

"My letters had my address on them, you know," I say once he has stopped talking and my anger has subsided . He huffs a laugh.

"I never got your letters Scar. When the first one came, I told them to return anything from that name to the sender."

"I know, I got them all back."

"I needed you to move on Scar. You deserved better than I could ever give you. I hurt you so badly. You almost died. I needed you to let me go. To be happy, and it worked. You look happy with Blake."

"Then why are you here now Vin? If you needed me to move on, if you needed me to be happy and you saw me smiling and laughing, why the hell come here now? You were planning on just moving on with your life and forgetting all about me."

"You think I forgot about you?" I look down at the sand, avoiding his gaze. "Scar, look at me. You think I just forgot about you? That I ever for one second stopped loving you, needing you like the air I breathe? I never moved on. Never forgot. I never stopped loving you. I just couldn't bear to see you hurt. I fucking hurt you. I stabbed you, Scar. You should never forgive me for that."

"And I killed your dad Vin, ME! I stabbed him in the back. I knew what I was doing. I grabbed that knife and I stabbed him until he stopped moving and I was sure he was dead. I wanted him dead Vin, I killed your father, and you should never forgive me for that."

That is the first time I have ever said those words out loud. The first time I spoke the truth of that night. I killed a man. I killed his dad, and deep down, I know that I did it on purpose.

Tears drown my eyes now, streaming down my cheeks. I stare up at him, and he tucks a loose strand of hair behind my ears and then swipes my tears with his thumb, one side at a time.

He truly is beautiful. He is different from what I remember, but he is still gorgeous. My anger subsides as I stare into his eyes. Eyes that are now also welling up with tears. I lose my train of thought altogether. Silence falls around us. I scan his body, seeing the tiny scars littering his arms, very faint raised white lumps, from years of abuse.

He has a new scar above his right eyebrow that I have not seen before. I knew every inch of him once. I forget all about what we were yelling about. I'm lost in him.

I reach out and trace the raised scar above his eye with my fingers, and he leans his head into my touch.

"That's new," I say, changing the subject before I completely lose it.

He gives me that halfway crooked smirk I remember so well and says, "Took me a while to adjust to prison." With that, my anger starts to return, and all the questions come flooding back in, swirling around my head.

"Prison, where you ignored me for six years," I snap. With that, I take my hand from his head and start running my fingers through the sand at my sides, trying to calm myself and take my mind off the anger.

"I am sorry, Scar. You saved my life that day. You were everything to me. Not just everything." He pauses and then corrects himself. "You were the ONLY thing. You are the only person I have ever loved." He is talking to me, but he isn't looking at me. He is staring out across the water as if he is talking to the darkening sky.

"I would have died for you that day, Scar. All I ever wanted to do was protect you, and I failed. I failed so badly that you were the one who almost died. By my hands. And you were the one who saved me. I couldn't let you go away for that. We were so young, and you still had a chance at life. A good life. At finding love again and being happy."

He keeps talking, almost as if it to himself. I sit dead still and listen to his version of events. I have longed to hear this from his lips for so long.

"I knew that if I let you see me, you would never have moved on. You would have never left and let me go. I needed you to let me go. I knew if I opened your letters, I wouldn't have been able to help myself from replying, and I couldn't reply. You would have waited for me, and I couldn't have you ruin your life waiting for me Scar. You had already sacrificed so much to save me. You deserved better than I could ever give you, and I needed you to move on."

He was rambling, talking so fast without taking a breath. Like he had to spit it all out or it would choke him. I was struggling to keep up. He paused for a bit and I stayed silent, just trying to process all he was saying. Replaying his words in my head over and over. 'Move on Scar.' He wants me to move on.

"And look at you." He starts talking again, but this time he turns to face me. He grabs my hands in his, and I feel a jolt of electricity running through my veins.

"You look…" He pauses, and a big smile spreads over his face. Even though it is dark now, I can see his eyes sparkling from the glow of the street lights up above in the car park. "You look amazing, Scar. You look happy." He continues to look at me, face to face. "You've travelled, have a boyfriend, you have a career. You've achieved everything we ever talked and dreamed about." He looks down at the sand between us. I can see sadness creeping all over his beautiful face. "You would have never moved on and done these things if I didn't let you go. I couldn't stand in the way of your happiness like that."

This idiot thinks I moved on. That I found love and just forgot all about him. He thinks that I just packed up and left and it didn't leave a hole in my heart. Like my soul wasn't sucked out of my body the day he was ripped away from me. Like I haven't been walking around soulless ever since. Did what we had mean that little to him that he thought I would just forget about it the moment I left town?

I was trying so hard to process my feelings and emotions. I didn't want my anger to bubble over.

"Was what we had real to you?" I finally ask. The question is laced with sadness and confusion. "I mean, we were so young, maybe it wasn't as real for you as it was for me." He looks at me with heartache, then he reaches for my hands again. They feel tiny in his, and even though years have passed, it still feels like home to me.

"You are the love of my life, Scar. There wasn't a day I didn't think of you. There is nothing I wouldn't do for you, and I couldn't have you waste your life waiting for me. It was and still is real for me. I will never stop loving you." He pauses to take a breath, and I just stare at him, getting lost in those beautiful eyes. "Even though it breaks my heart, I'm glad you have moved on," he finishes.

He looks down at our hands now and intertwines his fingers with mine. He finds his way to the little sparkling ring that sits on my ring finger. He looks back up at me with a smile, but tears are forming in his eyes. "Do you love him?" he asks. "Does he make you happy?"

I don't answer his question. Instead, I have my own that needs answering.

"Why did you come here Vin? If you HAD to let me go and you wanted me to MOVE on so badly, why did you come all this way?" I was so confused by his words and actions. He went to prison for something I did. Kept my secret for all these years despite what horrible fate that meant for him.

He proceeded to spend the entire time in prison ignoring my attempts to visit him. He returned every letter I wrote unopened. He is finally free. He travels to the one place I knew he always wanted to see, only to turn straight back around and head all the way here, across the world, to tell me I am the love of his life and that he never stopped loving me or thinking about me. In the same breath he tells me he is happy I moved on and asks if I love Blake. I am so confused.

"I thought I could let you go, I really did, when I was locked away it was easier. I had to believe you were happy and that you were living your life. It was the only way I survived. When I got out, I tried to move on too. I went back to work, organised to travel. Made it to Niagara Falls. I knew I had to move on with my life as well." He takes a breath, but his eyes don't move from my gaze the entire time. "After I saw you, it was like a live wire connecting us again. I couldn't let it go. I left straight away to get as far away from you as possible, to let you carry on living your life. But I just couldn't let it go. I had to make sure it was all real. That you were safe and happy. I told myself that once I knew for sure that you were ok, I would be able to let you go, for good this time." He pauses for a moment, staring at me with those piercing eyes. "Just say the word and I will leave," he says.

"Yes," I say as I break away from his gaze and stand up. Our hands drift apart, and he lets his fall to the sand. "I love him, and I am happy," I say as I turn and start to walk back to the car. I can feel his gaze following me, but he doesn't try to stop me or follow.

He is still sitting in the sand in the dark when I walk back from my car, carrying the box of letters I brought with me. I dump the box next to him in the sand. They hit the ground with a thud.

"Read my damn letters Vin. Read my letters and then come and tell me if you still want to move on," I say, and then I turn and walk away. This time I won't go back. I get in my car and I drive home.

He wants to know if I'm happy. If I love Blake. How my life has been all these years without him. It is all there. Laid out like an autobiography.

49

Have faith

"You ok?" Blake asks as he hands me a cup of coffee. I am sitting at the kitchen bench, swirling my cereal around in the milk. I have barely touched it. It has been two days since I saw Vin. Since I gave him my letters. I scribbled my new address on the box with my tinted lip balm, so he knows where to find me. I haven't heard a thing from him. Maybe he just took what I said at face value and didn't bother to read the letters. Maybe he felt like he didn't need to know any more and just left. Ahh, that would be so typical, wouldn't it? I spent years wishing I could see him one more time to tell him exactly how I feel. Only to have him here and to completely freeze up, slap him and then dump my entire life's story in his lap. It's probably going to take the poor guy a year to read them all. I'm such an idiot.

I should have just told him everything. Blake is GAY, and I am still in love with you. Please don't leave me ever ever again. There. simple. That's all I had to say.

"Not really, but I know I will be," I reply.

"Maybe he is a slow reader," Blake says half-jokingly, trying to lighten my mood. I can't help but chuckle. I told Blake everything when I came home that night. Well, almost everything. He sat with me while I cried. Comforted me as my emotions went from sad and hysterical to angry and frustrated. I don't really know what to do from here. I am absolutely regretting my impulse decision to give him the letters and leave.

I guess the letters will do a better job of explaining everything than I ever could in person. I thought it would be better to let my letters do the talking. Over the years I documented so much of my life in them. Once he read them, he would understand completely.

He would know that while I did move on, my heart never did. It always belonged to him. While I am happy, there is still a huge piece of me missing that no one but him will ever be able to fill. While I have travelled and have a job I love and friends, none of it feels one hundred percent right without him.

Blake grabs his cup of coffee and sits down next to me. He pushes my now very soggy bowl of corn flakes away.

"I know your past was painful, Scarlet. I know how you have struggled to really open up and talk about Vin and your relationship with him. I know how much he meant to you and how much you still love him." I grab Blake's hand. He has been the best friend and fake husband a girl could ever ask for. I couldn't imagine my life without him either.

"I did it you know, it was me," I blurt out the words I wasn't able to speak the night before when I poured my heart out to him.

"Did what, what was you?" he asks, flipping our hands so that he can give mine a squeeze.

"I killed him. It was me who stabbed and killed Mike. He was on top of Vin, he was going to kill him, and so I grabbed the knife out of my stomach and I stabbed him in the back. It was me, and Vin took the fall, and I never said a single thing. I let him go to jail for something I did. I let him hate himself for stabbing me even though I never blamed him. Not one single bit. I just let him rot for years for something I did."

I don't know why now, after all this time, I am suddenly speaking this truth. Something about finally speaking the words out loud to Vin opened the leak hole for the whole truth to flow out, and now I can't keep it contained. I sit in silence, waiting for Blake to shove my hand away or scream murderer and tell me to leave. He doesn't do either of those things.

He throws his arms around me, pulling me into his body.

"I love you Scarlet, and I also know for damn sure that you don't take the fall for something you didn't do and go to prison for someone if you don't love them with every single cell in your body. He will come back to you Scarlet. Just have patience and faith. God forgives you Scarlet, you just need to forgive yourself now."

Faith, I thought. God forgives me. What a funny notion. My life never really involved faith. I was never one to leave things up to faith. But he was right, I had to forgive myself. I had to let it go, trust that Vin will finally read my story and come back to me. That he will realise that a part of me waited for him and will never truly let go of what we had.

"Faith huh," I say as I look up from my coffee and into Blake's trusting, comforting dark eyes. "You really think God forgives me?"

"I know he does." All I really care about is if Vin forgives me.

I haven't really given much thought to what would happen to Blake if Vin comes back into my life. How would we explain everything? What would the small circle of friends we made over the years think or say? Is Blake willing and ready to come 'out,' so to speak? What would this mean for him? He stands to lose more than me if Vin comes knocking on that door. Yet here he is, supporting and loving me regardless. The thought of hurting him or potentially not having him in my life makes me feel physically ill. I can't lose Blake, but I can't lose Vin either, not again.

Blake hasn't brought the subject up, but it's one more thing I feel anxious about. My thoughts are getting away from me now, and I try to rein them back in before I let things get too far out of control.

"What will happen to us, Blake?" I ask, afraid of hearing his answer.

"I don't know," he replies quicker than I was expecting. He must have been thinking the same thing.

"If Vin comes back..." I pause, not really knowing what I am trying to say or ask. Not really knowing how to finish that sentence.

"You're asking if we will have to get divorced? If I will tell people I am gay? How will we explain it to our friends?" Blake basically lays out everything I have been wanting to say without hesitation.

Blake has always been like that though. He is never one to leave things unsaid with me. To so many others, he is very guarded and hidden, only showing them a small sliver of the real him. With me, he wears his heart on his sleeve, and I want to wrap it in bubble wrap. Protect it forever. The thought of it being me that hurts him is enough to send me crazy. I truly love Blake. Just not in the intimate way. Not in the way I love Vin.

"I guess, I just don't know how all this will work. What will we tell people, what will it mean for us? I don't want to lose you Blake," I say.

"You will never lose me Scarlet, no matter what, we will always be family. Let's just cross that bridge when we get there."

I nod at him, but inside, my stomach is churning. I hate that saying. We will cross that bridge when we get there.

I like to have a plan. I like to be organised. Waiting, not knowing makes me feel so out of control. The crossing of that damn bridge feels inevitable. Better to have a safety harness on or a backup bridge before we get to it.

Either way, I know things will change. If Vin stays, what will that mean, and how will we make that work? If Vin leaves, how will I ever go back to my life before now? How will I ever move on knowing he is out there living his life without me? Knowing that he knows I still love him with every fibre of my being. Yet he didn't choose me. He didn't choose to stay.

And as if he is reading my mind, Blake says, "I know the fear of the unknown scares you Scarlet, but just know that no matter what happens, you and I will be ok. We may not have a traditional marriage, but we are family. We will figure it out no matter which way it goes."

"You mean if he stays or goes."

"Exactly."

I nod as we sit there, letting our coffees go cold while the silence washes over us. Everything is so up in the air at the moment. Here we are, just waiting for it to all come crashing down, doing our best to catch things before they smash to the ground.

50

Go to her

It's taken me two days to get through most of the letters. I don't want to read them anymore. I want to smash down her front door, throw the gay guy out the window and wrap her in my arms. I want to kiss her lips and feel her hands on my body. I want to wrap myself in her scent and never let her go.

I fold up the letter I just finished and place it back into its envelope. I grab the next and open it up. She wants me to read them, and I'll be damned if I don't do what that girl wants from now till the day I die. Jesus, if that means a polyamorous relationship with her and Blake, I swear to a god I don't believe in that I'll do it.

I guess I owe him a lot. He sounds like he helped her heal after I pulverized what was left of her shattered heart when I ignored her. I really thought I was doing the right thing by her, but I only made everything so much worse for her. I didn't know how much she blamed herself. How much she hurt for what had happened to me. How much guilt she felt and how much she just needed to hear me say I forgive her. There was nothing to forgive. She saved my life. I owed her everything.

Every letter started the same.

'Vin,

You have to know how sorry I am. If I could take it all back I would. You have to know that I never forgot about you. Nor will I ever. I will never stop loving you.'

The first few went on to explain how much she hates herself for what she did. How much she blames herself. How she wishes she just stayed quiet and didn't start the entire thing. She tells me how much guilt she feels for not speaking up about what she did. How she was so out of it at the hospital, she didn't know what was happening until it all felt too late.

How she tried to visit me to set it right. When I wouldn't see her, she felt for sure that I blamed her and hated her as much as she hated herself.

I couldn't believe what I was reading. I had no clue she felt that way. That she thought it was all her fault. That she believed I hated her. My heart was breaking all over again with each new letter.

Around letter five or six, she told me about Blake. I lost count. By this time, I felt like I had gone ten rounds with Tyson. I didn't think I could physically stand to sit through one more letter. Then the pain reached a whole new level.

Because now, not only does she blame herself for everything, not only did she believe I hated her, but now I had to read how she met someone. She tells me about how he makes her laugh. How he doesn't try to pry her past out of her and is happy to let her be. Tells me how he is slowly putting little pieces of her back together.

I want to kill him and hug him at the same time. I can't be mad at the guy, he was exactly what she needed when I couldn't be. By the time she drops the punch line that the bloke is gay, I am ready to marry him myself. She goes on to explain their relationship in detail, and I find myself finally smiling at the thought of her finding joy again, even if it wasn't with me. She tells me about his parents. About her and Blake's plan to travel, how they plan to marry and their crazy thought process behind it all.

I've read enough to know that she still loves me like I still love her. That she never, not even for a moment, thought about moving on. I don't need to know any more. I want to go to her now and tell her how sorry I am. Crawl on my knees and beg her to forgive me for ever forcing her hand. For taking her choice away. For not seeing how much it would destroy her.

But she sent me these letters. She took the time to write them all, and they read like an autobiography of her life. The inner workings of her beautiful mind laid out raw. She wanted me to have them. She wanted me to understand and to know what she had been doing with her life.

I have spent enough time not respecting her wishes. If she wants me to read them all, then as she wishes. I will sit my giant ass in this chair and read them all. I have barely moved from the little kitchenette chair in my motel for two days. I only have a few letters to go, and then. Then I will go to her. Before the smear of her handwriting in lipstick on the box becomes completely unreadable.

51

Now, I never let you go

SCARLET

"Scarlet, SCARLET, get out here."

"I'm coming, hang on." I have just gotten out of the shower after coming home from work. Day three of not hearing from Vin, and I am crawling out of my skin. I can't remember a single conversation or piece of colour work or haircut I have done for the last three days. It is all a giant blur. I am going through the motions, but I am frozen. Completely numb.

None of it feels real. He is here in this town and what? Just ignoring me again. My life was finally feeling like I could have happiness. It may have never been a traditional marriage, and maybe we would have never had kids and the white picket fence, but I was happy. Then Vin comes into town and blows everything up, and then just proceeds to abandon me all over again.

I let down my hair from the top bun it was in so that it wouldn't get wet while I was in the shower. I run my fingers through the messy waves, then I quickly chuck on a pair of shorts and an oversized tee. I walk out towards the lounge room where Blake is still calling me.

I get to the end of the hall and I see him. He doesn't even wait for me to acknowledge him, he moves around Blake in the lounge room. Two big strides and he is sweeping me up into his arms. They wrap around me in a way that is so foreign yet so familiar at the same time. My body instantly melts into him as I wrap my legs around his waist and find his hair. It's too short to run my fingers through it now. The way I used to.

Our foreheads meet, leaning into each other, breathing each other in, and then his lips are on mine. We kiss for the longest time. I forget where I am. Forget that Blake is right there in the living room. Forget the pain, the heartbreak, the last six years. All of it gone in one kiss.

I pull away, needing to catch my breath. He doesn't want his lips to leave my skin, and they find their way to my forehead.

"I'm sorry Scar, I am sorry for everything. Please know, I never blamed you. Quite the opposite actually. You saved my life. I only did what I did because I thought you hated me for hurting you. I thought I didn't deserve you and that you would be better off without me. I was wrong to take your choice away. I was wrong to not trust you to make your own decisions. I should have been there for you. I didn't want you to waste your life waiting for me."

"I waited anyway Vin. I would have waited a lifetime."

I find his lips again, and this time we don't stop, fuelled by years of longing and missing each other. Years before that of only having each other. Growing up together. He walks me back down the hall, and his lips break from mine for a moment as he asks which room. Then they are on me again. He keeps me in his arms with my legs wrapped around his waist as he walks into my bedroom.

If he read all my letters, he knows that Blake and I don't share a room. It's clear he has. He lays me down on the bed before crawling on top of me. His hands find my face and brush the hair from my eyes. Then his thumb swipes my cheek, wiping a tear I didn't even know had escaped.

"My memories did you no justice. You are even more beautiful than I remember." I look up at him. He is resting on one elbow to the side of me with the majority of his body over mine, his broad shoulders all but swallowing me.

"I missed you so much Vin, you have no idea how much I have needed you," I say as I run my fingers down his back, finding the end of his shirt. I pull it up to bring it over his head, and he does the rest for me.

Holy hell, I forgot how amazing this man is. I mean, he was still a boy when I was last with him. We were only seventeen. He was gorgeous, but not like this, hard definition lining his shoulders and chest right down to the V that leads to the top of his shorts.

I have not been with anyone but Vin and no one since him. Years. I mean, I have become very efficient at doing it myself, and I have a nice collection of toys, but I have never wanted another man. I wonder if he has been with anyone since me. I still have no clue how long he has been out for.

Maybe a conversation is what we need right now. More than this. The sensible thing to do would be to talk it out before we jump each other's bones. The moment his hands find the bottom of my shirt and start slowly bringing it up, over my stomach and past my boobs, then over my head, I think, nah, screw that! I don't need to talk. I need him. I need to be in his arms, feel him, have his hands on my hips and lips on mine.

We can talk later. But then he stops, his eyes boring into mine. They trace a line down to my stomach. He shifts back onto his elbow to the side of me, and his big hands gently trace the angry raised scar across my belly.

"I did this." His eyes are low, looking at my scar, his soft fingers tracing it. He takes his hand from my body and runs it over his face, then back over his head. He pushes himself higher up onto his elbow, keeping his other hand behind his head.

The position makes him look like a god, and I don't want him to stop. I don't want him to stop touching me or kissing me, but he looks like he is in pain.

"Vin, it was an accident. I know you. You would have rather died that day than hurt me. It was bad timing and a very unlucky situation. What we both went through. It wasn't your fault."

"Well, it definitely wasn't yours either Scar, you didn't deserve to have this happen to you, and by my hands. I won't ever forgive myself."

His hand is back on the other side of my body now, and I grab it in mine, placing it over my scar.

"I forgive you Vin, I don't blame you. I would do it all again to keep you safe. Don't push me away again, please. Not when I barely have you back."

He moves his hand up to cup my face.

"You've always had me Scar, I'm yours. Forever." With that, I lean up and kiss him hard. He pushes back down onto me, kissing me back. I start to undo the button on his denim shorts, shuffling them down over his hips. He takes over and tosses them on the floor by the side of the bed.

He moves over me again and leans down to kiss my stomach. He traces kisses over and around my scar while his hands find my shorts and start to undo the top button and zip.

He slowly shuffles them down, following the path with his mouth. His hands never leave my body as he tosses the shorts to the floor and makes his way up my legs and thighs, kissing me as he goes, his mouth getting close to where I want him. He traces his mouth over my inner thighs, reaching his hand out to me and interlocking his fingers with mine. My hands feel tiny in his. He brings his mouth back up to my lips. Our hands stay interlocked as he kisses me, our bodies melting into each other. His knee finds its way between my legs, and I open them to give him better access, moving my hips to get friction in the right spot. If it wasn't clear to him where I want this to go before, it sure as hell is now.

He pulls his lips from mine, brushing his thumb over my bottom lip, wiping away the taste of him.

"I haven't been with anyone since you," I say as he is looking down at me with those piercing eyes. I don't know why I feel the need to make that clear. Maybe I am desperate to hear him say the same, although I can't blame him if he doesn't.

"You're all I've ever wanted Scar. I haven't been with anyone since you either." A sigh of relief washes over me, and then I lean back up to kiss him again, grinding into him with need as his hands gently rove my body and I am overtaken with want.

He gently wraps an arm around me and pulls me up with ease. His hand finds the back of my bra as he unclips it. His lips never leave my body. He kisses my neck and collarbone, and I lean into him more, running my hands over his broad shoulders.

He lays me back down, his eyes working their way up and down my body. His hands find their way to my boobs, caressing them in his hand. He swipes his fingers over my nipples gently, and the feeling makes goosebumps rise over my body. I arch my back, pushing my body further into his hand, desperate for more.

His fingers pinch my nipples, and it sends a current directly between my legs. He smiles and chuckles into my neck at how my body is reacting to him.

"God I missed you," he mumbles into my neck. His hands make their way back down my body and skim over the top of my underwear. They feel soaked through. He runs a finger up and down before hooking it into the top of my G-string and pulling it down.

I shuffle my legs, helping him get them free. My heart is racing, and I am desperate to feel him skin to skin. I stroke his bulge over his boxers; I can feel it twitch under my hand. His hand is now on my sweet spot, rubbing my clit with firm pressure. The feeling has me all sorts of worked up, and I want to feel him inside me desperately.

I push further into him as I hook my fingers into his boxers and slide them down. He takes his hand from my body for a moment to free himself and get the boxers all the way off. My breath catches at the sight of him. Like everything else on him, this is also big.

His fingers work their way to the exact place I want them. They slide between my lips, and then he pushes one finger inside me. The feeling has my back pushing off the bed. I want it deeper. He slides it out, spreading the wetness through my lips, and then pushes back in. This time he moves it back and forth, hitting my front and back walls, which has me all but dying for more.

I grab him in my hand, giving him a gentle squeeze before I start gliding up and down his shaft. He lets out a low moan and throws his head back in response.

"I want to taste you again. I thought I remembered what you felt like, smelt like, looked like, but you're nothing like I remembered. You're so much better. I need to taste you again," he says as he pulls his finger from me, leaving me empty.

He moves to between my legs. Grabbing my thighs, he pulls me towards his face. His nose slides through my lips and hits my clit at the same time his tongue finds my entrance. He makes slow, soft circles around, then up and down, before moving his mouth up to my clit and sucking. He uses more pressure as he slides two fingers deep inside of me.

I wrap my legs around his head, clinging to him. The feeling of his mouth sucking my clit, creating friction with his fingers sliding in and out of me has me spiralling. I move my hips to meet his face and create more friction as I reach my peak. Heat burns through me, and I push my hips further into him, squeezing my legs around his head as I come.

He looks up at me, our eyes locking on each other as he licks his bottom lip.

"Fucking hell, you have no idea how much I missed the sweet taste of you." He crawls up over me, his body weight lightly on me as he braces himself with his hands on either side of me. He pushes his body into me, his hard length pushing against my entrance. He moves his hips and slides into me, and OHHH MY GOOD GOD! I can't believe I really thought I would be happy the rest of my life without ever feeling this feeling again.

It's not just the fullness, the heaviness of his body, his hands gripping me. It's him. The way he holds me, the way he looks at me, the way he smells and feels and sounds. EVERYGODDAMNTHING. I don't know how I have lived without this man. Suddenly everything seems brighter. Like the world has been monotone and now it's been painted in vivid colour.

Having him back in my arms is like getting a sense back that I didn't even know I had lost. He starts grinding his hips into me, and I move my hips under him to meet his thrusts. He leans down and kisses me hard, and I pull him closer. It doesn't take long for me to feel that heat building again. I am so close.

He stops moving for a brief moment, and I greedily move my hips, trying to get him deeper again.

"Shit Scar, you're so tight. I have missed this so much. I am so fucking close. I want to come inside you." It takes me a moment to register what he is saying. FUCK! I used to be on the pill, but after Vin, there has really been no need. I am not on any contraception now, and Jesus Christ, I am not ready for a baby. That sure would complicate an already complicated situation.

"I am not on any contraception Vin."

"Shit, I am so sorry. I got so caught up and just fell back into how things used to be. I didn't think." He goes to pull out, and I grab a hold of him, wrapping my legs around his waist, pulling him back into me all the way.

He groans.

"Make me come and I'll finish you with my mouth. You used to love when I did that, remember?" He chuckles, a cheeky smirk across his face.

"Do I remember? Damn girl, I never dreamed I'd have this again. I never want to leave this bed or this pussy ever again," he says as he starts moving inside me.

"Good," I say as I push him back to roll over onto his back.

I climb on top of him, straddling him, and bounce up and down. He grips my ass, helping me move, his eyes on mine as I ride him.

"Fuck, you better stop that, or I am not gonna last. You look so good like that." I change to grinding back and forth to chase my own release, grinding my clit on him as he stretches me.

He grips my hips, his firm hands holding me like a vise as I move, his eyes roving my body, finding my eyes as I lose control. I have become pretty efficient at finding my own release, but this. Holy hell. I had forgotten what I was missing. My body convulses, and I feel myself clench around him.

He must feel it too, and it sends him close to the edge. He tries not to move an inch, waiting for me to ride the final waves of my orgasm.

He lifts me off him with ease. I quickly shuffle down him with my mouth. I waste no time with teasing as I wrap my hand around his base, stroking up and down while my mouth takes him deep. He thrusts up into me. A few more fast strokes with my hand and mouth, and he comes down my throat with a moan.

I climb back up to him and collapse onto his chest, our bodies heaving in sync. He blows down on my chest where I am dripping in sweat, cooling me down. He always used to do this when we finished. I would fall in his arms, and he would blow my chest to cool me down. I had all but forgotten about the sweet little gesture.

We lie in silence for a while, just holding each other. I have not felt this free, this myself since he left. I had been slowly pieced back together, but a part of me was always missing. Just like that, I am whole again.

"Jesus, we just forgot all about Blake," I say, slightly killing the mood, but now that the passion has passed, I am all too aware of the reality of the shit storm this is going to create. Vin just holds me close, stroking my hair as I lie in his arms.

"What happens now?" I ask, looking up into his beautiful eyes.

"Now," he says, "I never let you go."

52

Take my breath away

"Roooaar!" Blake is chasing the kids around the back-yard, pretending to be a lion. The kids are laughing and running around screaming. I walk out through the doors, holding the meat tray, ready to pass it to Blake's dad, who has taken the honourable position of master BBQ'er.

"I should turn the sprinklers on for the kids," I say as I pass the tray to Blake's dad.

"Yes Mum, yess!" tiny voices yell at me in between squeals of excitement as they run away from Blake… I mean, the lion. I connect the hose to the sprinkler and place it in the middle of the garden. The kids start running and jumping through it, and the squeals somehow reach an even higher pitch.

I am so caught up in the moment, enjoying the fresh air, my family, my two beautiful sons and my niece. Well, sort of niece. My sort of, adopted niece. I walk back inside to check on the Potato Bake I have cooking in the oven. Then I have to start making the salad. I grab the chopping board and salad bowl and start cutting the lettuce into strips.

I feel his hands slide over my hips and come together over my stomach as he holds me in a bear hug. I can feel him bending down, the hair on his face tickling my neck.

"How can I help?" he asks. I turn around to face him, forgetting all about the salad and the potatoes in the oven and even the guests we have outside. Everything fades into the background, a blur of white noise in the distance.

He smells good, like summer rain, and when I turn to look up at him, I know I am exactly where I am meant to be in life. He is my home. Still after all these years, Vin and those damn eyes take my breath away.

53

Till my last breath

VIN

My childhood wasn't a happy one. There was no uncle chasing me around the garden pretending to be a lion, no grandparents bringing me toys and squeezing my cheeks telling me how much they loved me. No big family BBQs and parties out in the sunshine on a summer day.

Before Scar came into my life, it was a pretty miserable existence. I mean, I do remember vague happy moments. But mostly I remember the rage, hate and pain. So, so much pain. She was the sun that warmed my skin. The rain that washed away my pain. She was everything to me, and now I am standing in our kitchen with her in my arms. My wife. My love, my Everything. As I watch our two boys play under the sprinklers with their uncle Blake, his boyfriend and their adopted daughter, Scar's mum is sitting at the table with Janet, Blake's mum, while Blake's dad is working the grill.

Somehow, although somewhat unconventional and with a very rocky beginning, it has all come full circle, and this is our life. I swore to her that I would never let her go. Ten years later, and I am still holding true to that. I will hold true to that till my last breath.

54

This moment

BLAKE

Oh my gosh I am tired. I have been chasing these kids around all afternoon playing this game. I swear their batteries never run out. Every time I hear them squeal or laugh, I am pulled back in. I can't stop. Seeing them smile and hearing them laugh is just too damn cute.

"Grant, help me!" I scream as I pretend to be taken down by Kia, Scarlet and Vin's eldest son. The rest stack on top of me, pretending to have caught the lion. I am fake roaring and pretending to fight as hard as I can while they all pin me down.

Grant rushes over roaring and starts wildly throwing children off me in the most gentle, playful way. The kids storm him, grabbing at his feet and legs. He pretend falls, dramatically toppling over and rolling next to me.

"This is the best," he says as he rolls up close enough for me to sling an arm over him.

"I'm exhausted," I say. He laughs and pecks me on the cheek.

Scarlet turns the hose on, and the kids jump ship to go and run through the sprinklers.

"Finally a reprieve," I say as I start to get up.

"You love it," Grant says as I reach a hand down to help him up. He's not wrong though. I do love it. All of it. I can't believe this is my life. Can't believe I almost held myself back from having this, all out of fear.

Telling my parents that I'm gay was the most gut-wrenching thing I have ever had to do.

While they were shocked beyond belief and didn't really understand it, they said that nothing would make them stop loving me. It took them a while to calm down and face the initial shock. Once they did, we had some hard conversations. It led to so much freedom that I barely remember the feeling of being caged up. I am completely free. That once caged, fearful animal now roams around proud, fierce and in love.

I met Grant on a night out with some of my friends from uni. I gradually told them I was gay, and none of them even baulked. Instead, they quite happily added gay bars to the list of places we visited on nights out. Grant and I hit it off straight away. He had known he was gay from a very young age. His parents were free spirited and open minded, and he told me that he never even told his parents he was gay. He just bought a boyfriend home in year ten, and no one ever questioned it.

I was attracted to his openness and outgoing nature, and I was infatuated with him. Eight years later, and I am still infatuated with him.

I look over at my mum happily talking to Scarlet's mum, to my dad cooking us dinner and Vin and Scar hugging in the kitchen where they think no one can see them. Our kids, growing up together, playing.

I wouldn't change a thing about what we did. It brought me here. To this moment. Exactly where I am meant to be.

55

Pure delight

SCARLET

Vin and I were holed up in my room for a week when he first came back. I don't think we ate or slept. I texted Blake, and he said he was going to stay with a friend near uni to give us some space. While my own heart was being stitched back together by Vin, I couldn't help but grieve for Blake and what this would mean for our relationship.

Vin and I finally made it out of the sheets and into some real conversations. I told Blake to come home so we could make our way out of this giant web of lies. Vin joked that we should all just move and start fresh, away from Blake's parents and our friends, and no one ever had to know a single thing.

While it was mostly a joke, we all seriously considered this as a viable option. In the end, we decided the truth was the only way forward, as scary as that sounded to all of us. Well, not quite the whole truth and nothing but the truth. Enough of a truth that we could all move forward.

Blake held my hand and told me that it was about time he stopped caring what everyone thought and started being true to himself. He told me how our relationship had given him the confidence and freedom to explore his sexuality more.

We lived in a little bubble for a few months, Vin hiding out in the house while Blake and I went about our normal lives. It was peaceful, and I started to think that maybe we should just keep Vin hidden forever, my dirty little secret. It wasn't like I didn't have others. But we knew we would have to face reality soon enough.

We invited my mum and Blake's parents around for dinner. I actually felt extremely guilty when I saw the look on my mum's face when she saw Vin. It hit me then how much I had pushed her away over the years, and I vowed to tell her my whole truth one day. Not today. But one day. With everyone around the dinner table, Blake came out of the closet, so to speak.

We explained everything and how Blake had felt, how we had used the relationship to protect each other and ourselves. Blake's parents were furious, but not so much for the reasons we had expected. Turns out they weren't the 'send him away to straight camp' type. They were mainly heartbroken and furious that he felt he had to hide it from them for so long. They didn't fully understand it, and it took them a long time to fully come around to it. But it sparked a lot of conversations about his future and what he actually wanted to do with his life.

He ended up finishing his degree but then moved on to psychiatry, which he found a real passion in. With the freedom to be himself, he met a guy on a night out that very quickly turned into something serious. They now live together with their adopted daughter Violet.

I eventually told my mum everything I had fought to keep locked up. She was nothing but supportive. I couldn't thank my mum enough for the love and support she gave Vin and me. She helped him start his own mobile mechanic's business, helping him to set up a website and booking system and helping him with his tax. She even lent him the money to purchase equipment and a Ute to set it all up so that he could drive to clients, recommending him to her work colleagues and friends until he was so busy he was turning clients away. He paid her back with interest.

We told our friends in drips and drabs, trying not to make a big deal out of it. We didn't go into the nitty gritty of our pasts. Blake said he was gay and that I had reignited a flame with a high school boyfriend.

The whispers died down fairly quickly. People were busy with their own lives, although the gossiping worried me to begin with. Once people started to see we were happy, they left us alone, and things developed into a new normal. Blake and my small group of friends welcomed Vin and our relationship, and Blake and his.

Blake, Vin and I lived together for a short while in the house Blake and I rented. Then, when Blake and Grant started getting serious, he moved in as well. Blake and I had to go through the proceedings of the divorce. Due to it being an uncontested divorce, we both applied, and it was granted within four months. Just like that, our fake marriage was over. However, the love we have for each other never died. He is still my best friend and the surrogate uncle to our kids, as I am to his. Vin never tried to come between that. I think he knew how much he owed to Blake. He had held me together all those years. After much convincing, Vin and I both went to counselling. We wanted to move on with our lives and one day have kids of our own without our trauma ruining it.

I'm glad we did.

Because as I look out from my kitchen at Blake and his boyfriend with their beautiful daughter, at Vin and my two children as they run around the backyard playing and squealing in delight, pure safety and happiness painted on their chubby cheeks, surrounded by family, surrounded by love, I am glad they will never have to suffer the way my Vin did. The way I did.

I am glad he got his happy ending. He deserves it. We all do.

The End.

MORE ABOUT THE AUTHOR

Hi, I am Nicole Bazley.
Ok, ok, I am going to be completely honest here. Nicole Bazley is a pen name. She is an alter ego created to gain the confidence to publish my first book.

It's not that I don't think my book is worthy. I do. It's just a daunting experience putting it out there. One I've held myself back from for many years. Ten to be exact.

While the name isn't technically my real name. Nicole embodies me in so many ways. She is me! She is the creative author who has so many love stories to tell. This name means something to me on a deep level.

A LITTLE ABOUT ME.

I love the beach, my family, being outdoors and staying active. I have always been a book lover and will read almost anything. My favourite authors are Jodie Picoult and Lee Child. I think I could read the Jack Reacher stories on repeat till the day I died.

I have always loved to write. Poems, songs and little stories, this is my first time actually putting my work out there.

I would say, I write contemporary romance stories that will have you free falling.

I hope you love my stories as much as I love writing them.

Nicole x

Catch me here

Website - www.nicolebazley.com

Email -nicolebazleyauthor@gmail.com

Facebook - @nicolebazleyauthor

Tiktok - @nicole.bazley.aut

Instagram - @nicolebazleyauthor

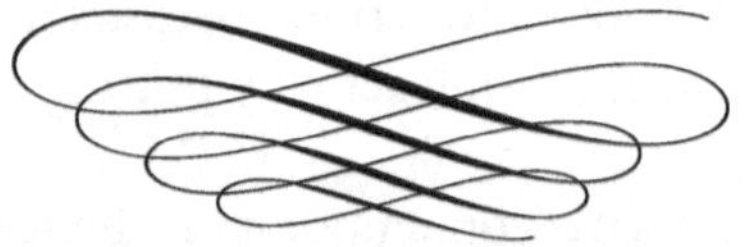